When the milk of
human kindness turns
sour, it is a singularly
unpalatable draught.

–Agnes Repplier

# MYSTERIES *of* LANCASTER COUNTY

# DAIRY DISASTER

MYSTERIES *of* LANCASTER COUNTY

*Elizabeth Ludwig*

**Guideposts**
Danbury, Connecticut

Mysteries of Lancaster County is a trademark of Guideposts.

Published by Guideposts Books & Inspirational Media
100 Reserve Road, Suite E200
Danbury, CT 06810
Guideposts.org

Cover and interior design by Müllerhaus
Cover illustration by Bob Kayganich, represented by Deborah Wolfe, LTD.
Typeset by Aptara, Inc.

Printed and bound in the United States of America
10 9 8 7 6 5 4 3 2 1

# Dairy Disaster

*To Anne:*

*You have always been there in my time of need. Thank you for always offering unfailing love and support, and for your willingness to visit a dairy farm when I asked! This book couldn't have been possible without you.*

# CHAPTER ONE

A buzz filled Secondhand Blessings. It bounced from the ceiling stretching high overhead and settled in the nooks between shelves. It was a mixture of excitement and energy and...anticipation? Yes, that was it.

Elizabeth smiled as she took a sip of her pumpkin-spice flavored coffee. October was always filled with anticipation, like the whole world knew change was coming and held its breath while it waited for the leaves to signal the season.

"*Guten morgen,* everyone." Rachel Fischer's clear voice quieted the women of the quilting circle who met at Secondhand Blessings every Thursday morning. Clad in a plain blue dress with a white prayer *kapp* holding her chocolate-brown hair firmly in place, she made a sweet picture framed against the barn's painted wall. She extended her hand toward the ring of chairs set up around a wide table at the center of the store. "If you would take your seats?"

Empty cup in hand, Elizabeth turned away to begin the day's tasks. She attended the quilting circle on occasion, but today would be especially busy since she and her sisters had decided to move the seasonal inventory toward the front of the store where shoppers could easily browse. Not only would it be visually appealing, it would encourage sales. It did, however, mean clearing space on the shelves, something Elizabeth had volunteered to do before she realized how much work it entailed.

She set her cup on the counter with a small click and rolled up her sleeves. She'd tackle the chore one shelf at a time. Slow and steady. Like running a marathon or eating an elephant.

Laughing at the direction her thoughts had taken, Elizabeth scooped up a stack of dishes and moved them into a box on the floor. Not wanting the box to get too heavy, she added some tablecloths, a lace-fringed dish towel, and several homemade aprons before sliding it to one side to be moved to the back room.

A voice rose from the women gathered around the quilting table. "Rachel, is there any word on Moses Troyer?"

The name registered in Elizabeth's brain. Moses had a daughter named Emma who usually attended the quilting circle. She was absent today. Was someone in the family sick? Hopefully not, but along with pumpkin bread and Indian corn, fall also typically brought with it the start of cold and flu season.

Elizabeth's hands closed around a valuable crystal punch bowl and a set of silver ladles. "No box for you," she said, lifting the bowl gently off the shelf. She carried the bowl and ladles to the back of the store and deposited them safely onto a shelf. When she returned to the front she heard Rachel addressing the group.

"We are in agreement, then? Leora, you will organize a schedule for meals, and Marietta, you will do the same for housecleaning? It will be several weeks before Moses heals from his injuries."

All around her, heads bobbed in agreement, some covered with prayer kapps, others not.

*Injuries?*

The word played silently in Elizabeth's brain. She didn't know Moses Troyer had been injured. Wondering *how* occupied her thoughts while she packed the next three shelves.

At the front of the store, Elizabeth's sister Mary blew in on a breeze and a mechanical beep from the sliding doors. Martha followed behind, a basket of cinnamon-scented baked goods balanced on one hip.

"Wow, you've been busy." Martha nodded toward the empty shelves then hitched the basket high enough to slide onto the glass display cabinet. "We were only gone a little while. You've gotten a lot done."

"I have, but I'm ready for a breather." Elizabeth ran her sleeve over her damp forehead. "Hey, did either of you hear about Moses Troyer being in some kind of accident?"

Martha pulled back the door of the display case and reached inside to make room for the new baked goods. "I didn't."

"Me neither," Mary said as she tied an apron around her waist. "Isn't that Emma Troyer's father? What happened?"

Elizabeth circled the display cabinet to help Martha. "Yes, that's him." She hefted the basket and moved it down to give Martha easier access. "I have no idea. Emma isn't at the quilting circle this morning. I just overheard Rachel and the others talking about ways they can help."

"Must have been a pretty serious accident," Martha said, putting the last loaf of banana nut bread in the display cabinet.

Mary checked her watch. "Maybe we could ask the quilters when they finish up."

Martha pushed the door closed and straightened. "I agree. If they're talking about helping the family, maybe there's something we could do."

Hearing them, Elizabeth's heart warmed. Before she could even ask, her sisters were considering ways they could help. Of course, that's how things worked in their little town of Bird-in-Hand. People cared for one another. It was one of the many reasons she loved living there.

"I'll make sure to ask Rachel before she leaves," Elizabeth said. Handing the empty basket to Martha, she nodded toward the next set of shelves with items to be moved. "If you need me, I'll be over there."

Elizabeth crossed to the shelf, where candlesticks, crockery, and an old electric clock stood side by side. Clearing the more delicate items took time, but eventually there was a space long and wide enough to accommodate several brightly colored pumpkins and a few fall wreaths.

Elizabeth had just placed the last item on the shelf—a vintage toolbox that had been converted into a table centerpiece—when the members of the quilting circle filed by. Some smiled at her and bobbed their heads in greeting. Others chatted about their plans for the Troyers, excitement making their voices bright. Rachel brought up the rear. Elizabeth reached for her elbow as she passed.

"Do you have a moment to talk?"

"Of course." Rachel waved to the members of the quilting circle and then moved out of the aisle next to Elizabeth. "The store looks lovely. You are doing a good job moving the fall decorations to the front where everyone can see the colors."

"Thank you, Rachel." Elizabeth motioned toward the chairs vacated by the quilting circle. "Did I overhear you say something about Moses Troyer being in an accident?"

Rachel's expression sobered. "Yes, that is right. His buggy was forced off the road late yesterday afternoon by a speeding car."

"Oh no." Elizabeth sucked in a breath. "Is Moses all right?"

"Thank *Gott*, he will be in time," Rachel said, nodding. "Besides some cuts and scrapes, he has a broken arm and a broken ankle. It will be several weeks before he is allowed to put weight on it, but at least he is home now, resting."

"And what about the driver of the car?"

"As of this moment, we still do not know who was driving the car."

"You mean they didn't stop?" Elizabeth exclaimed.

Rachel shook her head, her brown eyes darkening.

Elizabeth's thoughts sped to Moses's daughter. Moses owned a dairy farm, which meant the work of tending to the animals would fall to Emma, since she and Moses lived alone.

"I'm glad he's okay," Elizabeth said, then sucked in a breath. Buggies bore the brunt of accidents involving cars. "What about the horse?"

"Silas went by the Troyers' farm after he heard about the accident. He says the horse will be fine, just a few scratches. He will tend it while Moses heals."

Relieved by the answer, Elizabeth let out the breath. Too often, the result of such an accident was far different. "I heard you all discussing plans to help."

"*Ja.* Since Emma will be tied up with the farm, several of us will be taking meals to them during the week. And others will go by to help her with the housework and tending to Moses."

All of this sounded hopeful, but worried lines still furrowed Rachel's brow. "I am concerned about the farm though. I am going to stop by on my way home to see if Emma needs help with the cows."

Elizabeth's thoughts raced. Rachel's son owned a dairy farm. Would he be able to help? "Are you thinking of contacting Adam?"

"Ja, if Emma and Moses approve. I will speak to them first to see what they think."

Elizabeth glanced at the shelves she'd been working on and quickly made up her mind. Reorganizing the store could wait.

She reached back and tugged her apron strings loose. "Do you think Moses and Emma would mind if I come with you? Maybe there's something I can do."

Pleasure beamed from Rachel's face. "That would be *wunderbar.* I'm sure the Troyers would appreciate a visit." Her brows winged upward. "But the store?"

"Mary and Martha are both here. They won't mind, and they'll be glad we're looking after our neighbors," Elizabeth said. "Give me a moment to let them know where I'm going. Then I can drive us out to the Troyers'."

At Rachel's nod, Elizabeth folded her apron, stored it under the counter, then wandered the aisles in search of Mary and Martha. When she found them, Mary offered to finish moving the fall inventory, so Elizabeth happily made the drive with Rachel out to the Troyers' farm.

A long gravel drive split the pastureland in front of the Troyers' white farmhouse. Hemmed with fence posts and barbed wire, it wound like a ribbon past a large barn, worn gray with age, and two silos that towered over it like sentries. Here and there, black and white Holsteins polka-dotted the rolling hills, their bawling echoing off the line of trees that were just beginning to don their fall robes.

"There," Rachel said, pointing toward a spot near the door. "We will park and see if Moses is well enough for visitors."

Once they rolled to a stop, Rachel pushed open the car door, its dinging adding to the chorus created by the cows and one lone basset hound, whose low howl mustered fear in a murder of crows. They took flight as one, their glossy black wings stark against the leaves of a golden maple.

The screech of the screen door as Emma Troyer pushed through added the final note to the symphony. Elizabeth might have chuckled over it all had not worry and fatigue lined Emma's pretty face as she greeted them.

"We have come to check on your *daed*," Rachel said, "and see if there is anything we can do to help around the farm while he is laid up."

Emma's shoulders sagged beneath the pretty pink cotton of her plain dress. Her fingers sought the handle and then she pulled the screen door open again. "Daed is sleeping now, but please, come inside. I know he will be pleased that you thought of him." As they passed, she added, "I have a pot of coffee brewing. Would either of you like a cup?"

Rachel nodded, but Elizabeth held up her hand. "None for me, thanks. I've had my quota for today. Any more and I won't be able to sit still."

Emma led them past a sparsely furnished living room and down a narrow hall to the kitchen. As in most Amish homes, the wide room invited company and conversation. A sturdy table draped with a floral tablecloth dominated the center, and around it, six chairs waited to be occupied. Stirred by a breeze from the open window above the sink, a kerosene lamp suspended from the ceiling swayed, and against a cheery, robin's-egg-blue wall, a gas refrigerator hummed. It was from this Emma took a small pitcher of cream to set on the table next to a matching sugar bowl.

Rachel skirted the table to sit in the chair closest to the window. "So, tell us. How is Moses?" she asked in a quiet voice.

Taking her cue from Rachel, Elizabeth lowered her tone to match. "My sisters and I were very sorry to hear about your father's accident."

Emma's head dipped as she carried the coffeepot to the table. "*Danki.* He is mending, but the doctor says it will be some time before he is back on his feet."

Concern pulled at the corners of Rachel's mouth. "And that means more work for you."

Emma nodded, her knuckles white around the handle of the pot. "But we are making do. Daed has taught me everything there is to know about caring for the cows."

"That is as may be," Rachel agreed quietly while Emma poured her a cup. "Still, it is no chore to hold out a helping hand. Silas and the boys will be glad to pitch in whenever you need them."

Pride was something the Amish frowned upon, yet something akin to it was reflected in the angle of Emma's upturned chin. "Danki, Rachel. I will keep your offer in mind." She said the words carefully, firmly, then set the pot down with a thump that rattled the lid.

Her answer obviously did not please Rachel, whose lips thinned. Her gaze dropped toward the dark liquid swirling in her cup.

"Perhaps we can help out another way," Elizabeth offered, her words breaking the awkward silence that enveloped them.

Curiosity shone in the gazes Rachel and Emma turned to her.

Elizabeth leaned forward to rest her hands on the table. "I've never milked a cow before, but I'd be willing to learn."

Gratitude suffused Emma's face, and for a moment, Elizabeth thought she might accept, but then she smiled and shook her head.

"Danki, Elizabeth, but it is not the milking that troubles me. It is finding time to track down additional buyers. We have a few, but with prices being what they are, it has been harder and harder to break even."

Elizabeth chewed her lip as another idea struck. Most of the milk they bought for the store came from Rachel's son, Adam, but Martha's baked goods sold well, so they could always use a little more. She looked at Rachel. "Do you think Adam would mind if we bought a few gallons of milk from Emma and her father while he is on the mend? Just to help out, I mean."

"Of course not," Rachel said.

Elizabeth turned her gaze to Emma. "It wouldn't be much, but it would be something."

"Having a new customer would be a big help, even if you cannot buy a lot of milk," she replied shyly.

"Good, then I'll talk it over with my sisters and let you know what we need."

"That would be wonderful, Elizabeth." Gratitude warmed Emma's voice. Her fingers shook as she reached up to smooth a wisp of hair that had escaped from her kapp. Poor thing. She was obviously more worried than she let on.

Throughout the exchange, Rachel sat quietly. Though she nodded when Elizabeth glanced her way, something in her gaze still whispered of concern.

Elizabeth wondered if the situation was more dire than Emma was letting on. Would the help they were offering be enough to get Moses and his daughter through this crisis?

# CHAPTER TWO

Mary swiped her finger over the spoon Martha laid on the counter and stuck it in her mouth. "Mmm."

"Hey, I wasn't finished with that," Martha scolded gently, shooing Mary from the counter with a flutter of her apron.

Laughing, Mary pulled open the silverware drawer and took out a clean spoon to replace the dirty one. "Here you go. And since you're not going to use this…"

She plucked up the spoon, frosting still clinging to the sides, and took a lick. The flavor was puzzling—sweet but oddly pungent at the same time. "Did you do something different to this icing?"

"No, why?" Martha grabbed the clean spoon and used it to scoop a large helping of frosting from the bowl. "Doesn't it taste good?" She brought the spoon to her nose and took a whiff. "I can't tell. My sinuses are all stuffed up."

"It's good. Just…different." Mary took another lick, shrugged, then dropped the spoon into the sink and ran cold water over it. "I didn't know you weren't feeling well. Did you go see the doctor?"

Martha shook her head and plopped the frosting over the top of the cake she was icing. "His office is always packed on Fridays. Besides, it's nothing. Just a little sniffle. I took some vitamin C this morning, so that should take care of it."

Martha picked up an icing spatula and began expertly smoothing the frosting over the top and sides of the cake. "Emma Troyer came by today. I'm so glad we are able to help them out a little by buying some of their milk."

"So, that explains all the baking." Mary waved her hand over the cupcakes, cookies, and custard pies cooling on the counter. "Looks like you've had a busy morning."

Martha laughed and added another dab of icing to her cake. "Yes. I sure hope all of this sells. Emma is bringing more milk tomorrow, so our display case is going to be stuffed full."

"That won't be a problem. Your baked goods always fly off the shelves." After helping herself to a s'mores cookie cup, Mary sauntered toward the end of the counter and picked up her cell phone. "I'll be in the office if you need me. I'm gonna give Michael and Heidi a call before I start working on the invoices that came in yesterday."

"Tell them I said hello, and ask them to give that sweet baby a kiss."

Thinking of her grandson always made Mary smile. She nodded to Martha, took a bite of her cookie cup, and then wandered to the ornate writing desk perched next to the window in their office.

After swallowing the bite, Mary frowned. Apparently, she was coming down with the same thing Martha had, because the normally mouthwatering treat had an odd flavor. Either that, or her taste buds were out of whack.

"Looks like it's vitamin C for me too, eh, Tink?" Mary said, bending to slip the remainder of the cookie cup to the dachshund warming herself in a patch of sunlight on the rug. Tink didn't seem to think the treat tasted strange. She gobbled it in one bite and then waited for more, her ears perked expectantly.

"Sorry, that's all I've got." Mary scrubbed Tink under the chin and then tapped Michael and Heidi's phone number on her cell screen. Her daughter-in-law answered on the fifth ring.

"Hi, Mary."

Heidi sounded out of breath, and in the background, Mary could hear Nick's piercing cries. "Hey, sweetie. Is this a bad time?"

Heidi's sigh seemed weighted with care. "Actually, the last few days, there's never a good time."

"Uh-oh. The baby's still not feeling better?"

"No. I was hoping the new medicine the doctor prescribed would help, but so far, I feel like it's only made things worse. He's not sleeping well, which means Michael and I aren't sleeping well. We're all pretty cranky and tired."

Compassion swelled Mary's heart. "Have you told your pediatrician the medicine hasn't helped?"

"I called her today. She told me to wait another day or so to give it more time to work." She sighed again, only this time, there was a watery edge to the sound. "I'm at my wits' end. I hate that I don't know how to help him."

"Be patient, sweetheart," Mary soothed. "I'm sure you and your doctor will figure it out. In the meantime, try putting a warm water bottle on his tummy. And have you tried adding some lavender to his bathwater? Sometimes a little soothing fragrance before bedtime is all they need."

"My mom suggested that, and it does seem to help a little." Heidi cleared her throat, her voice gaining strength. "But I haven't tried the water bottle. I'll do that now, see if I can get him to calm down and take a nap."

"Okay. I'll ask around too," Mary said. "Maybe our neighbor, Rachel, or one of her Amish friends knows of a good home remedy for tummy trouble we can try. I'll let you know."

"Thanks." She paused, Nick's crying growing louder in the background. "I'm sorry. I'd better go. He's getting wound up again."

"Okay. Love you, sweetie. I'll be praying for you all."

"Thanks, Mary. Love you too."

There was a chime as the call disconnected. Mary put her phone down with a sigh. Poor Heidi sounded exhausted, and with Michael working, he probably wasn't as much help as she would have liked.

Closing her eyes, Mary spent a moment in silent prayer before tackling the stack of invoices piled on the corner of her desk. Before long, the pile had dwindled to about half, with several more set aside to be paid later in the month. Which reminded her...

She glanced at the calendar. Elizabeth's birthday was coming up, and she and her sisters had yet to discuss how they would celebrate.

Almost as if she knew Mary had been thinking of her, Elizabeth appeared and nodded toward the invoices. "Hey, good job on those. I meant to start on them today, but I got wrapped up fixing this for Emma and Moses." Her eyes shone as she set a basket on the larger desk she shared with Martha.

"What is it?"

"A care basket. I put a couple of puzzle books in here for Moses because he loves crosswords, and some simple jar meals for Emma." She held one up proudly. "I got the idea off the internet. This one is all the spices for a hearty homemade chili. All Emma will have to do is add beef, canned tomatoes, and water."

"Hey, neat idea."

"Thanks." Elizabeth replaced the jar and closed the lid on the basket. "How are Heidi and Michael doing? Martha said you were going to call them?"

"I did." Mary relayed the details of the call and then wagged her head sadly. "Poor Nick. I wish we could figure out what's causing his tummy aches."

She shrugged and pushed up from the desk. "I told Heidi I would ask around for some good home remedies. I thought maybe Rachel could recommend something."

"Do you want me to check?" Elizabeth offered. "I'm going out to see the Troyers today to deliver the basket. I could stop by the Fischers' farm on my way back."

Like most of the surrounding Amish families, the Fischers did not keep a phone in the house. Instead, they used a phone connected to an answering machine inside a small shack at the edge of their property. Callers could leave voice mails, but often it was several hours or even the next day before Rachel got the message.

"Would you? That would be awesome," Mary agreed. "Save me from having to go over after the store closes."

"Be glad to." Elizabeth flashed a sympathetic smile and patted her shoulder. "Try not to worry. This is probably just something he'll outgrow in time."

Yes, but what if it was something else? Instead of voicing the fear, Mary shoved down a niggle of apprehension and moved to the filing cabinet. No sense borrowing trouble, as their mama used to say.

The drawer screeched open with one pull. "So, Elizabeth, have you thought about what you'd like to do for your birthday? It's coming up fast, you know."

"I know." Her cheeks flushed a pretty pink. "John did mention taking me out to celebrate, but we haven't made any definite plans yet."

A smile chased away the last bit of unease from Mary's heart. She was happy for her sister, happy that she and John were getting closer, even if they did still have some things to resolve. She and Bill had made progress in that area as well.

Mary nodded and resumed her seat. "Are you thinking a small party at home, or would you rather go out?"

"I'll leave that to whatever you and Martha decide. I'm happy either way."

That was true. Sweet, unassuming Elizabeth never wanted anyone to be put out on her account, which of course only made people want to please her more.

"I'll talk it over with her," Mary said. "And if we go out, would you mind if I invited Bill?"

"That would be lovely."

"Great. In the meantime, be thinking about what kind of cake you'd like Martha to bake."

Elizabeth nodded and slid her arm under the basket handle. "I'll let you know what Rachel says about Nick."

"Okay. Thanks again."

She waved goodbye to Elizabeth and then lowered her head to the task of finishing up the invoices. The work was tedious and time-consuming, but it was a distraction, albeit a temporary one. The minute she filed the last one, concern for Heidi, Michael, and Nick came creeping back.

Elizabeth was right. Nick's tummy trouble was probably just something he would outgrow. At least she hoped so. Because she dreaded to think what she would do if it were anything else.

# CHAPTER THREE

Emotions too exuberant to be contained bubbled up inside Elizabeth and spilled out from her mouth in the form of a cheerful tune.

*This is my story, this is my song*
*Praising my Savior all the day long.*
*This is my story, this is my song*
*Praising my Savior all the day long.*

Martha closed the drawer on the cash register and nodded to her. "Someone's in a good mood this morning."

Elizabeth pushed a pillar candle onto the pin of a candlestick and set it on the shelf next to another one just like it. "And why not? It's Saturday, and this fall weather is gorgeous."

Mary poked her head around a display of books and grinned. "Not to mention she has plans with John. Where did you say you were going? Arthur's in Lancaster?"

"Arthur's?" Martha lifted her brows. "Fancy. Sounds like a date."

"Not a date. Just dinner with a friend," Elizabeth corrected, her cheeks warming.

Mischief sparkled from Mary's eyes as she looked at Martha. "I'm in the mood for some good seafood. What about you, Martha?"

Martha circled the cash register and pretended to think. "Hmm…seafood sounds kinda good."

"Oh, you two." Elizabeth waved them off with a smile. "I am looking forward to seeing John, but that's not what has me in such a good mood. I'm just thinking about how thankful Emma and Moses were when I dropped off the care basket yesterday afternoon."

*Thankful* was a poor representation of the humble gratitude she'd witnessed on Moses's face and the relief and pleasure on Emma's, but it was the best description Elizabeth could find.

"Giving to others always makes me feel so good. Thank you both so much for covering here at the store for me so I could do that," she continued, then motioned to Martha. "Oh, and Emma told me to tell you she would bring more milk this afternoon."

"That's good. We'll probably sell out of everything I baked yesterday, so I'll get to work on stocking up for Monday." Martha bent to peer into the display case, her finger wagging as she counted the items still on the trays. When she finished, she straightened and laid her arms atop the case. "Do you suppose it's too early to start planning for Thanksgiving? I was thinking about taking cake and pie orders and donating the proceeds to Emma and Moses for their farm. Maybe some homemade rolls too."

"Oh, Martha, I think that's a wonderful idea," Elizabeth said. Leave it to Martha to find a practical way to contribute to the Troyers' needs. Hardworking and earnest, her middle sister looked on every problem as merely a task to be solved, and the more hands-on the job, the better.

Mary set to work cleaning the bookshelves with a feather duster. "It is a good idea, Martha, but make sure you don't overdo it." She directed a pointed glance at Elizabeth. "She hasn't said much, but she hasn't been feeling well the last couple of days. I heard her coughing in her room late last night."

Elizabeth frowned. "Martha, I didn't know you felt bad. Would you like me to handle some of the baking this afternoon?"

"Oh, pooh." Martha shut the door on the display case with a sharp click. "It's just a little cold. Nothing a hot bath and some chicken noodle soup won't fix."

Unwilling to be put off, Elizabeth shook her head. "Well, I'm available to help. After we close up today, I'll run up to the house and get started on some pumpkin bread. Maybe some cookies and a carrot cake too. Those usually sell pretty fast."

"Oh, and speaking of fast—" Mary paused, touched the handle of the feather duster to her lip, then shrugged. "Actually, one doesn't have anything to do with the other." As if to shoo away her wayward thoughts, she fluttered the feather duster in the air then chided herself with a roll of her eyes. "Anyway, I heard talk around town this morning about the car that ran Moses off the road. People are saying it belonged to Beau Hegel."

Martha's lips pulled into a frown. "Hegel. Why does that name sound familiar?"

"Because his uncle is a judge," Elizabeth supplied. "And his aunt heads the Friends of the Library over in Lancaster."

"Of course." Martha snapped her fingers. "Judge Clyde Hegel. His wife's name is Jocelyn."

"That's them." Mary's head bobbed. "From what I understand, their nephew is kind of wild. People are saying this isn't the first time he's gotten into trouble, but it's always been stuff like driving too fast or rolling through stop signs. But he's always had his uncle to bail him out."

Indignation flared in Elizabeth's chest. "Rachel said the driver of the car didn't stop, even after Moses was forced off the road. Are they sure it was Beau?"

"It was him," Mary stated. "A witness said there was no mistaking the Penn State decal on the back window of the bright red Mustang he got for his birthday. Plus there's a dent in the rear fender from where he backed into a parking sign at school."

"Well, then he's for sure in a whole heap more trouble than just speeding," Martha said. "It might do him some good if his uncle doesn't bail him out."

"Maybe." Elizabeth's brows rose. Teens weren't helped by overindulgent relatives who focused more on helping their kids avoid consequences rather than teaching them to own up to their mistakes. She sighed heavily and glanced over at the door as the chime signaled a new customer. Spotting Rachel, she lifted her hand and then looked back at her sisters.

"Well, for Beau's sake and Moses's, I do hope they get all of this settled quickly. It has to be weighing on both of them having it hanging over their heads."

Her sisters nodded in agreement, and Elizabeth left the candles she'd been arranging to go meet Rachel. But instead of the warm smile she expected to see, Rachel greeted Elizabeth with a troubled frown. "Hello, Elizabeth. I am glad you are here."

Rachel was too young to have many wrinkles, but today, deep furrows plowed her brow. Even more concerning was the fact that she rarely hesitated to voice her opinion, choosing instead to speak plainly and let love season her words. Yet her jaw worked as she mulled the thoughts brewing inside her head, a grimace making her skin tight.

"Rachel, is everything okay?"

"Actually…" Rachel maneuvered a dark wicker basket off her arm onto the counter next to the cash register and fumbled nervously with the rim. "I am afraid I bear unpleasant news. It is about Martha's baked goods."

She nodded toward the display case where Martha still stood. Clearly hearing her name spoken, Martha circled the cabinet and came to stand next to Elizabeth.

"About me? What is it? What's going on?"

Rachel's hand lowered to her side. "I am very sorry to tell you this, Martha, but I overheard several women at the farmer's market complaining that the items they bought from your store this morning tasted bad. I would not have repeated it except…"

Her slim fingers plucked at a checkered cloth inside the basket. Pulling it back, she revealed several banana nut and cinnamon muffins Elizabeth remembered selling to her earlier that morning.

"Rachel, are you saying there's something wrong with your muffins?" Elizabeth asked.

Rachel's grimace deepened as she took one of the muffins from the basket. "Try it for yourself. It is not bad, exactly. It just does not meet your usual standards. I thought you would want to know."

Elizabeth took the muffin, but before she could sample, it, Martha grabbed it from her hand and brought it to her nose.

"Doggone cold. I can't smell a thing." She pinched off a bite and stuck it in her mouth. "It...I mean...I can't..."

"Let me try." Elizabeth took the muffin back and pulled off another piece. It certainly looked all right—moist, perfectly baked to a golden brown. She sniffed it. Hard to tell without tasting.

Martha watched intently as Elizabeth put the bite in her mouth and chewed. "Well?" Her gaze flitted to the muffin and back. "How is it?"

Knowing the truth would hurt Martha's feelings, Elizabeth winced. "I'm sorry, Martha. It does seem to have a bit of an odd flavor."

"What!" Martha grabbed the muffin and stared hard, as though she could tell what was wrong with it simply by looking. She set the muffin aside, reached for the basket, and took out one of the cinnamon muffins. Her hand jerked out, and she held the food under Elizabeth's nose. "What about this one?"

Elizabeth took a tentative bite then shook her head sadly. "The same, I'm afraid." She brushed the crumbs off her fingers and took the basket from Rachel. "We'll give you your money back, of course."

"I am not worried about that," Rachel said. "I am more concerned with the muffins." She looked at Martha. "Did you do something different with your recipe? Maybe you forgot to add an ingredient?"

"But we're talking two different batches," Elizabeth pointed out with a frown. "Martha, can you think of anything you might have done different to these?"

"Well, I mean, other than the milk?"

Catching her meaning, Elizabeth groaned. "Surely it wasn't the milk we bought from the Troyers? What else did you use it for?"

Martha's wave encompassed the length of the display case. "In there? Just about everything." She pushed open one of the doors and took out a package of apricot custard turnovers. "These, for sure."

Elizabeth's fingers shook as she ripped open the plastic. A small bite confirmed her fears. "It *was* the milk. It had to be. These have the same odd flavor."

Worry lines pinched Martha's features. "Then we need to pull all this stuff off the shelves. We can't sell poor product to our customers. This will all have to go in the trash."

Martha opened the display case door wide and immediately began removing trays.

"Do you need to throw it all away?" Rachel asked, laying her hand on top of the case. "Your shelves will be empty."

"It's that or risk having someone get sick." Martha's movements slowed, and her face reflected horror at the thought. "Oh no. Do you think someone might get sick?"

"Now, now, let's not go borrowing trouble." Elizabeth gave her arm a pat then motioned her aside. "Move over and let me help. While I'm doing this, maybe you can get started on baking replacements?"

Martha ran her hands nervously down her apron. "In the meantime, we'd better let Mary know what's going on in case anyone complains about something they bought."

Compassion swelled in Elizabeth's heart at the misery darkening her sister's eyes. Martha took pride in her baking. It had to hurt knowing that people were talking about her food in this way.

She leaned closer, her shoulder bumping Martha's. "Don't worry. It'll all be okay. I'm just glad Rachel let us know so we can get this problem fixed."

"Me too." Martha flashed a grateful look at Rachel over the glass. "But now, I suppose I'd better get back to the house and get to work."

"Go," Elizabeth said, angling her chin toward the door. "I'll talk to Mary."

Needing no further encouragement, Martha bustled out of the store. Once she was gone, Elizabeth focused on Rachel.

"I need to talk to Emma, ask if she has any idea what might have happened." Remembering what Emma had said about delivering more milk, Elizabeth groaned. "It needs to be sooner rather than later, though. She's coming by today. I hate to embarrass her, but we certainly can't buy any more milk unless we can figure out what's wrong with it first."

Rachel plucked absently at her bottom lip. "It would be better if you went out to the farm rather than speaking to her where people might overhear, ain't so?"

"I agree."

Elizabeth grabbed two more trays out of the display case and carried them to the trash can. As much as she hated seeing food go to waste, she hated the extra work it would mean for Martha even more. Reluctantly, she tipped the trays and watched as an entire day's worth of baking tumbled into the garbage.

Which was fitting. Her day had started on such a bright note. But after hearing Rachel's news, it only seemed right that her mood, along with the baked goods, should get dumped in the trash.

# CHAPTER FOUR

Once again, the Troyers' basset hound greeted Elizabeth and Rachel with a rousing refrain as they stepped out of the car.

"Sugarpie, hush," Rachel scolded, putting her finger to her lips to silence the dog. "You will wake Moses."

Elizabeth's gaze slid to the hound loping down the porch steps. His ears didn't quite drag the dirt, but his belly definitely did. He plopped to sit at their feet, his tongue spilling from the side of his mouth and his bloodshot eyes begging for a treat.

Elizabeth reached for the milk sample she'd brought with her and raised her eyebrows skeptically. "The dog's name is Sugarpie?"

"Emma named him when she was a *kind*." Rachel patted the dog's head then moved around him toward the porch. "Do not worry, he will not bite. He is a good watchdog. He barks at people he does not know, but he does not have a mean or ferocious bone in his body."

At the word *bone*, Sugarpie let out a low howl, triggering another round of shushes from Rachel.

"Rachel! Elizabeth!" Emma waved to them from the milking barn, a long, low structure open on two sides to let the crisp October breezes blow through. Cupping her hand to her mouth, she called, "I will be right there."

Rachel raised her hand over her head to signal she'd heard and then turned to Elizabeth. "Emma was very happy when Moses decided to add a processing plant to their farm. For several years, they struggled to break even. Moses even considered selling his herd, until Emma read of another farm that raised their profits after they began processing their own milk." She pointed to another building just south of the milking barn. "It took some convincing but eventually Moses agreed to give it a try."

Elizabeth looked where she pointed. "Has it helped?"

"Enough. Moses is no longer talking of selling his cows. And they have been able to hire a couple of extra hands to help with the processing."

"That is great news," Elizabeth said.

Rachel smiled. "Emma is still not satisfied. Now she is trying to talk her daed into opening a small market here on the farm."

"Direct to consumer, like a farm-to-table type thing."

Rachel nodded. "Like most people, Moses does not like change, but he is a reasonable man. If Emma can convince him that a store makes sense, he will listen."

"Good for him." Elizabeth's gaze slid to the building Rachel said housed the milk processing plant. "How long did you say they've been processing their own milk?"

Rachel put her finger to her temple and tilted her head. "Just over a year, I think. Why?"

Elizabeth bit her lip and looked down at the jug in her hand. "I was just wondering if the problem with the milk could be due to a hitch in the processing." She nodded toward the barn. "Do you think Emma would mind showing me how it's done?"

"We can ask."

Rachel held out her hand and followed Elizabeth down the porch steps. As they walked, the milk grew heavier in Elizabeth's hands, not because it was full—the jug was more than half empty—but because she had no idea how Emma would react when she told her there was something wrong with it.

At the entrance to the milking barn, Elizabeth and Rachel stood blinking while they waited for their eyes to adjust to the dim light. Though they entered at the same time, Rachel spotted Emma before Elizabeth did and signaled toward the far end of the barn.

"There she is. It looks like she is just about done feeding the cows."

Her skirt swishing, Rachel moved forward with Elizabeth on her heels, past a long trough interrupted every couple of feet by metal stalls and a cow poking its nose through to eat. Along with the sweet scent of grass and hay, Elizabeth caught traces of grain and corn and other less pleasant smells that made her glad for the open walls, despite the chilly draft inching under her pant legs.

Emma looked up as they approached, the puzzled lines creasing her brow growing deeper as she caught sight of the jug Elizabeth carried. She set her bucket down and wiped both hands on the dark apron covering her plain dress. "I am so sorry to keep you both waiting. I was just finishing up in here."

"We weren't trying to rush you," Elizabeth said quickly. "We just need to speak to you, and since it was about the cows..."

Or rather, their milk. Elizabeth fell silent.

Emma's gaze skipped from the cows, to Rachel, then Elizabeth, and settled finally on the jug in Elizabeth's grasp. "Is...is there something wrong?"

She didn't say more, or perhaps couldn't. Her brown eyes widened, worry making her pupils overlarge.

Elizabeth stepped forward, her tone as gentle as she could make it, despite the news she bore. "Emma, I'm afraid there's a problem with the milk we bought from you. Martha didn't notice it at first, but it has an odd flavor."

"It cannot be s-spoiled," Emma said, her words coming out so fast they tripped over themselves. "Everything fresh—I mean—what I took to you was fresh."

Elizabeth twisted the cap off the jug and held it out. "Not spoiled. The flavor just isn't good. I brought some in case you wanted to taste it for yourself."

Emma licked her lips then took the jug and brought it slowly to her nose. "I don't..." She hesitated, her hand shaking around the handle of the jug.

"Taste it," Rachel urged gently.

A shuddering breath escaped her lips as Emma tipped the jug for a sip. A second later, dismay shot over her face and she stared at the milk in disbelief. "Rancid."

"No, it's not spoiled—" Elizabeth began.

Rachel cut her off with a hand to her arm. "For dairy farmers, tainted milk is often called rancid, even if it has not gone sour. It means simply the milk has an unpleasant taste or odor."

"Oh." Elizabeth shot a sympathetic glance at Emma. The poor girl had gone pale, and her eyes had taken on the glassy look of unshed tears. "Emma, tell me about the way your milk is processed. Is it possible that something went wrong during the handling of it to cause it to taste so bad?"

She shook her head before Elizabeth finished speaking. "I do not see how. We have not changed a single thing."

"What about their food?" Rachel pointed toward the long troughs. "Is their meal mixture the same?"

"Meal mixture?" Elizabeth interrupted.

"A cow's milk can be affected by what they eat," Emma explained, and to Rachel, she said, "I have not changed a thing. I am feeding the cows the same mixture that Daed uses—corn, soybean, hay, molasses"—she ticked the items off on her fingers—"and then we add the vitamins and a protein supplement. Everything is measured. We make sure the food is the same every time."

"We?" Elizabeth said. "You mean the men your father hired when he put in the processing plant?"

"Well, one of them. Abel." Color crept into Emma's cheeks. "Zach Vogel is a neighbor. He's just helping out."

Rachel cleared her throat upon hearing the words. Emma paid no attention and pointed toward the building where the milk was processed. "Abel is bottling the milk we collected yesterday right now."

"Would it be okay if we talked to him, and possibly Zach?" Elizabeth asked. "Maybe one of them could explain why the milk has such a strange taste."

"I do not mind."

Emma reached for the handle of her bucket, swung it over her arm, and then led them out of the milking barn to the processing plant. Inside, the buzz of machinery filled the air.

The machines were allowed in the district the Troyers belonged to since it was part of their business. Still, the number of pipes and steel vats caught Elizabeth by surprise. She paused in the doorway, blinking.

"This is…wow."

Emma's eyes brightened happily. "It is small. We are only milking eighty cows right now, but I hope that number will grow." She pointed to her right. "The cows are milked twice a day, morning and evening. Once the milk is collected, it is stored in a vat until it can be processed, usually the next day, but no more than forty-eight hours."

She said this earnestly, as though it was very important that Elizabeth understand how fresh the milk was they sold, and then continued walking, explaining the process as they went.

"The milk is tested before it goes any further." She pointed to a small room with a row of tall windows on one side. "That is also Abel's job. From there, it is piped into silos, where it undergoes pasteurization and homogenization."

Elizabeth blew out a breath. "I had no idea it was so complicated."

Emma shrugged. "Not complicated, just meticulous. We are very careful about how we handle the milk, and every-thing must be thoroughly cleaned after every use to prevent contamination."

If that was true, what happened to the batch the Classens had received?

Elizabeth gestured back toward the room where Emma said Abel worked. "I didn't see Abel when we passed."

"No, right now he is getting the milk we packaged yesterday ready for distribution."

"But if the milk is bad..." Rachel trailed off, her meaning made clearer in the arch of her brows.

"Ja. We should go." Emma swallowed and pointed the way.

Abel was a wide barrel of a man. The suspenders clipped to his trousers appeared ready to snap, and the buttons on his shirt bulged over his belly. He had a full beard and a thick mop of graying hair that poked out in every direction. Right now, he was plowing his fingers through it as Emma explained the trouble. After a moment, she handed him the jug, which Abel promptly tipped back for a swig. The look on his face said it all. He grimaced as he swiped his sleeve over his mouth and then pulled a handkerchief from his back pocket to mop his brow. When at last he turned to look at Elizabeth and Rachel, Elizabeth felt herself pinned under his direct gaze. In several long strides, he was in front of them, his brown eyes no less imposing up close.

His deep voice rumbled up from his chest. "You are Miss Classen?"

"I am. My sisters and I own the Secondhand Blessings store on the other side of town."

He nodded and held up the jug of milk. "Thank you for bringing this to our attention. I am very sorry for the inconvenience." He scratched his scalp. "I cannot understand how it happened."

He looked genuinely humbled and contrite. Elizabeth shook her head. "My sisters and I are more concerned about the Troyers. We want to make sure they figure out what is wrong before any more milk gets shipped out."

He dipped his head and motioned toward the jugs of milk he'd been loading in the back of a refrigerated pickup. "This milk is from a different batch. Every day, we rotate the milk we ship to make sure our customers are getting the freshest product. Hopefully, it was just one batch that was ruined, but I will sample several jugs just to be sure."

"That's a good idea." Elizabeth glanced at Rachel then back at Emma and Abel. "Do you have any idea what might have caused it to be bad?"

Abel's large shoulders rose as he held up the jug. "This milk was tested for bacteria before it got shipped out, but I will test it again. That might give us a clue."

"If it is bacteria, we will need to empty out all of the equipment and make sure everything is properly sterilized," Emma said, lifting her chin.

Elizabeth's stomach sank. "By 'empty out,' you mean—?"

"We will need to throw everything away. Two days' milking."

Two days! Elizabeth glanced at the truck. Of course. They would need to throw out everything that had already been packaged plus everything still in the vats and silos.

"We will pray it does not come to that," Rachel said softly.

"In the meantime, would it be wise to check the animals' food?" Elizabeth asked. "I know you said you have not changed anything, but is there a chance the food may have rotted? I heard you say earlier that a cow's milk is affected by what she eats," she finished, her cheeks warming under the sudden attention turned her way. Emma and Abel were the experts, after all.

Emma's eyes widened, her head and Abel's both bobbing. "Ja, we should check." Emma looked at Abel. "You get started on sampling and testing. I will inspect the food stores."

"Is there anything we can do to help?" Elizabeth glanced at Rachel.

"We will be glad to do anything you need," Rachel said.

"Danki," Emma said, a hitch in her voice. Blinking rapidly, she cleared her throat and motioned toward the barn. "I do not think there is anything you can do to help, but if you would like to learn more about how we do things, you are welcome to walk with me."

"I would like that." Elizabeth looked at Rachel. "Do you mind?"

"Not at all." Rachel gestured for Emma to lead the way and then fell in step next to her and Elizabeth. "So, Emma, how is your daed doing? He is staying off his foot as the doctor recommended?"

Emma grimaced. "You know my daed. Getting him to obey all of the doctor's orders would require a gunnysack and a rope. He is at least keeping to the house, which is more than I expected, but that may be a mixed blessing."

"What do you mean?"

"I fear he is in more pain than he is admitting."

"I am sorry to hear that."

"Me too," Elizabeth added.

Emma reached out to yank open a wide metal gate. Just past this was an enormous white bag. To Elizabeth's eye, it extended the length of a soccer field and towered over her head by at least a foot, possibly two.

"What on earth is that?" she asked.

"That is one of our feed bags," Emma said, a hint of laughter in her voice. "It is where we store the silage we harvested over the summer. During the winter months, we cut the end off and feed the silage to our cows."

"Amazing. I've seen those long bags. I just never knew what they were for."

Emma laid her hand on Elizabeth's arm. "Just so you are aware, the silage will ferment the longer it sits. It may smell bad, but that is normal."

Elizabeth nodded. "Now that is something of which I was already aware. My family has always kept animals, so I'm familiar with the smell. We just never had to store this much food." She motioned toward the silage bag snaking the length of the fence. "Is this what you are feeding the cows now?"

"Not yet. It is still early in the season." Emma pointed toward another long, low building—or rather, a roof perched atop four poles. There were no walls. Were it not for the large size, it would have resembled a carport. Inside, a young man in a baseball cap drove a Bobcat tractor with a large shovel attached, pushing silage into a pile. Earbud wires dangled from his ears, and he wore a cell phone clipped to his belt. At Emma's shout, he yanked the earbuds out.

"Zach, could we speak to you?" Emma cried, yelling to be heard above the noise of the Bobcat. She waved the young man over and then repeated the process of explaining Elizabeth and Rachel's visit and the problem with the milk. Zach listened patiently all the while, his head wagging in disbelief when she finished.

"Wow, Emma, that's…I'm so sorry."

"*Ne*, it is not your fault," she said quickly.

Perhaps too quickly? Her behavior seemed suddenly shy and, for lack of a better word, earnest.

Emma's gaze softened with her voice. "I am very grateful that you are helping out, Zach."

"Of course. Anything I can do." He cleared his throat and flashed one more glance at Emma before shoving his hands into the pockets of his blue jeans.

Elizabeth eyed him curiously. There was no mistaking the flush that crept up from his collar and over his ears. This boy had a crush on Emma, which was surprising, because unless Elizabeth was mistaken, he was an Englischer. Theirs would be a relationship the Amish strictly forbade.

"Anyway, I should probably get going," Zach continued. "My dad is expecting me back at our place."

"Zach's family also owns a dairy farm. That's why I asked him to come," Emma explained, though the fact she felt the need to do so only solidified Elizabeth's notion that there was something between the two that they weren't telling.

"It is kind of you to help in this way, Zach," Rachel said. Her gaze flitted to Emma. "But where is the other man your father hired?"

Emma's shoulders squared. "Ezra was called away on a family emergency. He will only be gone a couple of weeks. Zach is filling in until he returns."

Was it her imagination, or did Elizabeth read an unspoken challenge in Emma's eyes? She looked at Rachel to be sure, but Rachel either didn't see it or she wasn't taking the bait. Pressing her lips together tightly, Rachel inclined her head and said nothing.

"Okay, well, I'll just get going then." Zach nodded to Elizabeth and then Rachel in turn. "Nice to meet you, Miss Classen. Mrs. Fischer. See you later, Emma."

"Goodbye, Zach." Emma waited until he'd gone and then, as though she was anxious to get back to the topic at hand, she gestured to the silage Zach had been working on. "This is what we are feeding the cows. Once it is used up, we will start on the bags outside."

Elizabeth bent to scoop a handful of the silage and bring it to her nose. It still smelled fresh with only the faintest sour whiff to say it had started to ferment. Frowning, she let the chopped bits of corn and hay tumble through her fingers.

"I'm no expert, but this seems fine to me," Elizabeth said, sweeping her hands across her pants to dislodge the last clinging bits. "And you only feed the cows in the barn?"

Emma crossed her arms, her chin rising defensively. "Some farmers limit what and where their cows eat to protect certain foods from affecting the flavor of their milk. We cannot afford to do the same...yet. We still need grass to supplement the TMR we give them. Eventually we hope to get there, but for now, we allow our cows to graze in the pasture next to the house."

"TMR?"

"Total mix ration." Emma gestured to the silage.

Elizabeth tapped her bottom lip, thinking, then hitched her thumb toward the gate. "Would it be all right if we took a look at the pasture?"

"As long as you do not mind getting a little muddy," Emma warned. "The rain we have had the last couple of days has made the ground soft, and the cows' hooves leave some pretty big holes."

Elizabeth smiled and hiked up her pant legs, glad she'd thought to wear boots. "I'll be careful."

Shrugging, Emma turned and led the way. Rachel followed, but instead of walking with them when they reached the edge of the pasture, she stopped and motioned them on.

"I will wait here." She pointed to her shoes. Though they were a sturdy style, it was clear that she didn't want them filling with mud.

After the first sucking step nearly pulled the boot off Elizabeth's foot, she wondered if maybe Rachel had been right to wait.

"Wow, you weren't kidding about the ground being soft." She paused to readjust her toes before forging ahead. "This is like walking through oatmeal."

Emma laughed and pointed to a tall metal cage. "That is one of the feeders." She swept her hand out. "We have them all over the pasture."

Puzzled, Elizabeth eyed the wide bars. "I thought you said they come out here to graze on grass?"

"Grass, yes, but we give them hay too." She reached up to grasp the top of the feeder. "The hay is put in here"—she pointed down—"and the cows reach it there. The rungs are just far enough apart for the cows to eat through."

Hay only. Elizabeth frowned. It didn't look as though the problem with the milk had anything to do with their food. "You said you have several feeders like this?"

Emma nodded. "Do you want to see them all?"

Did she? Elizabeth debated the question and then shook her head. "I guess not. I mean, if you're only using them for hay, what's the point?"

She turned to go back, but her boot didn't come with her. Elizabeth threw out her hand and grabbed on to the feeder, only barely catching her balance in time to stop herself from pitching forward into the mud.

Emma seized Elizabeth's other arm with a gasp. "Oh my goodness! Are you all right?"

"I'm fine." Hopping on one foot, Elizabeth twisted to look for her boot. After spotting it, she gestured to Emma. "Would you mind?"

"Of course." Emma let go of her arm and bent to wrestle the boot out of the ground. It gave, inch by inch, finally popping free with a muddy slurp. "Ugh. Here you go." She held the boot out. "Do you want me to hold it while you put your foot in?"

"No, that's okay. If you set it down I think I can—" Elizabeth paused, her eyes arrested by a thick blob clinging to the heel. "What is that?"

Emma lifted the boot and followed Elizabeth's gaze. "What?"

"Right there." Elizabeth hopped closer to point. "It doesn't look like just mud. There's something white in the middle."

She ran her finger across the muddy blob, exposing more of the white before it plopped off the boot onto the ground. Despite her sock, Elizabeth gingerly lowered her foot and bent to retrieve the blob.

"What are you two looking at?" Rachel called.

Holding the blob between two fingers, Elizabeth scraped away more of the mud. "It looks like an onion," she called back.

"A what?" Emma asked.

Elizabeth pierced the side of the blob with her fingernail and brought it to her nose. Yep, it was definitely an onion. She scanned the ground and spotted another similar blob. And then another. And another.

She sucked in a slow breath. "Emma, do you and your dad have a problem with wild onions growing in your pasture?"

Furrows formed across Emma's brow. "Ne. Why?"

Elizabeth held up the onion. "Because I think this may be what your cows ate that made the milk taste funny. And if they didn't get them from growing wild here on your farm…"

Emma's face took on a stricken look at the implication. Eyes wide, she stared at Elizabeth. "If they aren't growing wild, then how and when did they get here?"

Exactly. Figuring out when the onions got into the feeders was a mystery. Figuring out who put them there and why…that was a problem.

# CHAPTER FIVE

Emma carried two cups of coffee to the kitchen table, setting one in front of Rachel and the other, Elizabeth.

Like a little bird, she hovered, an indecisive frown turning her lips down. "Would either of you like milk or…no, not milk…I could get you some sugar if you would rather."

Rachel patted the chair next to her. "Emma, come sit. Black is fine."

A breath puffing from her mouth, Emma slid into the chair Rachel indicated.

Elizabeth pulled her cup close, its warmth chasing the chill from her fingers. "You're sure you don't want us to talk to your father for you?" she asked.

Resting her arms on the table, Emma leaned forward and bobbed her head firmly. "Ja, I am certain." Her gaze skipped to Rachel. "You know my daed. It's hard enough getting him to stay off his feet as it is. If he thinks I cannot run the farm without his help, it will be impossible keeping him out of the barn." She looked at Rachel and Elizabeth in turn. "Which is why I have decided not to tell him about the onions. I would like the chance to figure out what is going on for myself, before involving him."

Elizabeth glanced around the wide kitchen. "Where is your father?"

"Sleeping." Emma rubbed her hand wearily over her face. "I think his leg bothers him more at night. I hear him rustling about at all hours, which is why he slips into his room during the day to catch quick naps."

Rachel tapped her finger against the side of her coffee cup. "I've known your father a long time, Emma. I know he can be stubborn when it comes to his health." She thought a minute and then looked at Elizabeth. "Emma is probably right about Moses not giving his body a chance to heal if he thinks something is wrong with the cows."

Elizabeth shook her head. "So then, what can we do to help?"

Rachel looked at Emma. "I could talk to my Adam, see if he has any advice. Maybe see if he could come by a couple of times next week?"

Emma's lips pursed. "Thank you, Rachel, but if I am going to make this farm as productive as it could be, I need to try and work out these problems on my own."

"But this isn't about the farm producing," Elizabeth reminded her gently. "The cows are *giving* milk. The problem is figuring out who might be trying to hinder what you're already doing."

Emma's gaze darted away while she pondered Elizabeth's words.

"Maybe that's something we could do to help," Elizabeth said. "My sisters and I are pretty good at solving mysteries. Maybe we could help you figure out who's behind this one."

Emma bit her lip, thinking, and then gave a slow nod. "If you think someone put the onions in the pasture on purpose, then ja, I could use your help figuring out who."

"And why," Rachel prompted.

Again, Emma nodded, but this time, with worry in her gaze.

Elizabeth cleared her throat. Though she hated to ask, the two people with the most obvious opportunity worked right outside Emma's door. "Emma, how long has Abel worked for your family?"

"Over twenty years." She blinked in confusion. "Why?"

Elizabeth avoided answering her question by asking another question. "What about Zach? How long have you known him?"

"Well, our families have known one another a long time, and I have known Zach my whole life." She paused, the concern in her dark eyes growing. "You do not think it was one of them who put the onions in the cows' food, do you?"

"Is it a possibility?"

"Ne." Emma's gaze swung to Rachel. "You also have known these families a long time, ain't so?"

Rachel nodded in quiet agreement. "Abel and I both grew up in Bird-in-Hand. I do not know Zach as well, but I know his father. I do not think it was either of them."

"We'll figure it out," Elizabeth said, responding to the unspoken questions she read flashing across Emma's face. "Hopefully, it'll turn out to be nothing more than a bad prank."

"And if it is more?" Emma asked, a tremor in her voice.

"What do you mean? What are you thinking?" Rachel asked.

Emma's shoulders inched upward, a clear indication of the stress building inside. "What if someone doesn't want me running the farm? Or what if they are angry with me, or Daed, or..." She shrugged. "I don't know."

Her words stirred an idea in Elizabeth's head. Beau Hegel had been driving the car that forced Moses off the road. What was it Martha had said about his uncle, the judge, possibly not bailing him out this time? If that was true, could it have motivated him to pull an awful stunt like feeding onions to the Troyers' cows once he did get out? Could the threat of a trial or even jail time have prompted Beau to act out of spite, or worse, an attempt at intimidation against the Troyers? She didn't know Beau well. Her acquaintance with him was limited to having seen him a handful of times around town. By all appearances, he seemed like a nice guy, but then again, looks could be deceiving, especially if he was the type to commit a hit-and-run.

"I have an idea I'd like to check out," Elizabeth said, picking up her cup and holding it in both hands while she braced her elbows on the table. She turned her gaze to Emma. "While I'm doing that, maybe you could speak to Abel and Zach about keeping an extra eye on the cows' food?"

"I will, for sure and for certain." Emma eyed Rachel meekly. "And maybe you *could* ask Adam what I should do about cleansing the taste of the onions from the milk?"

A smile spread across Rachel's face. "I will be happy to. And Emma, I know you want to prove to your father that you are capable of running the farm, but do not let pride get a foothold in your heart, ja? There is no shame in admitting you need help."

Emma's head bowed. "Danki, Rachel. Your words are wise. I will think on them."

With that settled, the conversation turned to more pleasant things, and Elizabeth enjoyed the rest of her coffee while Rachel told Emma about some of the ideas the members of the quilting circle had come up with to help out while Moses mended.

"I cannot thank you all enough," Emma said, happy tears making her eyes shine. "I will tell Daed about the meal train and let him know there will be someone coming by to deliver the food."

"*Goot.*" Rachel pushed back from the table. "And I will send Hannah on Thursday to help with your wash day."

"You are certain you can spare her?" Emma asked, rising at the same time as Elizabeth.

Rachel gave a quick nod. "It is no hardship. My Hannah is a good worker. She will make sure the laundry is done to your liking."

A soft laugh burst from Emma's lips. "At this point, my liking is just to have fewer clothes piled on the floor."

There was plenty of truth in the wry statement, Elizabeth realized. Housework had a way of piling up when there was a sick loved one to look after. She rounded the table and walked with Rachel and Emma to the door.

Pausing when they reached it, Elizabeth glanced over her shoulder. "Goodbye, Emma. I'll stop in a day or two to let you know how things are going."

"Danki, Elizabeth." Emma took hold of Rachel's arm and gave it a pat. "Please thank the ladies from the quilting circle again for us. Daed and I will always remember their kindness."

"Of course."

Rachel's answer carried such conviction that it warmed Elizabeth's heart. Here again was another example of the people of their community caring for one another in times of need. Now, if she and her sisters could do their part and figure out how the onions had gotten into the Troyers' feeders, she'd feel much better.

After dropping Rachel off at home, Elizabeth returned to the farm, where she was greeted by a herd of Classen family pets. Though not as boisterous as Sugarpie, Mary's dachshund, Tinkerbelle, let loose a string of happy howls that made Elizabeth smile as she pushed past the family border collie, Pal, to hang her coat on a hook near the door.

Hearing a clatter rise from the kitchen, Elizabeth stepped out of her boots and moved down the hall. Martha was hard at work, elbow-deep in a sink full of suds.

"What's all this?" Elizabeth motioned to the mountainous pile of baking pans stacked precariously next to Martha. "Where did all these dishes come from?"

Martha lifted her arm to brush away a damp tendril clinging to her forehead. "I've been baking, trying to make up for the stuff I had to throw away this afternoon."

Elizabeth's shoulders sank. "Oh, Martha, I would have helped. You should have waited for me."

Martha shrugged and went back to scrubbing. "I figured there was no sense putting it off. Any luck finding out what happened at the Troyers' farm?"

"Maybe." Elizabeth took the scrub brush from Martha's fingers and bumped her aside with her hip.

"And?"

"It's not good, I'm afraid. It looks like the Troyers' cows may have gotten ahold of some onions."

Martha grabbed a towel and a baking sheet and started drying. "What does that have to do with their milk?"

"According to Emma, if the cows eat onions it will give the milk a bad flavor. But that's not the worst part."

"Oh? What's the worst part?"

Elizabeth slid the clean pan into the rinse water then rested her arms on the edge of the sink. "Apparently, someone put the onions into the feeders on purpose."

Martha slowed the towel over the baking sheet. "What? Why would anyone do that?"

"That's what I came home to try and find out." Reaching for another pan, Elizabeth frowned. "What was that you were telling me about Beau Hegel?"

"The young man the witness says forced Moses off the road?"

Elizabeth nodded. "How much do you know about him?"

Martha's brow furrowed thoughtfully as she put the baking sheet away. "Well, he works at Russell's Feed and Supply, the feed store over in Lancaster. I only know because I ran into him one time while I was there buying food for the goats."

Elizabeth made a mental note of the place and went back to scrubbing. "You said something about his uncle. What about his other family? Know anything about them?"

"Not much. His mother is a teacher, I think, and his father passed away several years ago."

Elizabeth stopped scrubbing to tip her head, thinking. "Several years ago" meant Beau had lost his father at a young age, which might explain why his uncle felt compelled to keep bailing him out of trouble. In the absence of his brother, Clyde Hegel would have wanted to watch over his nephew, maybe protect him in a misguided, fatherlike way.

Elizabeth finished up the stack of pans then rinsed out the dish towel and got started wiping down the countertops. "You know, Martha, I think I'm going to drive out to Lancaster tomorrow, just to see if I can have a word with Beau. I'm not saying he was behind the onions in the Troyers' field, but I would like to meet him face-to-face, maybe get my own impression of him. If possible, I'd like to find out what he's like and who he hangs around with."

Martha finished storing the last of the baking pans and then pushed the cupboard door closed. "Okay. Anything you need me to do?"

"I don't think so, other than keeping an ear open for news of the case." Elizabeth turned to rest her hip against the sink. "I'm curious if Beau's uncle will get involved, or if he really will let his nephew deal with this mess on his own."

"I'll see what I can find out," Martha said, giving a nod as she ducked out of the kitchen.

Left alone, Elizabeth shook the crumbs out of the dish towel then draped it over the edge of the sink to dry. Talking to Beau and learning about his friends wasn't a whole lot to go on, but at least it was a start. And in a case this peculiar, that was something.

Even if it wasn't much.

# CHAPTER SIX

The sun settled warmly on Mary's shoulders as she exited the church doors and started down the steps. With the sermon still ringing in her ears, the air seemed crisper and more inviting, the call of the birds more cheerful and lilting. She picked out a sparrow warbling from a nearby tree, his round little body stark against the branches aflame with orange leaves, and watched as he took flight.

*Behold the fowls of the air: for they sow not, neither do they reap, nor gather into barns; yet your heavenly Father feedeth them. Are ye not much better than they? Which of you by taking thought can add one cubit unto his stature?*

The verse was a familiar one, but in light of the trouble with her little grandson, the pastor's message had held particular meaning this morning. And the last part of the passage, even more so.

*Take therefore no thought for the morrow: for the morrow shall take thought for the things of itself. Sufficient unto the day is the evil thereof.*

She dragged in a deep breath and blew it out. "Okay, Lord. I hear You." She frowned. "I guess that's not the same as listening, is it? Help me to do both."

"Mary, hold up."

At the sound of Gladys Turner's voice, Mary paused and glanced over her shoulder. Gladys was a choir member and frequent visitor to Secondhand Blessings.

"I'm glad I caught you," Gladys said, huffing as she lumbered down the steps, one hand gripping tightly to the railing. "I was afraid you would scoot out before I could put my choir robe away."

"Well, good morning." Mary held out her hand to help Gladys down the final step. "The choir sounded wonderful today."

"Thank you, Mary, but we missed your sweet voice up there. Will you be joining us again soon?"

"Maybe next week," she agreed.

"Good." Laying her hand against her chest, Gladys took a couple of deep breaths and then tossed a quick glance around. "Do you have a minute to talk? I really wanted to ask you about what's been going on at the store."

"Our store?" Mary's eyebrows rose and just as quickly settled back into place. "Oh, you mean the baked goods. You must have bought some of the ones that came out of the bad batch."

She chose her words carefully, preferring not to reveal the root cause of the "bad batch." To her surprise, Gladys shook her head.

"No, I didn't buy any. I've been out of town visiting my daughter the last few days or I certainly might have. I just love Martha's baking. But I did see the review some lady posted on your Facebook page. It wasn't exactly complimentary."

Mary's heart sank. It had taken her months to convince Elizabeth and Martha that they should have a Facebook page, and now this had to happen. Bad reviews were a hazard of any business, but so far, theirs had managed to avoid negative feedback, mostly because she and her sisters only stocked quality merchandise but still agreed to let people return things they weren't happy with. It all came down to good customer service.

She swallowed hastily and shook her head. "No, I'm afraid I haven't seen it, Gladys."

"Oh? Some lady posted that she was very disappointed with some muffins she bought there. Said she wouldn't be back and couldn't believe people actually recommended Martha's baking. I assume that was a reference to comments other people had left."

Gladys's lips thinned, her arms folding like pretzels inside the sleeves of her jacket. "Well, I hopped on right away and posted a positive review so her comments aren't the first thing people see when they look up your store. I also made sure to let people know that rotten muffins weren't typical for you all. Of course, that's not what I called them. That was the word the other lady used in her review. I would never say something so rude about Martha's cooking. Goodness, talking about it has me flustered all over again." She pulled the church bulletin out from the pages of her Bible and fanned her face with it.

Gladys's remarks and the tone of her voice had begun to draw attention. Mary grasped her arm and guided her away from the crowd and onto the sidewalk.

"It was very nice of you to post a positive review, Gladys. I sure appreciate you looking out for us."

"Of course. I just love all three of you Classen girls." Her eyes widened. "You'll look up that review I told you about?"

"I'll do it as soon as I get home."

"Good. And maybe we can ask some of our church friends to go online and post some positive reviews as well. I hear that kind of thing can be a big help to a struggling business."

*Struggling?* Mary bit back her protest. Secondhand Blessings wasn't struggling. Plus, she wasn't so sure she wanted everyone in Bird-in-Hand talking about their minor mishap and tracing it back to the Troyers. But Gladys had a good heart, and her intentions were kind. Mary offered a smile.

"You're very sweet, Gladys. Thank you."

"No problem." Gladys lifted her chin. "Whoever posted that mean review obviously isn't from around here."

"She was just stating her opinion," Mary reminded Gladys gently, "but I appreciate you sticking up for us. I'll talk to you later, okay?"

She eased away and set off in search of her sisters. Poor Martha! Mary hadn't seen her since Sunday school, but hopefully she hadn't been bombarded with news of the review as well. Martha was very proud of her baking, and something like this would likely hurt her feelings.

Back inside the church, the people lingering in the halls had dwindled to a few handfuls. Mary had heard John offer to drive Elizabeth home. Figuring Martha had headed there too, Mary returned to her car and made her way there as well. As she thought, Martha was already puttering around the kitchen preparing lunch when Mary went inside.

"There you are. We were wondering where you went." Elizabeth stepped out of her shoes and pushed her arms into the sleeves of a thick sweater. "What were you and Gladys Turner talking about? It looked pretty serious."

"That's because it was." Mary hung up her coat, grabbed Elizabeth's hand, and pulled her into the living room. "Did anyone talk to you about someone posting a bad Facebook review?"

"Someone posted a bad review about the store?" Elizabeth shook her head. "No, I didn't hear anything."

"The store...and Martha's baking in particular."

"Uh-oh." Elizabeth frowned. "Does Martha know?"

"That's what I wanted to ask you," Mary said.

"If she does, she didn't say anything." Elizabeth thought a second and then shook her head. "No, she's in too good a mood to have heard anything about it this morning. Stuff like that really bothers Martha."

"I know." Mary opened the browser on her phone. "Let's see what it says."

Mary navigated to Facebook and found the review Gladys had been talking about. She and Elizabeth hunched closely together while they read silently to themselves.

*This was my first visit to this quaint little store. The exterior was cute and everything was laid out very well.*

Elizabeth drew back to look at Mary. "That first part sounds promising."

"Keep reading." Mary pointed to the second part of the review.

*Unfortunately, that is the only good thing I can say about Secondhand Blessings. The staff seemed distracted and it took a while for me to get checked out. That may have been due to the number of customers. It was pretty busy when I went in.*

Mary ground her teeth as she read. "At least she admits we didn't ignore her on purpose."

"Shh. I'm not done yet."

Mary wasn't either. She read the last few lines with a lump in her throat.

*The worst part was the muffins I bought for my first book club meeting. They looked delicious, and I had really high hopes but was sorely disappointed when I brought them home. Don't buy the baked goods from Secondhand Blessings unless you don't mind rotten muffins spoiling your plans! As a side note, the rest of the store was nice. The management may just want to look into hiring a different baker.*

"Wow," Elizabeth said when she finished.

"No kidding." Mary slid her phone back into her pocket. "No wonder Gladys was so upset. I am too. This lady didn't even give us a chance to try and make things right."

"In her defense, it was her first book club meeting that was ruined. She probably didn't have time to run back to the store and didn't want to risk getting another bad batch even if she did."

"You're right." Mary snapped her fingers. "Why don't we leave a comment offering to give the lady her money back?"

Elizabeth sucked a sharp breath through her teeth. "I don't know. Everything I've ever read says not to respond to bad reviews."

"Except this is a little different. We won't try to explain what happened. We'll just apologize and let her know we'll make every effort to make it up to her. I've seen businesses do that before."

After a moment, Elizabeth nodded. "I guess that would be all right."

"Good, that's settled. Now, should we tell Martha?"

"I'd rather it be us than someone springing it on her around town, and eventually, someone will."

"You're right." Mary sighed and combed her fingers through her hair. "I guess I should be the one to tell her since Gladys talked to me, and it might as well be now."

"No sense putting it off," Elizabeth agreed.

Mary took a breath and turned into the hall, Elizabeth's steps a dull echo behind hers against the wood floor.

"There you two are." Martha set a tray of sliced meat on the table next to a loaf of homemade bread and a jar of mayo. "I hope you're both okay with sandwiches. I've got lettuce here, tomatoes and onions sliced on the counter, and cheese in the fridge."

Elizabeth nodded. "Sandwiches are fine, Martha."

"Good. Is Bill or John joining us today?"

"Not today," Mary said. "Bill is helping set up for the youth lock-in at church."

"And John already had other plans," Elizabeth said, then directed a nod of encouragement to Mary.

Mary grabbed the cheese out of the refrigerator and handed it to Martha. "Thanks for getting everything ready, but before we get started, there's something I need to show you." She motioned to the table. "Okay if we sit down for a minute?"

Martha shot her a quizzical glance and another at Elizabeth. "I guess so. What's going on?"

Mary explained about the review then pulled it up on her phone for Martha to read. When she finished, Mary covered her hand and squeezed. "I'm really sorry, Martha. Try not to take that review personally."

At her words, pinched lines formed around Martha's lips. Her reputation as a baker was at stake. How could she not take the reviewer's words personally?

Mary pushed on. "If it helps, Elizabeth and I already talked about responding to the person and offering to give her money back."

"Yes, that would only be right." Martha took a deep breath in through her nose and blew it out of her mouth. "Well, that's a bummer, but I guess I shouldn't be surprised."

"What?" Mary and Elizabeth asked in unison.

"The muffins must have been pretty bad, though I would say calling them rotten is a little extreme."

"That's true," Mary said, carefully. She pulled her hand from Martha's and laid it in her lap. Her sister was taking this much better than expected.

Elizabeth's face mirrored the same doubt Mary felt. "Are you sure you're okay, Martha? Mary and I didn't want to hurt your feelings. We just thought we should say something to you before somebody else did."

"I'm fine." Martha's chin lifted, and she tilted her head stubbornly. "Bad reviews are just words, and that's nothing compared to what the Troyers are going through." She looked at Mary. "I really do like the idea of offering this lady her money back, but maybe we could go one step further and give her store credit for her trouble on top of that. She may not buy any more baked goods from us, but at least she'll know we are genuinely sorry about what happened."

"I think that's a wonderful idea, Martha," Mary said.

"Me too," Elizabeth seconded.

"Good. Then let's eat." Martha pushed up from her chair and grabbed the mustard and mayonnaise from the refrigerator. "Elizabeth, are you still planning on driving over to Lancaster today to talk to Beau?"

Elizabeth nodded and grabbed a knife to slice the bread. "I thought I'd head out after we're done with lunch." She paused midslice and looked up. "Are you thinking about coming with me?"

"If you wouldn't mind." Martha set the lettuce down and pressed her hand to her hip, her fingers drumming thoughtfully. "You know, it's been pretty muddy with all the rain lately. If we can figure out which vehicle belongs to Beau, maybe it wouldn't hurt to check it out."

"See if maybe he's taken it down some long gravel driveways, you mean?" Mary shot a wink at Elizabeth.

Martha smiled. "Exactly."

Mary smiled back, a feeling of relief filling her. No doubt Martha didn't like hearing she'd been the object of a bad review, but she wouldn't let it keep her from focusing on the real problem—which was pinpointing anyone who might have a grudge against the Troyers. Apart from that, only one other thing mattered...and that was figuring out what she and her sisters could do to stop them.

# CHAPTER SEVEN

The first thing that hit Elizabeth's senses when she walked into Russell's Feed and Supply was the sweet, earthy odor of sawdust. The second was a conglomeration of deer corn, hay, pet food, and…unpackaged cookies? She picked one out of a bin and brought it to her nose. Molasses.

"Smells good, right?" Smiling, a woman in blue jeans and a fuzzy beige sweater topped by an apron bearing the Russell's logo signaled to the cookie in Elizabeth's hand. "That's one of our most popular homemade doggie treats."

"Homemade, you say?" Elizabeth dropped the treat back into the bin and brushed the crumbs from her fingers.

The woman nodded. "They're made right here in Lancaster. All organic. And they're on sale." She pointed to a sign fixed to the side of the bin. "We sell them by the pound."

Elizabeth glanced at the figure, then looked again, her eyes widening. She loved their pets, but Pal and Tink wouldn't be getting any organic doggie treats anytime soon. "Um, okay. Thank you."

"No problem. Let me know if you need help finding anything."

"Actually—" Elizabeth stopped her before she could leave. "Would you mind telling me if Beau Hegel is working today?"

"Beau? Yes, he's here. He works in Lawn and Garden. That way." The woman's ponytail swung as she half turned to jab her thumb over her shoulder.

"Thank you," Elizabeth said, her gaze following in the direction the woman pointed. Behind her, the double doors slid open. Martha ducked inside and wound past the rows of cash registers to Elizabeth's side.

"Well, I found the employee parking lot, but Beau's red Mustang wasn't in it. Are you sure he's working today?"

"According to the lady I just talked to, he is." Elizabeth motioned toward the lawn and garden area. "Let's go see if we can find him."

She skirted a tower of tomato cages and proceeded down a long aisle stocked with weed killer, seed starters, and all manner of hoses.

"So, have you thought about what you're going to say to him if we find him?" Martha asked, hurrying to match Elizabeth's stride.

"Not really," Elizabeth admitted. Mostly, she just wanted to get a look at him. Not that one could tell everything about a person just by glancing at them. There was a saying about a book and its cover, after all. Still, she had inherited some of her father's keen sense when it came to feeling a person out. Maybe talking with Beau would give her an idea of the kind of man he was—one who'd made a mistake and regretted running a man off the road, or one who'd made a mistake and would do anything to cover it up.

Elizabeth spotted Beau the second she emerged from the aisle. He was helping a woman load a large bag of birdseed into a shopping cart. Grabbing Martha's arm, Elizabeth pointed.

"There he is."

"Huh. I wonder what he's driving."

Elizabeth blinked and looked at her.

"It's not the Mustang," Martha prompted gently. "It wasn't in the parking lot."

Elizabeth shrugged and directed her attention back to Beau. "He's a lot younger than I expected. I was picturing someone in his midtwenties."

Beau's gaze swung their way, and both Elizabeth and Martha shrank against a display of garden pavers. Elizabeth quickly realized he wasn't looking at them. He tilted his head and listened patiently while the customer with him explained what she wanted.

"I'm thinking something in ground, with maybe a layer or two of brick surrounding it to keep the children from accidently tripping into it," the woman said. "The fire pit we have now is one of those cast-iron jobs, but it's just too small. I want something a little bigger and heavier duty."

"Have you had a chance to check out our displays?"

"Not yet. Would you mind showing me what you've got?"

"Not at all. Right this way."

Beau stepped around the woman's cart and made a beeline for the aisle where Elizabeth and Martha stood. Once again, his gaze swung their way, only this time, it connected with Elizabeth's. She managed a slight nod then grabbed Martha's arm and moved a few steps down the aisle. For several minutes, she perused bags of lava rock and pretended not to listen while Beau explained the different types of fire pits the store carried in stock.

Mostly, he was knowledgeable and patient, two characteristics that struck Elizabeth as unexpected—a reaction she immediately chided herself for. She didn't know Beau, but she had let herself form a poor opinion of him, however subliminally. Another part of her argued that he'd driven off and left another man injured, which said something of character. Or did it? She wasn't privy to the details of the incident that forced Moses off the road. What if the witness was wrong? Or what if Beau had an explanation for what happened they simply had not heard yet?

She angled her head toward Martha to whisper. "We should go."

"I thought you wanted to talk to him?"

"I do. I did. What I mean is—"

"Can I help you, ladies?" Beau's voice made both of them jump. Whirling, Elizabeth faced him first, and then Martha.

"No, thank you," Elizabeth said.

"We're just looking," Martha added. And then, "You're Beau Hegel, aren't you?"

"I am." He looked from Martha to Elizabeth. "Do I know you ladies?"

Elizabeth shook her head. "Probably not. We own Secondhand Blessings."

"I know that place." He wagged his finger at them. "The store in the old Classen family barn."

"Yes, that's us," Martha said.

Beau stuck out his hand, his grip confident but not too firm as he shook Elizabeth's hand, and then Martha's. "Nice to meet you ladies. I've heard good things about your place."

Not recently, Elizabeth thought, grimacing as the words from the review Gladys shared with them popped into her head. Beau's eyebrows rose, and she realized he'd been speaking to her. Her gaze flicked to Martha and back. "I'm sorry?"

A smile spread across his face. Winsome. Charming. Infectious. "I was just wondering if you two were looking for anything in particular?" No trace of irritation laced his voice at having had to repeat himself.

"To be honest," Elizabeth began, and then stopped when a man with a decided limp approached, jangling a set of car keys.

"Beau. Hey man, here are your keys. I put the Mustang back by the loading docks where I found it."

Dressed in worn denim jeans with holes at the knees and a plaid shirt under a dirty brown Carhartt jacket, the man looked too casual to be an employee of the feed store. He flipped the keys to Beau, who smiled and caught them midair.

"Thanks, Jack." Beau angled his head at Jack and narrowed his eyes. "Did you remember to polish the rims like I asked?"

"Dude, of course." Jack actually looked offended before his wide mouth stretched in a grin. "But I gotta say, your ride was covered in mud. Never seen it like that before. I should have charged you extra." He elbowed Beau playfully and then turned to Martha and Elizabeth. "Apparently, I'm going to have to introduce myself." He flashed a droll look at Beau and extended his hand. "Jack Byler, of Byler's Detailing."

He removed two business cards from an inside coat pocket and held them out smoothly. Shooting a glance at Martha,

Elizabeth took one and read the front. "Auto Detailing Specialist?"

"That's me." Jack's chest puffed proudly. "Been in business almost ten years. If either of you ladies would like to have your car detailed, give me a call. I'll work you a deal, seeing as you're friends of Beau's." He jerked his sleeve up to glance at his watch then shook his head. "Well, I'd better be going. I've got two more cars I gotta squeeze in before supper. And Beau, let me know the next time you decide to take the 'stang off-roading, eh? I'll be sure to leave myself a little extra time to get 'er done."

Rather than answer, Beau merely snorted and shoved his keys into the pocket of his jeans. "See ya later, Jack."

"Later, Beau. Ladies." Jack tipped his head and spun, disappearing around the corner as quickly as he'd appeared.

"Sorry about that." Beau's lips curled in a wry grin as he shot a glance both ways down the aisle. "We're really not supposed to handle personal business while we're on the clock." He hitched his thumb down the aisle Jack had taken. "The boss doesn't complain too much about it since Jack cleans his car too, but I don't want to press my luck."

"A man who comes to you to wash your car." Martha scratched her head. "I've never heard of such a thing. Windshield repairmen, maybe."

"It's a pretty smart move, actually. His business has almost doubled since he started what he calls his pickup service." He nodded to the card in Elizabeth's hand. "You just call to schedule your appointment, and then he picks up your car, takes it to his shop and gets it all cleaned up, then parks it right back where you left it."

"That is interesting," Elizabeth said. "I'll have to keep him in mind the next time I need my car washed."

From the corner of her eye, she saw Martha cast her a knowing glance. It wasn't the washing part that had captured Elizabeth's attention, it was what Jack had said about the mud on Beau's car and the joking comment about taking it off road.

*Off road* could mean a lot of things—across a pasture. Over a two track.

Or down a long gravel drive like the one that led to the Troyers' farm.

# CHAPTER EIGHT

Mary pushed away the pile of bills she was sorting and smiled as her tablet lit up and Nick's round, chubby face filled the screen. After swiping it up, she answered the video call with a cheery hello.

"How's my favorite grandson this morning?" Mary asked, cooing with delight as Nick giggled and stuck his fingers in his mouth, drool running down his wrist onto his sweater.

Michael's face popped into the picture next to Nick's. "Mom, he's your only grandson."

"That makes him my favorite," she replied, then glanced at the clock in the corner of her screen. "Why aren't you at work?"

"Who, me? Or Nick?" Michael snorted and pulled Nick close to bounce him on his knee. "Just kidding. I took the day off to let Heidi rest."

"Uh-oh. Nick still not sleeping through the night?"

"No." Michael sighed and rubbed his knuckles over the scruff on his cheek. "Poor little guy. He always wakes up around the same time, then stays awake screaming his head off for at least an hour."

"Ugh. I'm sorry. Did the warm water bottle help at all? I told Heidi to try putting it on his tummy."

"Yeah, it helped a little."

"Good. And I talked to our neighbor, Rachel Fischer. She said peppermint or ginger are good natural remedies. Maybe you can ask your doctor?"

"I'll pass that along to Heidi." Nick began to fuss, so Michael picked him up and switched him to his shoulder. "How are things at the store? Heidi said she saw a bad review someone posted. What was that all about?"

"Yes, that's true." Mary explained about the milk and the resulting effect on Martha's baked goods, which had led Elizabeth to the discovery of the onions. "It's so sad. After all the trouble the Troyers have had, I would hate to think that someone might have done this on purpose."

Nick reached for Michael's nose. Michael avoided his grasping fingers and frowned. "Any idea who?"

"We have a couple of leads. Nothing concrete." She shook thoughts of the Troyers away and touched the screen. "When is Nick's next doctor's appointment?"

"Next week…if we make it until then." He mugged for Nick and then snuffled the baby's belly—his smaller, less pudgy belly.

Mary leaned closer to the screen. "Um, Michael, has Nick been losing weight?"

Guilt flashed across her son's face as he flipped Nick around to settle him on his lap. "Uh…yeah. A little. We didn't tell you because we didn't want you to worry."

Mary waved dismissively. "How much has he lost? He looks so thin."

Michael hesitated and lifted one shoulder in a sheepish shrug. "Only a couple of pounds so far."

"So far!" Mary sat up straight then forced a calming breath into her lungs.

"The doctor is keeping a close eye on it," Michael assured her quickly. "We're worried too, Mom. We're doing everything we can."

"I know you are." Mary blew a breath through her lips then grabbed a pen and fiddled with the clasp on the top. "Do you think I should come spend a few days with you and Heidi? I could help with the baby, maybe give you both a break."

"You know we always love having you visit," Michael began, and then shook his head. "But I don't want to pull you away from the store. Plus, we'll see you over Thanksgiving."

"That's weeks away," Mary protested. She set down the pen and fingered the edge of the tablet. "You know I don't mind coming, Michael."

"I know you don't, Mom."

He said it firmly, but with a warmth that brought tears to Mary's eyes.

"Okay," she said at last. "But you will let me know if the baby gets any worse?"

"Of course we will."

Mary's gaze settled on her beloved grandson's face. Something was definitely wrong. Why couldn't they figure out what?

Rather than giving in to the fear nudging her heart, Mary said goodbye, blew several kisses to Nick, and then spent the rest of the morning praying while she went about her business at the store. Fortunately, foot traffic was light, so she could focus on asking for answers for her grandson while she straightened shelves and swept the floor. By noon, she was tired and hungry, but her peace had been restored.

"Ready for a break?" Martha took the broom from Mary's hands. "I made a big pot of potato and cheddar soup if you're hungry."

"Starving." She glanced toward the door. "Aren't you coming?"

"Nah. Emma Troyer is supposed to be coming by with another order of milk. I figured I'd wait until she gets here before I head back up."

Elizabeth had already taken her lunch with John, so Mary pulled her apron over her head, laid it on the counter, and made her way up to the house alone. As soon as she stepped into the kitchen, the savory aroma of garlic and bacon filled her nose, making her mouth water and her stomach rumble.

She dished up a bowl and carried it to the kitchen table, but the doorbell rang before she could sit down to enjoy it.

"Coming," Mary called above the chorus raised by Tinkerbelle and Pal as they scrambled to see who was at the door.

Scooping up Tink, Mary urged Pal to sit and then reached for the knob. Emma stood on the porch, a crate packed with milk jugs in her arms.

"Oh, Emma, Martha said you were coming." Mary pushed the door wide and stepped back to make room for Emma to pass. "She's still down at the store."

Emma hesitated on the stoop. "Is this okay? I can take it down—"

"No, no, bring it inside," Mary urged, setting Tink down.

The dachshund scurried down the porch steps with Pal hot on her heels. On a day like today, with a breeze sending leaves scuttling across the yard and only a slight nip in the air to mark the season, it would be a while before she could coax the two back inside.

"Come on in," Mary said again, holding the door wider. "We can take that straight back to the kitchen."

"I appreciate you and your sisters trusting me enough to purchase more milk and cream," Emma said, following Mary down the hall. "I simply cannot believe someone would put onions in our cows' food."

"It is a shame," Mary agreed. "I hope you and your father have taken some precautions?"

"Other than keeping a closer eye on the cows, there is not a whole lot more we can do," Emma admitted. She set the lug on the counter and then shook out her hands. "We have already cleaned all of the feeding cages and thrown away any food we thought was affected. We even made sure all of the milk we sent out for delivery is from the cows not exposed to the onions. We'll continue milking the others, but it may be a few days before they give good milk again."

"Sounds like a good plan."

"Ja. Abel is making a few extra rounds before he goes home for the night, and I have been getting up earlier than normal to check the food before I give it to the cows."

Extra labor the Troyers didn't need. Mary shook her head sadly. "Is there anything my sisters and I can do?"

Emma patted the milk jugs. "You are already doing it." Her brows rose. "Can I put these in the refrigerator for you?"

"No need. I'll take care of it," Mary said. "I'm still on my lunch break, so I have plenty of time."

Emma's gaze drifted past her to the stove and then the bowl of soup still steaming on the table. "Oh, I am so sorry."

She quickly removed the milk jugs and then grabbed the lug off the counter. "I will not keep you."

Remembering what her sisters had said about Beau getting his car detailed, Mary put her hand out to stop Emma from leaving. "Um, if you have a second?"

Eyes wide, she nodded.

"Emma, have you, by chance, noticed Beau Hegel's car around your farm?"

Her brow furrowed. "You mean besides the time he came by to speak to Daed?"

"Beau came to talk to Moses?" Mary angled her head curiously. "Was that before or after the accident?"

"After."

"Do you know what it was about?"

"He said he wanted to apologize." Her tone and her pressed lips said she didn't quite believe him. "They only talked a moment, and then Beau got upset and left."

"But you don't know what he said?"

Emma shook her head. "Daed refused to speak of it."

"So he was upset too."

"Very."

Mary placed a light touch on Emma's arm. "Thank you."

Emma's head dipped in a hesitant nod. "Will you please tell Martha I will make another delivery on Thursday—that is, if she still wants me to."

"I'll tell her."

"Danki. And…" She bit her lip and dropped her gaze.

"Emma? What is it?"

She looked up. "Rachel told me your grandson has been having trouble with tummy aches."

Mary nodded. "Yes, that's true."

Emma seemed to think a moment and then sucked in a deep breath. "When we were *kinner*, my *maam* used to mix a couple of drops of vinegar in half an ounce of water before each meal. She said it helped with digestion."

"Really." Mary grabbed a pencil and scribbled the information on a scrap of paper. "I've got it. Thank you so much, Emma."

"You are welcome. I hope it helps," she added shyly.

Mary smiled. "Me too."

Giving a wave, Emma set off for the door. Rather than returning to her soup, Mary called Heidi and relayed the simple home remedy Emma had shared.

Vinegar and water. It wasn't much, but at this point, they were all willing to try anything. As she hung up, the irony didn't escape her.…

Every now and then, a person had to swallow something bitter in the hope that something sweeter would follow.

# CHAPTER NINE

Elizabeth felt a happy little tingle in her middle as John swung the car door wide and reached in to take her hand and help her out. Dinner with John was always a fun, relaxing time, but she was especially looking forward to the cozy little restaurant he had found nestled in a corner of an old warehouse in downtown Lancaster.

Around the eaves and tucked into vintage barrels, white lights twinkled from grapevine garland. Across the window fixed to the top half of the entrance, the name Jillian's glinted in gold lettering, but before they could even reach it, the door swung open and a man in black slacks and matching shirt and tie welcomed them in. He held out his hands to Elizabeth.

"May I take your coat?"

"Yes, thank you."

In the blink of an eye, the man slipped the coat from her shoulders. As he strode toward the coatroom, Elizabeth angled her head to whisper, "Oh, John, this place is wonderful. How have we never heard of it before?"

A smile twinkled in the depths of John's blue eyes. "A friend told me about it. I hoped you'd like it."

Elizabeth inhaled deeply, her stomach rumbling at the smell of butter and garlic, sizzling steak, and marinara. "Italian? How could I not?"

Smiling, John gave the name on their reservation to the hostess and then took Elizabeth's elbow as they were led to their table. Already, several couples occupied the tables dotting the polished marble floor, but the one nearest the fireplace still sat vacant, and it was to this their hostess led them to be seated.

Elizabeth motioned to the chandeliers glinting overhead and the beautiful artwork hanging from the walls, which should have been at odds with the exposed beams and black ductwork, and yet was so perfectly complimentary. "All of this *and* a cozy fire?" She sighed happily and picked up her menu. "I'm going to enjoy this."

Her words seemed to delight John, who went to great lengths to keep her entertained throughout their meal—which was in fact delicious—and regaled her with stories of the calls the police station had received over their dessert and coffee.

Finally, Elizabeth set down her fork and pushed away the last few bites of her molten lava cake. "That's it. If I eat one more bite, I won't fit in the car."

John reached across the table to place a light touch on her hand. "That may have been my plan all along, you know."

Her heart fluttered at the slow smile that curved his lips.

He angled his head toward a couple of patrons seated alone at the bar. "I've been noticing several glances directed this way. I may have been trying to ply you with food just to keep all those other fellows at bay."

He was joking, but even so, Elizabeth had never been comfortable with compliments about her looks. A blush warmed her cheeks as she pulled her hand away and laid it in her lap.

"If they're looking," she began softly, "it probably has nothing to do with me and everything to do with the review some lady gave the store."

"What?" John frowned and picked up his coffee cup. "What review?"

Elizabeth explained about the Troyers' milk and the review that had followed about Martha's baking.

"That couldn't have made Martha very happy," John said when she finished.

"Actually, she was more concerned about the Troyers, as are we all." Elizabeth plucked at the edge of her linen napkin. John was a police officer for East Lampeter Township. If anyone knew the kind of trouble Beau Hegel was capable of, it would be him. "John, how well do you know the Hegel family?"

He took a sip of his coffee then set his cup down and leaned forward to rest his elbows on the table. "Clyde Hegel, you mean? I've known him all my life. Clyde, his brother Blake, and I used to play ball together in high school."

"Blake Hegel…was that Beau Hegel's father?"

John's gaze dropped to his cup, and he ran his thumb slowly around the rim. "That's him."

"I heard he passed away when Beau was young."

"Yeah. Cancer. It was a hard time for the family." There was more than sadness in John's voice. Regret lingered there too.

"You really like that family," Elizabeth said quietly.

John paused, and after a second, gave a slight shrug. "Let's just say I'm sorry for the trouble they're going through now."

"Do you know Beau well?" Elizabeth pressed, matching his posture by placing her elbows on the table.

"Not really. He followed in his dad's footsteps by playing football. I went to several of his games. He was good."

This was news. Elizabeth raised her eyebrows. "How good?"

"He landed a scholarship to Penn State, if that tells you anything."

But he'd never attended, so far as Elizabeth knew. "I don't understand. What happened? Why didn't he use his scholarship?"

John appeared to think a moment, then pushed his empty coffee cup away. "It happened two years ago, after he graduated high school. He went out drinking with a couple of his buddies. They were in a car accident, and Beau tore up his knee pretty good, broke his ankle too."

"Oh no."

John nodded. "He wasn't the same after he recovered, lost some of the blazing speed that made him such a prize."

"And the scholarship?"

"He lost that too."

Elizabeth bit her lip, thinking. "So, the accident. Was this one of the times that Beau's uncle bailed him out of trouble?"

"Clyde never would admit to it, but that's the rumor," John said, his face hard.

Sensing he didn't want to answer any more questions and unwilling to spoil what remained of their time together, Elizabeth decided to change the subject to a more pleasant topic.

Extending her arms, she smiled and pushed back against the table. "So, about my birthday."

John's face brightened, the glow from the flickering fire reflected in his eyes. "Have you thought any more about how you would like to celebrate?"

"I have, actually." Elizabeth smiled and clasped both hands under her chin. "Do you remember that flea market over in Lebanon you told me about?"

He grinned. "The Dancing Dutchman."

"That's the one."

Laughing, John grabbed a packet of sugar and slid his cup to the edge of the table for the waitress to refill. "Okay, I get it. I'll take a look at their calendar and pick out a Saturday when we can go. I've heard that place is huge. We'll leave early and make a day of it."

"Great. Thanks, John."

Glad to see his good humor restored, Elizabeth basked in the warmth of the fire at her back and the soft music swirling around them. Not that John was ever ill-mannered or cross, but he wore the mantle that came with his position at the station humbly and took his responsibilities seriously. Sometimes too seriously, which made Elizabeth wish she could lift some of the weight from his shoulders when he looked especially weary.

She blinked at the rush of emotion that accompanied the thought and took a hasty swallow from her coffee cup. John was a kind, moral man and a good friend. Which was nice except…she wanted more. But did he?

# CHAPTER TEN

Elizabeth put the final polish on a pair of brass candlesticks and then placed them on a shelf next to a row of vintage Christmas stocking holders, also done in gleaming brass.

"That looks beautiful," Martha said, scooting around Elizabeth, a basket of homemade clover rolls in her arms.

"Thanks." Giving the candlesticks one final flick with the polishing rag for good measure, Elizabeth smiled and followed Martha to the bakery counter. "Are those proceeds going to the Troyers?"

Martha nodded and set the box on the counter. "I took the order yesterday from a woman up in Lancaster. She's supposed to be coming by this afternoon to pick them up."

Tucking the invoice into one corner of the box, Martha smiled. "That's the third order so far."

"Apparently that review didn't hurt your reputation as an excellent baker too much."

"Maybe not," Martha said, a slight blush coloring her cheeks. "Anyway, between orders and counter sales, I have almost two hundred dollars to deliver to the Troyers." She frowned. "Not sure when I'll have time to take it to them though. I still have several batches of cookies and cupcakes I need to get done for tomorrow morning."

"That's a big order," Elizabeth said.

Martha nodded. "One of the churches is having their harvest festival tomorrow night and asked me to help out with the goodie bags."

"That's awesome."

"It will be if I can get them all done."

"I'll be glad to help," Elizabeth offered. "What time do you plan on getting started?"

"Actually..." Martha slid an envelope from the pocket of her apron. "Would you mind delivering this to Emma for me instead? It would save me a trip. Plus, I could get started on the baking as soon as the store closes."

Elizabeth took the envelope and tucked it into her pocket. The store closed early on Tuesdays, so she would have plenty of time to drive out to the Troyers' farm and still get back in time to help Martha. "I'll be glad to."

"Thanks, Lizzie."

The shop's sliding glass doors opened, and Elizabeth looked up to see a tall man enter wearing a faded baseball cap with a green and yellow logo above the brim. Just inside the door, he paused and stood, blinking, while he looked around.

"He looks lost," Martha said.

"I'll go see if he needs help," Elizabeth replied. She circled the counter and approached the man with her hand extended. "Hello. Welcome to Secondhand Blessings. I'm Elizabeth Classen."

The man shook her hand, his grip rough and callused but not too tight. "Jeff Thompson. Pleasure to meet you, Ms. Classen."

"The pleasure is mine," she said, smiling. She gestured around the store. "Something I can help you find?"

He fidgeted at the question, his starched jeans rustling. "Actually, I was hoping to speak with the owner, if he or she is available."

Elizabeth angled her head up at him curiously. "That would be me, I suppose. My sisters and I are co-owners. What can I do for you?"

"I'm hoping there is something I can do for you." He swiped the cap off his head and held it clutched in both hands. "It's about the review someone left last week. Do you have a moment to talk privately?"

Now, her curiosity was really piqued. Mary was working in the office, so Elizabeth nodded and pointed toward the stockroom. "We can go in there if you'd like."

"That would be perfect." He held out the hat. "After you."

"Okay." Sweeping past him, Elizabeth made her way to the stockroom. At least it would offer a bit of privacy with the door half-closed. Once they were both inside, she turned and faced Mr. Thompson squarely. "So, I'm curious. What is all this about?"

Ruddied by the sun and wind, Mr. Thompson's cheeks took on an even rosier hue as he shuffled from foot to foot. "Well, I suppose I don't know how else to do this but to come right out and say it. I heard you and your sisters might be buying milk from the Troyers. Is that true?"

Confusion swirled through Elizabeth's head. "I'm sorry, I don't understand what that has to do with the review."

"You're right. I'm not explaining this well." Slapping his hat against his palm, he cleared his throat and began again. "I own one of the local dairy farms around here. You may have passed it? It's on the old Mill Road, down past the school."

Understanding clicked in Elizabeth's head. "Oh, I see. I'm very sorry, Mr. Thompson, I'm afraid we don't need any more milk—"

He cut her off before she could finish. "No, no, it's not about that."

*Then what?* She motioned for him to go on.

"Several farmers and I belong to the local Dairy Farmers Association. Maybe you've heard of us?"

She shook her head.

"Well, at any rate, a group of us work together to oversee milk production and safety here locally. We also see to it that the herds on local farms are healthy and happy, not mistreated in any way."

Still unsure of his point, Elizabeth waited silently.

"Ms. Classen, were you aware that the Troyers are not a part of any local dairy association?"

"I...um...I wasn't aware that participation in such organizations was mandatory."

"Oh, it's not," he replied quickly, "but it does help keep all of us accountable to one another. And it gives us a place to ask questions, seek out answers whenever there's a problem, for lack of a better word, with the milk our cows are giving."

His meaning clear, Elizabeth clasped both hands tightly. She hadn't said anything about the onions to anyone but her sisters. "Like the problem the Troyers are having."

"Exactly." He let his arms fall to his sides, the cap dangling from his fingertips. "This is a small town, Ms. Classen. Word travels fast, especially when it involves one of the local businesses. When I heard that the Troyers were pulling back some of their deliveries, and saw the review left on your website after you started buying their milk, well…" He shrugged. "I just thought maybe you would want to know."

She searched his face for clues to the thoughts lurking behind his steady, hazel gaze. Was it genuine concern that had driven him to come, or something else? Her gut instinct said there was more he wasn't telling, but what?

"I appreciate you making us aware of your concerns," she said. "I'll certainly let my sisters know you came."

He reached into his shirt pocket and pulled out a business card. "No problem. And one last thing, the Dairy Farmers Association is holding its monthly meeting on Thursday night at six thirty. I wrote all the details down for you on the back of this card. You're welcome to come if you'd like to check us out, maybe get to know a little more about what we do. In the meantime, if I can answer any questions for you, please don't hesitate to give me a call."

Taking the card he offered, Elizabeth thanked him once again for stopping by and then walked with him to the door. Rachel was shaking a fine mist from her cloak when they reached the entrance, and smiled at Mr. Thompson as he passed.

After he'd gone, Elizabeth turned to Rachel. "You know him?"

"Jeff Thompson?" She nodded. "He is the head of the Dairy Farmers Association my son belongs to."

Adam. Of course. Elizabeth glanced down at the card in her hand. "About that. Do you think Adam would be available to answer a few questions for me?"

Rachel shrugged. "I do not see why not. I was heading that way after I leave here. You are welcome to join me, if you like."

"Actually, I have a stop to make first." She patted the pocket containing the envelope Martha had given her. "It should be quick. I just need to give the proceeds from Martha's bakery orders to Emma."

"No problem. It is on the way." Rachel raised the basket on her arm. "I'll just give these things to Mary and then we can head over."

Elizabeth went with her to explain where they were going, and then led Rachel to her car for the short ride to the Troyers' farm. When they got there, she was surprised to see a familiar red Mustang with a Penn State decal in the back window parked in the driveway.

Straining against the seat belt, Rachel leaned forward to point out the windshield. "Does that car belong to...?"

"Beau Hegel," Elizabeth finished, slipping her car into PARK. "I wonder what he's doing here."

*Again?* She left the question unspoken and reached for the door handle. Before she could exit the car, the Troyers' front door flew open, spilling raised voices into the otherwise peaceful morning air.

"It's not my fault your horse bolted! The Amish have no business driving slow-moving vehicles on paved roads. This isn't the 1800s."

"That is Beau Hegel's voice," Rachel said, eyes wide.

"Let's go." Elizabeth jerked on the handle and scrambled from her car. With Rachel on her heels, she hurried to the porch just as Beau stormed from the house. Moses hobbled after him on one crutch, waving the other in his hand like a sword.

"The Amish have just as much right to travel the road as you *Englisch*," he said, his tone lower than Beau's but no less firm. Behind him, Emma clutched at his arm, pleading something in Pennsylvania Dutch that Elizabeth couldn't understand.

"That's crazy!" Beau roared, his face glowing an angry red. "Your buggy didn't have lights. How was I supposed to see you?"

"Perhaps if you slowed that car down, instead of tearing around the county, menacing innocent people going about their business." Moses jerked the crutch around to point at Beau's red Mustang. With each word, his voice rose and his face flushed redder.

"Whoa, what's going on here?" Elizabeth asked, hurrying up the steps to stand between Moses and Beau.

Emma hurried to her, eyes wide and her cheeks pale. "Thank goodness you are here."

Elizabeth nodded to her, her courage bolstered when Rachel came to stand next to her. Lifting her chin, Elizabeth turned to Beau. "What are you doing here?"

"What am *I* doing here?" he repeated. He jerked several folded sheets of paper from his back pocket and waved them at Moses. "Why don't you ask *him*? I'm sure he could tell you."

"Because I'm asking *you*," Elizabeth replied firmly, staring hard at Beau until he swung his gaze back to meet hers. She pointed to the papers in his hand. "What is that?"

"It's court papers," he growled through white lips. "I was served this morning."

Rachel swung toward Moses. "I do not understand."

Neither did Elizabeth. It wasn't the Amish way to hash out their legal troubles in courts. Of course, Beau wasn't Amish.

But now wasn't the time to ask why Moses had chosen to press charges.

Elizabeth cleared her throat, drawing Beau's gaze back to her. "If those are court papers, then obviously you shouldn't be here. A public argument won't look good for you, especially with so many witnesses."

She crossed her arms and waited for her meaning to sink in. Beau's frown deepened, but slowly, his shoulders fell and he whirled to pound down the steps to his car.

Emma blew out a breath that Elizabeth echoed before turning a questioning gaze to Moses. "What was all that about?"

Moses cut his hand through the air in disgust. "Aargh, youth. Amish or Englisch, they are all the same. Hardheaded and rash."

"Perhaps we should go inside," Rachel suggested, her even tone layering a sense of calm where before there had been none.

"That is a good idea," Emma said, reaching for her father's hand. "Please, Daed. You are not supposed to be on your feet."

Moses shrugged from his daughter's grasp. "Bah. I have been *off* my feet too long." Even as he spoke, a pained grimace creased his features. "But I will go inside. It is too wet to keep our guests standing on the porch."

He shot a glower at the gray sky before spinning to lumber awkwardly inside, the crutches banging against the jamb.

"Give me a moment to get him settled," Emma begged, tossing a glance at her father's retreating figure.

"We will wait for you downstairs," Rachel replied quietly.

Emma nodded hastily before hurrying after Moses.

Inside, Elizabeth wiggled out of her jacket. "Thank goodness we arrived when we did."

Rachel agreed with a nod. "Ja. I do not like to think what might have happened had we been later. I have never seen Moses so angry."

"I was just about to ask," Elizabeth said, lowering her voice. Not that the Amish didn't get mad. They were human, after all. But it was rare to see a man of Moses's age and stature lose his temper like he had.

Realizing adrenaline from the unexpected confrontation still coursed through her veins, Elizabeth sank onto the couch next to Rachel rather than pass the minutes pacing the floor. Finally, Emma's footsteps sounded in the hall. She ducked into the living room a moment later, her face no longer pale, but still apologetic.

"Thank you both for waiting."

"How is Moses?" Rachel asked, rising to her feet. "He did not reinjure himself, I hope."

"I do not think so, though how he managed not to is beyond me. Anyway, he is resting now." Emma motioned Rachel back onto the couch and slipped into the padded wooden rocker across from them with a sigh. "I knew I should not have allowed Beau to speak with Daed again. He was so upset after the last time."

Elizabeth leaned forward to interrupt. "Emma, what happened before we got here? And what did Beau say to make Moses so angry?"

Emma lifted her hand to press against her chest, her eyes wide, anxious tears darkening her lashes to a sooty brown. "Angry words passed between both of them, Elizabeth. And I am afraid none of them were good."

# CHAPTER ELEVEN

Elizabeth forced herself to sit still while Emma explained how Beau had shown up on their doorstep, demanding to speak to Moses, ranting something about false charges of reckless driving.

"He was very angry," Emma said, clutching her apron, her knuckles white. "I would not have let him in except Daed heard him grousing about and hobbled down the stairs before I could send Beau away."

"Did you hear what they said?" Rachel asked.

"Mostly they just argued about the papers Beau brought with him. He kept waving them around and saying the accident was not his fault. Well, not his only."

"And what did your dad say?" Elizabeth asked.

"Daed claimed he had no idea what Beau was talking about."

"That's it? They were both so angry when we got here," Elizabeth said, splaying her hands over her knees. "What happened?"

Emma dropped her gaze, her shoulders slumping beneath the plain cotton dress she wore. "Beau offered to give my father some money. It was not a lot. I think he just wanted to help pay for expenses while Daed recovered from his injuries."

"But Moses did not take it that way."

"Ne." Emma lifted her gaze to Rachel. "Daed said the love of money was the root of all evil and told Beau he would not be able to buy his way out of trouble this time. I think Daed was just in pain and irritated with Beau's attitude," she added quickly. "I do not think he meant to be insulting in any way."

Rachel dipped her head in understanding, and Emma spread her hands wide and turned back to Elizabeth. "The rest you saw for yourself."

Elizabeth sighed as a clear picture of all that had taken place formed in her head. Elevated emotions, misguided intentions, angry words. How many times had the same scenario played out in exactly the same way with exactly the same result?

No, not the same. Worse. And poor Emma looked like she wanted to sink into the floor. She was already carrying such a heavy burden.

Reminded of the reason for their visit, Elizabeth reached into her purse and took out the envelope Martha had sent. "I'm glad we showed up in time to help, but that wasn't why we came." She held out the envelope to Emma with a smile. "It's the proceeds from the orders Martha took."

"Oh." Fresh tears welled in Emma's eyes. "Danki, but I do not think I can accept this."

"Of course you can," Elizabeth responded, with a gentle pat on Emma's shoulder. "We want to help. It's what neighbors do for one another."

Her head bowed, Emma pondered this silently and then slid the envelope into her apron pocket without another word.

"Good. Now, there is one more question I would like to ask you," Elizabeth said, returning to her place on the couch. "I ran into someone at the store today, or rather, he ran into me. A man by the name of Jeff Thompson. Do you know him?"

"The man who owns the dairy farm on the old Mill Road? Ja, I know him." Emma's face crinkled in a perplexed frown. "Why?"

"He came by the store today to talk to me about the Dairy Farmers Association. He said your father refuses to be a part of it. Any idea why?"

Emma's chest rose and fell with a sigh. "Ja, I know. It has been a long-standing disagreement between Mr. Thompson and my father. Daed thinks the association wants to micromanage all the local farmers into doing things their way. Mr. Thompson argues they are just concerned with the quality of milk produced in this area. He says one farmer with a bad reputation can affect them all. It has led to many run-ins, I am afraid."

"What kind of run-ins?" Elizabeth urged.

Emma fidgeted nervously in the rocker. "Let us just say my father has been vocal in his opposition...but so has Mr. Thompson."

*Interesting.*

Elizabeth rubbed her bottom lip, thinking. "So then, would you say Mr. Thompson has been pressing Moses to join the association?"

"Pressing?" Emma blinked in confusion.

"What do you mean?" Rachel added, angling on the couch so she faced Elizabeth. "As in trying to coerce him to join?"

"Coerce is a strong word," Elizabeth admitted. She turned to Emma. "But does it fit?"

"I..." She struggled for a moment and then shrugged. "I do not think I can say. Emotions on both sides have been strong."

"What are you thinking, Elizabeth?" Rachel asked quietly.

What, indeed? Elizabeth took a moment to sort her thoughts and then leaned forward. "Emma, Jeff Thompson invited my sisters and me to a meeting of the Dairy Farmers Association Thursday night. Now, it's a long shot, and I have absolutely no proof that he's involved at all, especially given Beau's tirade a moment ago."

"But?" Emma prompted.

"I think we need to at least consider the possibility that Jeff might have tried sabotaging the cows in order to force Moses into seeking outside help, possibly even from one of the members of the association."

Emma straightened, her spine stiff, shoulders rigid. "Which would give him another tool to encourage my father to join."

"Exactly."

Rachel leaned in to the conversation too. "Would that not be an extreme measure to take? Organizations like this are voluntary, after all. And I have always known Jeff Thompson to be a reasonable man."

"Maybe so, but given what Emma told us about the history between him and Moses, we can't discount him," Elizabeth pointed out.

Rachel thought about this and then pressed her lips together and sat back against the couch.

"So then, I should think about attending the meeting," Emma said, waving her hand. "I might overhear something, or see something that would give us a hint as to who put the onions in the cows' food."

"Like I said, it's a long shot," Elizabeth reminded her, "but it can't hurt. I'll talk to my sisters about attending as well. The more of us there, the more likely we'll stumble across something—assuming there's anything to stumble across," she added quickly.

After fishing Jeff Thompson's card from her purse, Elizabeth copied the information for Emma and then walked with Rachel to the door.

"We'll see you Thursday," Elizabeth said, flashing Emma an encouraging smile. "Let me know if there's anything you or Moses need before then."

Emma agreed, and then Elizabeth and Rachel continued on their way to see Adam. He was in the barn when they arrived. Like Rachel, he had only good things to say about Jeff Thompson, though mindful of their promise to Emma, Elizabeth was careful to leave the Troyers' name out of the conversation.

"What can you tell us about the Dairy Farmers Association?" Elizabeth asked. "Mr. Thompson said they are meeting Thursday night."

"Ja, that's right. They meet the third Thursday of every month."

"And how long have you been a member?" Elizabeth asked, walking alongside Adam as he prepared the cows for milking. Bucket in hand, Adam washed each cow's udder before attaching the milking machine and moving on to the next cow.

"Let's see." Adam paused, the water in the bucket sloshing as he set it on the ground. "I joined the year after I married Leah."

"So it's been a couple of years."

He nodded.

"Have you found it to be beneficial?"

He shrugged. "It is always nice to have somewhere to go if I have questions. For example, adding the walk-through foot-baths one of the other farmers recommended last summer has been very helpful in preventing foot rot."

Elizabeth motioned toward the barn. "So then, what would be the reason for not joining?"

Adam looked from her to Rachel and back. "Well, some farmers in the area are not so keen to have other farmers poking their noses into their business. Others say there is no point in joining since they can search the internet for any information they need."

"That's a valid argument, but there must be some questions an internet search can't answer. In that case, wouldn't it be easier to ask for help?"

"True, but the chasm between the two sides is wide. Neither one is willing to concede the other's point of view." Adam reached for the handle on the bucket and continued down the line of cows. "Fortunately, around here, many farmers have family members they can turn to."

"Hmm." Elizabeth pursed her lips as they continued to walk. "I suppose it all boils down to personal preference. Some people want an organized group to belong to, others don't."

"That is the root of it."

Adam worked in silence while Elizabeth pondered everything he'd said. When he finished with the last cow, Elizabeth followed him as he walked outside. He dumped the water onto the ground, forming soapy rivers the brittle grass quickly lapped dry. He turned to Elizabeth, his hands propped on his hips.

"Is there anything else I can help you with?"

"Maybe one last thing, though it's not related."

At his nod, she plowed ahead. "Rachel talked to you about cows eating onions and giving rancid milk. And you said the time it would take to purge the flavor from their system and give good milk again would depend on the animal and how long they had been eating onions."

"That's right."

"Any ideas on how someone could speed that process up?"

He looked at Rachel. "Is something going on at the farm?"

"Ne, not us. A friend of ours is having some trouble." She didn't say who and fortunately, Adam didn't ask.

He removed a pair of work gloves from his back pocket and wiggled his fingers inside them. "The best thing to do would be to change the cow's food and check its environment carefully. Make sure it doesn't still have access to the onions. After that, I would say just keep an eye on the animal. Hopefully, the problem will clear up on its own in just a few days."

Surely that wasn't too much to ask. Emma, Abel, and Zach could keep an eye on the cows for that long. In the meantime, Elizabeth, Martha, and Mary would keep searching for clues that would lead them to the culprit.

And hope that nothing else happened before then.

# CHAPTER TWELVE

Elizabeth picked at the flaky croissant on her plate while she waited for John at the Bird-in-Hand Bakery. It was after eight in the morning, but the overcast sky on this Wednesday morn made it feel much earlier.

"Looks like it might rain."

Elizabeth startled as one of the bakery employees, an older woman named Judy, motioned toward the window with the coffeepot in her hand.

"Outside. Looks like rain."

"Oh, right." Elizabeth shook free of thoughts of Emma, Beau, and Jeff and focused on Judy. "Yeah, I think the forecast said we'd see a few drizzles the rest of this week, but then have clear skies over the weekend."

"Hmm." Judy gave an exaggerated shiver that jangled the hoop earrings dangling from her ears. "It's too early in the season for it to be so gray and dreary." She clicked her nails against the side of the coffeepot. "Lucky we have plenty of this stuff to keep us warm. Can I refill your cup?"

Elizabeth thanked her and pushed her cup to the edge of the table.

"Should I fill this other cup yet?" Judy asked while she poured.

Elizabeth had asked for a second cup when she arrived. It still sat empty on the opposite side of the table, waiting for John.

"No, my friend's not here yet," she said, her head swiveling toward the door when a jingle and a cold blast of air signaled someone's arrival. "Oh, there he is now."

Because he was on duty, John was in his police uniform. He wore it well. And that was all Elizabeth would let herself think about that.

"Looks like I'm just in time," Judy said, giving a wink as she nodded hello to John and then filled his cup as well. She set the pot on the table then reached into her apron for an order pad and a pen. "Anything else I can get for you?" she asked while he slid into the booth.

"Just coffee for now," John said, blowing into his hands. He smiled at Elizabeth. "It's getting chilly out there. Should've worn my gloves."

The comment of course made her look at his hands— strong, capable, trustworthy were adjectives that came to mind.

"No problem. I'll check back with you in a couple of minutes in case you change your mind," Judy said, shooting Elizabeth another quick wink and grabbing the coffeepot before flitting off to check on her other customers.

"So, what's up?" John rubbed his palms together briskly. "Your message said you had a few more questions you wanted to ask about Beau?"

"That's right." Elizabeth looked around, but the other people in the bakery showed no interest in the two of them. One had his nose buried in his tablet. Another peered at her laptop, the glow from the screen reflected in a sparkly pair of cat eyeglasses. Farther down, an older couple chatted quietly over a shared cheese Danish.

Elizabeth cleared her throat and then rested her clasped hands on the tabletop. "John, I hope asking you to come doesn't make you feel like I'm taking advantage of our f-friendship."

She stumbled over the word, but why should that be? John *was* just a friend. Wasn't he?

She cleared the thought from her head and wriggled closer to the table. "What I mean to say is, I do have more questions, but I don't want you to feel as though you have to answer them. I actually told myself I wasn't going to press you the last time we talked, so I will totally understand if there is some information you can't give me."

John braced both elbows on the table and peered at her, humor glinting in his blue eyes. "Why don't you go ahead and tell me what it is you want to know and then let me decide?"

He was teasing. Of course he was. Feeling silly, she puffed out a breath, releasing the unease knotting her stomach. "Okay, so I know you said Beau's uncle bailed him out of trouble a few times. Any chance you could tell me what kind of trouble?"

John shrugged then curled his fingers around his coffee cup. "Traffic violations mostly, parking tickets, speeding, stuff like that. Nothing too serious, and it's all public record."

"What about other things? Has he ever had issues with incidents not related to his driving?"

"I could check. Why?" He brought the cup to his lips, but not before she glimpsed a lopsided grin. "Don't tell me you're working on another mystery. What is it this time? You trying to do the district attorney's job for him?"

The last part caught her off guard. "Wait. Who?" She frowned. "What are you talking about?"

John swallowed a gulp of coffee and sat back, confused lines bunching his brow. "The district attorney. I thought you knew Beau was facing charges for his part in Moses's accident."

"I do, but what does the district attorney have to do with that?"

"He's the one pressing charges." John shook his head. "Who did you think it was?"

"So you're saying it's not the family. Is that common?"

"Well, sometimes the families of the victim hire their own attorney. That's mostly civil suits. In this case, because there were injuries and Beau allegedly fled the scene, the DA did."

She leaned forward. "John, does Beau know it's the district attorney who filed against him?" She held up her hand. "Wait, let me rephrase that…is it possible that Beau thinks the Troyers are the ones pressing charges?"

John scratched the back of his hand absently. "It's possible, I suppose." He narrowed his eyes to study her. "Why? What's going on? Is there something you haven't told me?"

"Actually…" She bit her lip hesitantly. She hadn't *exactly* said she wouldn't tell anyone about the onions, just that she wouldn't tell Moses. And she *was* trying to figure out who was behind the onions by talking to John—something she'd told Emma she would do.

Elizabeth sucked in a breath and briefly explained about the Troyers' cows and why she had placed Beau as number one on her suspect list.

"Not that I have any proof," she finished. "In fact, that was one of the reasons I wanted to talk to you."

"Beau certainly does have motive," John said, fingering the handle of his cup. "He's young, impulsive. And based on his penchant for trouble, something like this would be right up his alley."

Doubt twined with the regret in his tone. Elizabeth arched an eyebrow. "But you're hoping it wasn't him?"

John's gaze fell. "I didn't say that."

"No." She reached out to cover his hand. "But you didn't have to. I could hear it in your voice."

He chuckled ruefully. "The truth is, I was really hoping Beau would turn his life around after this latest incident. I know it doesn't sound like it after everything I've told you about him, but he really is a good kid. He just needs…"

He swallowed hard and turned his hand over to grip Elizabeth's. She held her breath while she waited for him to finish. He needed…what? Jesus? A year ago, John would have argued that people didn't need a strong faith to get them through life. Law and order. Strength and integrity. Those were the things he believed in. He'd come a long way since then. *They* had come a long way.

He released her hand and smiled, but it looked forced. "Enough about Beau. I checked my calendar. What are you doing Saturday?"

"This Saturday?" She shrugged and laid her trembling hands in her lap. "Just the store, but I can ask the girls to cover for me. I thought you had to work?"

"I have vacation time coming. I asked for it off." He leaned forward to rest his arms on the table. "Anything else you'd like to do besides visit a flea market?"

He'd used his vacation time for her? John had a son in college and a daughter in high school. His vacation days were precious. "You didn't have to take the day off just for me."

"I wanted to. I'm really looking forward to spending an entire day with you."

He said it so firmly, and his gaze was so steady, it brought a blush to her cheeks. She swallowed nervously and said, "In that case, let's add dinner."

He grinned. "Of course."

She hesitated. "Maybe a movie after? There are several new ones I've been wanting to see."

"Done." He checked the item off in the air. "What else?"

"John." She laughed. "How much do you think we can do in one day?"

"I dunno. Anything you want." His gaze softened, and his grin changed, became warmer somehow, like he meant it just for her. "I want to make sure you have fun. Feel special. You deserve it."

There was a roughness to his voice as he finished that raised pleasant little shivers on her flesh. It felt good. Nice. And yet...

She drew back as far as the seat behind her would allow. Needing something to do with her hands, she reached for her croissant and began crumbling it into even smaller pieces. "On second thought, maybe we ought to just stick to dinner and the flea market. I really need to get back so I can, you know, figure out what's going on over at the Troyers."

Was that disappointment flickering in his gaze? Her heart cramped a little at the thought. And that was a problem. Because it shouldn't. They were just friends. But with each passing day, it was becoming harder and harder to keep reminding herself of that fact.

# CHAPTER THIRTEEN

Lights glowed brightly from the town hall, and brightly colored mums and a cluster of pumpkins decorated both doors, welcoming the members of the Dairy Farmers Association and anyone else wishing to attend the meeting. By the time Elizabeth, Mary, and Martha showed up, the room was pretty full, even though the meeting wasn't scheduled to start for another fifteen minutes.

Glad for the warmth that greeted them as they stepped inside, Elizabeth took a deep breath as she reached for the buttons on her raincoat. The scent of coffee lingered on the air, and several people milled about with Styrofoam cups in their hands, chatting about everything from the chill in the air to a recent outbreak of bovine mastitis.

Mastitis in cows. Elizabeth shook her head. The idea would never have occurred to her.

"There's Emma," Mary said, pointing. "Who's that with her?"

Though he was missing the baseball cap and earbuds, Elizabeth recognized the tall, strapping young man instantly.

"That's Zach Vogel," she said, folding her umbrella and leaning it next to the door. "He's a neighbor of the Troyers. Emma says one of their hired hands was called away on a family emergency, and Zach is helping out until he gets back."

Martha draped her jacket over her arm and then held out her hand for Elizabeth's and Mary's coats. "I'll go find us a seat."

"I'll go with you," Mary said.

Elizabeth nodded to them both. "Okay, thanks. I'll be there in a minute. I'm going to look for Rachel and Adam first."

As her sisters moved away, the door behind Elizabeth opened, shepherding in a blast of damp night air that raised goose bumps on her neck and arms. Rubbing them away briskly, she turned as Rachel entered, Adam at her back.

Elizabeth smiled and moved toward them. "There you are. I was just about to look for you."

Water droplets dotted Rachel's black cloak and bonnet. Elizabeth eyed them with a shiver. "I sure hope the forecast for this weekend is right. All this rain is depressing."

Behind Rachel, Adam removed his hat and coat and stored them, along with Rachel's cloak, on a long row of hooks near the door. "Has the meeting started yet?"

"Not yet." Elizabeth motioned to where Martha and Mary sat. "We just got here ourselves. Would you like to join us?"

Rachel looked past her and shook her head. "Actually, I thought we would sit next to Emma so she is not alone."

*With Zach.*

Rachel didn't say this, but Elizabeth thought she could read the implication in the worried glance Rachel aimed in Emma's direction.

"About that." Elizabeth laid her hand on Rachel's arm and lowered her voice. "I keep getting the impression there's something going on where Zach is concerned. Am I wrong?"

Rachel opened her mouth then shut it again quickly. "It is not Zach. There is a history with the Vogels. His father, Simon, used to be a member of the Amish church."

All manner of thoughts flashed through Elizabeth's mind at the news. Though the practice wasn't as common now, in Simon's day, people were often shunned for leaving the church after they took their vow.

"I didn't—" Elizabeth began, only to be cut off when Jeff Thompson moved to the front of the room and held up his hand.

"Okay, folks, thank you all for coming. We're going to get started here in just a few minutes, so if you haven't done it already, grab yourself a cup of coffee and make your way to your seats."

At that moment, Jeff seemed to notice Emma Troyer. His brows rose, and his gaze drifted past her as though he were looking for someone. Then the smile returned to his face, and he took his seat at a long table beside a couple of local farmers Elizabeth recognized, and two more she did not.

"You started to say something?" Rachel whispered.

Elizabeth shook her head. "We'll talk after the meeting."

Agreeing with a nod, Rachel moved with Adam toward Emma while Elizabeth eased into a squeaky chair next to Mary and Martha. The hour-long meeting passed quickly, with lots of banter and laughter passing back and forth between the farmers assembled. Most of the attention was focused on a large promotion the association was putting together for all the area farmers, which incited a few differences of opinion.

All were resolved quickly and with minimal discussion, thanks to Jeff's skilled leadership.

"That didn't seem so bad," Mary said when the meeting ended.

"No it didn't," Martha agreed. "And I didn't get the feeling there was a lot of micromanaging going on the way Moses claims. I wonder why he's so averse to joining?"

"Maybe just digging in his heels?" Mary offered.

"That, or they toned down the meeting because they had visitors present," Martha said.

"One way to find out." Elizabeth nodded toward Emma. Rachel and Adam stood chatting with another Amish couple some distance away, but Emma still lingered, so now was the perfect time to talk with her.

"You go," Martha urged. "She might feel a little intimidated if we all descend on her at once."

Mary agreed, so Elizabeth walked over alone. When she spotted her, Emma's face lit with a relieved smile.

"Hey, Elizabeth."

"Hi, Emma." She looked around but saw no sign of Zach. "Where's your friend?"

Emma didn't ask who Elizabeth meant. A flush reddened her cheeks, and then she shrugged. "He…uh…he's still around somewhere."

Sensing she did not want to discuss Zach further, Elizabeth motioned around the room. "So? What did you think of your first meeting?"

"It was amazing."

A spark of excitement flickered in Emma's eyes. Obviously, she didn't share her father's point of view where the Dairy Farmers Association was concerned.

"I had no idea they handled promotional projects along with everything else they do. Did you see they have a monthly newsletter? There is a sign-up sheet by the door for anyone who wants to subscribe."

Elizabeth could almost hear the wheels turning inside Emma's head. Promotion from the Dairy Farmers Association would certainly help if she and her father decided expand the farm. But all of this would be very foreign for someone who didn't use email or who had no experience with online promotions.

"Emma, has your father ever attended a meeting of the association before?"

"He has, but it was several years ago," she admitted. "At the time, they were discussing joining a co-op to help distribute their milk."

Understanding dawned. "Let me guess, Jeff Thompson was for it."

"And my father against. Firmly." Her lips curved in a wry grin. "That wasn't the only thing. They have disagreed plenty over the years, but I am pretty sure that is when Daed decided he wanted no part of the association."

"Hmm."

Emma's gaze drifted over Elizabeth's shoulder, and sadness seemed to grip her. Her mouth closed, her shoulders drooped, and even her eyes seemed to lose a little of their luster.

Elizabeth turned to see what had captured her attention. In a far corner stood Zach, and he looked to be in deep conversation with a pretty young girl with luminous brown eyes and dark, silky hair.

"Who is that?" Elizabeth asked.

Emma answered in a pained whisper. "Lillian Murphy. Her father and Zach's are friends."

Elizabeth cleared her throat, drawing Emma's eyes back to her face. "Speaking of Zach's father, is he here?"

"That is him, over there." She pointed to a tall, stout man with a gray speckled beard and ruddy face. Like many of the Amish farmers, he was dressed in dark trousers, suspenders, and a plain shirt, but his beard wasn't trimmed like theirs, and he had a full mustache.

"He's quite a bit older than I expected," Elizabeth remarked, studying him. "Does he have any other children?"

"One son, but he is several years older than Zach."

Was it Elizabeth's imagination, or did Emma's voice soften every time she spoke his name? Making a mental note to pay more attention, Elizabeth pressed on.

"Rachel told me Simon used to belong to the Amish church."

"Ja, that is so."

"How long ago was that?"

"I'm not sure. It was before my time or Zach's. I only know because Zach has mentioned it."

So, at least eighteen or nineteen years ago. "Did he happen to mention why his father left?"

"Ne. Sorry. Zach says his father never talks about it."

Elizabeth pondered this information. There were many reasons people didn't speak about things. Some were too painful. Others were awkward, embarrassing, or uncomfortable. Sometimes, it was simply because the person had a secret they didn't want to come out.

The question lingering in Elizabeth's brain was, which one applied to Simon Vogel?

# CHAPTER FOURTEEN

Mary took her foot off the accelerator as she neared the Troyers' farm and strained to see out the windshield past a steady rain and stiff breeze that appeared determined to rob the trees of their fall color.

"It's only October," she muttered, flipping on the turn signal. "Too early for all this dreary weather."

As she wound her way up the driveway, her artist's eye noted how the dark-spotted Holsteins stood in stark contrast to the line of trees decked in orange, yellow, and ruby red. Looking at them meant taking her eyes off the driveway just long enough to bump through a deep mud puddle. Dirty water splashed the windshield, but running the wipers only made matters worse.

"Great."

If there was one thing she hadn't missed about living in Bird-in-Hand, it was wet, dirty roads. By the time she reached the farmhouse, tension and nerves had caused her stomach to cramp. Grimacing with discomfort, Mary climbed out of the car, hiked up her pant legs, then picked her way to the porch. Reaching it, she gave three quick knocks on the door and stepped back while she waited for Emma to answer. After several seconds, she tried again, with the same result.

Maybe she was in the barn? Mary circled around to the side of the house, where a basset hound, and not Emma, bounded up the hill to greet her, baying so loudly he scared a flock of swallows from a nearby tree.

"Sugarpie, no!" Emma emerged from the barn. Giving a wave to Mary, she hurried after the dog, her booted feet slipping more than once. At last she reached the porch, out of breath and her cheeks rosy from cold.

After they exchanged greetings, Mary gestured toward the barn. "I'm sorry to pull you away from work. I was actually hoping I would catch you on your lunch break."

"Ne, ne, it is no trouble." Once she'd reached down to snag Sugarpie by the collar, Emma pulled the dog away from Mary and eased toward the door. "Would you like to come inside?"

"Only for a minute," Mary said, rubbing her hands briskly over her arms as they moved into the hall. "Martha asked me to come by for some more milk. She didn't want you to have to get out in the buggy in the middle of this."

"That was so kind of your sister," Emma exclaimed. "I admit, I have been a little worried about how bad the storm is getting. But I wasn't planning on taking the buggy. Zach offered to drive me to make our deliveries."

Mary smiled. "Well, I saved him a trip."

Being inside the warm house made both of their noses run. Emma grabbed a tissue from a box on the hall table, handed it to Mary, and then grabbed another for herself. "Would you like to sit down for a minute? I was just about to make a sandwich to take up to Daed."

"Please, don't let me stop you from doing what you have to do," Mary said. "I'm in no hurry."

"Danki. I will just be a second." Emma scurried to the kitchen. A short time later, she reappeared with a tray and smiled as she bustled toward the stairs. "Be right back."

Poor girl, Mary thought. Watching her scramble to run the farm and care for her father at the same time made all of Mary's own problems seem small in comparison.

"There," Emma said, shuffling down the stairs with a weary sigh. "I have to get Daed his lunch promptly at noon or he is tempted to help himself and come down the stairs."

"How is your father?" Mary asked.

"Better. Still not one hundred percent, but he will get there."

"I'm glad to hear it." Mary motioned toward the kitchen. "Listen, I don't want to keep you from your lunch. If you want to just show me where the milk is, I can load it up myself."

"Oh, you do not need to do that," Emma protested. "In fact, I was just about to make a sandwich. Would you like one? I have turkey and fresh bread."

Thinking about food made Mary's stomach rumble, but not in a good way. She slid her hand to her middle and hoped she wasn't coming down with a bug.

"That's sweet of you, Emma, but I probably should get going before the weather gets too bad."

Her eyes widened. "Of course. It is in the kitchen. I will fetch it for you."

She left and returned quickly, a gallon of milk in each hand. "Here you go."

Mary took the milk she offered and then raised an eyebrow. "How are the other cows doing? Are they still giving bad milk?"

"Unfortunately, ja. We are still milking them to get the bad milk out of their system, but it will probably be at least another day or two before we can begin using what they give."

Which meant more work in the meantime, and less profit. "Say, you wouldn't happen to have two more gallons sitting around, would you? I've been craving milk lately. And it's a lot healthier for me than sugary drinks."

Emma's face brightened with a pleased smile. "Yes, I'm sure I can find you another couple of gallons."

"Great. I'll just go put these in the car."

While Emma returned to the kitchen, Mary crossed to the door. She switched one of the jugs to her hip, reached for the knob, and yanked the door open. To her surprise, Zach stood on the other side, his hand raised to knock.

"Oh, sorry." He jumped back out of her way and then seemed to catch himself. He held out his hands. "Can I take those for you?"

"Well, yes, that would be nice." She handed over the milk and pulled her keys from her pocket as she led the way back to her car. "So, you're Zach Vogel, right? Emma said you offered to help with deliveries today."

"Actually, Abel handles most of the deliveries in the truck. I just offered to help with the ones Emma makes to people's houses."

"I see. Well, that was nice of you to offer."

He shrugged and nodded to her car. "You want these in the back?"

"Yes, please. On the floor is fine. Emma is bringing me another couple of gallons."

Mary hurried her steps, but Zach shifted the milk to one hand and had the door open before she could reach it.

"I've got this," he said, an amiable smile on his face.

Impressed, Mary stood back and watched him work. He seemed like a nice young man, very willing and eager to help out.

"So, Zach, my sister Elizabeth tells me your family owns a dairy farm too?"

"That's right. Ours is just a couple of miles east of here."

"Then you must know a lot about the dairy business."

He straightened and rested his arm on top of the car door. "Some. My dad is really the one who runs the place."

The house door opened and Sugarpie came bounding out, followed by Emma. This time, instead of barking at Mary, the dog made a beeline to Zach. Zach crouched and gave the dog a generous rub behind the ears before hurrying to the stairs to help Emma with the extra milk.

"That's perfect. Thank you, Emma." Mary held the door while Zach deposited the jugs next to the first two gallons on the floor. "And thank you for your help, Zach."

"No problem."

He backed up a step, giving Mary room to shut the door, and stuck his hands in his jeans pockets. "It's nice of you and your sisters to help the Troyers this way."

Mary grinned wryly. "Ah, well, it's not much."

"Every little bit helps," Emma said, moving to stand next to Zach. As in...right next to him. And Zach didn't seem to mind one bit, if the longing glance he shot her way was any indication.

Mary lifted an eyebrow. Maybe Elizabeth was right. Maybe there was something between them.

She shifted her attention back to Zach. "So, we were talking about your dad's dairy farm. Are you thinking about running your own farm someday?"

Which would make sense, given his interest in Emma.

"It's a possibility. I've learned a lot from my dad, but I haven't really decided if farming is what I want to do with my life. I thought about taking a couple of classes at the community college to see if anything hooked me, but so far, nothing really interests me enough to look into it."

"Have you thought about going away to school?"

"Nah. I'd rather stick close to home."

Zach's gaze slid to Emma. Though she staunchly refused to look at him, color crept to her cheeks. Mary remained silent, watching the interaction going on between them with interest.

"My dad needs me," Zach continued. "Besides, I haven't found anything I like more than what I have right here, in Bird-in-Hand."

"In that case," Mary said, breaking the sudden, awkward silence, "community college might be good for you. Maybe if you took classes, you *would* find something."

"I dunno. I go back and forth. Sometimes, I feel like school is the answer. Then I second-guess myself and wonder if it's not just a big waste of time." His posture shifted, and he reached down to give the adoring basset hound resting against his leg one last pat. "I mean, if you already know what you want, you should go after it, right? Just like old Sugarpie here."

Mary narrowed her eyes thoughtfully. Was he talking about farming, or something—make that some*one*—else?

"Maybe you're right," Mary said. "Anyway, I should get going. The rain has let up a little, but that won't last. It's supposed to get a whole lot worse tonight."

She looked at Emma. "If you're going out to make deliveries, you might want to keep that in mind."

"We will. Thank you, Mary."

"You're welcome. Goodbye, Zach. Thanks again for helping me with the milk."

"Sure thing." He moved toward the car along with Mary and held the door while she climbed in.

Such a gentleman, Mary thought, as she pulled away from the farm. In her rearview mirror, Zach and Emma gradually grew smaller. Though they remained side by side, Zach made no move to close the distance between them, and Emma kept her hands by her sides.

A gentleman, yes. But was he the right gentleman for Emma?

# CHAPTER FIFTEEN

Elizabeth drew her spoon absently through a bowl of beef stew while she listened to Mary describe everything that had taken place at the Troyers' farm earlier that afternoon. From the living room, a cozy fire radiated warmth all the way to the dining table. That, along with Martha's savory stew, chased the chill from even the deepest corners of the house. Well, almost every corner. Right here, where Elizabeth sat, a chill settled squarely between her shoulders while she listened to Mary talk.

"I guess there's no doubt about it," she said when Mary finished. "Zach and Emma obviously have feelings for each other."

"Which presents a problem, since he's Englisch and she's Amish," Martha said, crumbling a cracker into her stew.

Elizabeth put down her spoon, indignation building in her belly at the idea that she might have been duped. "Actually, it presents more of a problem than that."

Mary tilted her head questioningly. "What do you mean?"

"Emma asked Rachel and me not to tell her father what was going on with the cows. She said it was because she wanted a chance to figure out what was going on first. Now, I have to wonder if maybe it had something to do with Zach as well."

"Hiding their relationship from her father?" Mary pursed her lips. "That wouldn't be good."

Mary had kept plenty of secrets of her own over the years, and Elizabeth knew she'd lived to regret most of them. She reached out to give her sister's hand a squeeze.

"I may be wrong. It may not have anything to do with him," Elizabeth said. "He did look a little chummy with that other young woman at the Dairy Farmers Association meeting the other night. Remember?"

"Lillian Murphy." Mary closed her hand around a half-empty glass of juice, her fingernails tapping a quiet rhythm against the side. She hadn't eaten much of her stew, because she said her stomach was bothering her, but at least she'd managed a few sips of juice.

"He and Lillian did spend quite a bit of time talking." Mary looked at Elizabeth. "But what if you're right, and Emma hasn't told her dad about her feelings for Zach? Are we obligated to let Moses know what's going on?"

Elizabeth bit her lip, thinking, and then shook head. "We may not like it or even agree, but Emma isn't a child. Her personal life and her relationship with her father are none of our business."

"True. What about the farm, then?" Mary asked. "What is our next step in figuring out what's going on there?"

"Well, since we found the onions in the feeders, nothing else has happened, right? And we haven't seen any sign that whoever put them in the cages has come back. Maybe the Troyers were just the unlucky recipients of a poorly played prank."

Even as she spoke the words, Elizabeth wasn't sure she believed them. She couldn't say why, but the feeling in her gut persisted.

"I'm not so sure, Lizzie." Martha balanced a butter knife in one hand, a slice of homemade bread in the other. "The onions were a pretty specific prank."

Elizabeth was almost relieved to hear that Martha had doubts too. Still, she needed more. "What do you mean?"

"Well, who but another person familiar with dairy cows would even know to do something like that?"

"That's true," Mary said, sitting up in her chair. "I wouldn't have."

"Me neither," Elizabeth admitted.

"And why the Troyers?" Martha continued. She dipped the knife into the butter and spread a thin layer over her bread. "Can it really be a coincidence that they were targeted and nobody else?"

Elizabeth widened her eyes. "You've checked? When did you have time to do that?"

"Earlier today." A sheepish smile crossed Martha's face. "I got the idea at the meeting last night and meant to ask around, but I forgot all about it until this morning. I called a couple of farms nearby to check, but nobody else reported having the same problem, either before or since."

"That's awesome, Martha. That was a good idea," Elizabeth said, then looked at both her sisters. "So, if we agree the Troyers were targeted, what do we do now? If nothing else happens, do we assume whoever had it in for them has moved on?"

Instead of answering, Mary grimaced and stood up from the table, her hand on her stomach. "Sorry, girls. I'd like to stay and help hash this out, but I'm afraid I'm going to have to lie down."

"Your stomachache is getting worse? I thought you took something for it before supper," Martha said.

"I did." Mary shook her head, her other hand sliding down to cover the first. "Not helping."

Lines of worry creased Martha's brow. "Have you thought about going to the doctor?"

"I was hoping it was just some kind of twenty-four-hour bug, but I might have to go get checked out if it doesn't get better," Mary said.

"Don't put it off," Elizabeth urged. "Martha and I can handle the store tomorrow. Call in the morning and see if you can get an appointment."

"Tomorrow is Saturday," Mary reminded her gently. "You and John are going to Lebanon to the Dancing Dutchman. And anyway, the doctor's office is closed on Saturdays."

"Fine, Monday then. Unless you start to feel worse. Then we'll drive you to Lancaster to one of those urgent care places if we need to."

A grateful smile pulled Mary's lips. "Okay. I'm sure I'll be fine by morning, but I'll let you know if I'm not."

"All right. Good night, Mary."

Mary grabbed her glass, carried it to the kitchen, and poured the juice in the sink before heading up to bed. Meanwhile, Elizabeth and Martha finished their supper and then talked some more as they cleared the dishes. Still, after more than an hour of exchanging ideas, they were no closer to solving the problem than before. Martha offered to think on it more and then proceeded to her room to watch TV.

Discouraged, Elizabeth shut off the kitchen lights and followed Martha up the stairs.

More than anything, she wanted to believe the incident at the Troyers was an isolated event, but deep down she didn't think so. And that meant they had to figure out what was going on before something else happened. But between little Nick's illness, and now Mary's, plus the Troyers' cows, what they had on their hands were too many questions and not nearly enough answers.

# CHAPTER SIXTEEN

Elizabeth applied a pale gloss to her lips before giving her hair one last pat and pushing up from her dressing table. It wasn't much in the way of makeup, but then again, she'd never been one to spend much time in front of the mirror. Still, the powder she'd applied earlier and the gloss now gave her the small boost of confidence she was oddly in need of today.

"You're being ridiculous," she chided her reflection with a frown. "This trip is just John's way of doing something nice for you for your birthday."

With that thought fixed firmly in her head, she headed down the stairs to wait. As promised, John arrived promptly at ten, and they made the drive to Lebanon in just under an hour.

"This place looks promising," Elizabeth said, eyeing the massive beige and brown metal building while she unbuckled her seat belt. On either side of the main building stretched a wing housing garage-like stalls with even more booths. Crowds of people flocked to every vendor, drawn by the subtle scents of cinnamon and woodsmoke that lingered in the air, and the gaiety that made the bright rays of sunshine even brighter.

"You were right, John. This place is huge. It'll take us most of the day just to get through it."

"If you think this is big, you'll have to come again in the summer." He pointed toward a wide-open field just beyond the store. "When the weather's warm, I hear they rent out spaces back there as well."

"Wow."

"They even bring in food trucks and a couple of carnival rides for the kids."

"That's neat," Elizabeth said, but imagining what the crowds would look like then, she shrugged. "Maybe I'll see if Mary and Martha want to come back with me. For now, I'm glad there aren't so many people here."

Because that would mean John would be on high alert, scanning the crowds for any sign of trouble. It was the life of a police officer, Elizabeth knew, but for just a little bit, she wanted them both to relax and enjoy the day.

She smiled and reached out to pat his hand. "Come on. Let's go check it out."

John's answering smile made her feel warm inside, despite the chilly breeze that greeted them when they stepped out of the car.

John buttoned his coat and pointed toward the wings. "We'd better do those first before it starts snowing."

Fortunately, each vendor in the garage stalls furnished space heaters, so even with the temperatures outside dropping, Elizabeth and John could duck in and out of the cold with ease. Right away, Elizabeth found a metal sign for the Troyers that read BE HEALTHY, DRINK MILK and bore a picture of a Holstein on the front. Thinking it would look perfect in the market Emma hoped to add, Elizabeth purchased it. John found a wooden toolbox filled with vintage tools and snatched it up to give to a friend on the force who collected them.

"Look at that," Elizabeth said, pointing to a large antique stove with porcelain handles. "Martha would love it."

"Except I don't think it'll fit in my car," John said, laughing.

"Or our kitchen," she joked back. "Still, it's pretty. I'm going to take a picture so I can show it to Martha."

"Okay." He held out his hand. "Give me the sign you bought."

She gave it to him, and John held up the toolbox.

"While you get the picture, I'll take these things out to the car."

Elizabeth agreed and sidled closer to the stove to snap the picture. That done, she moved on to check out an old printing press. With her hands free, she could examine all the little drawers and dies and even leaf through one of the original papers printed on the press. Another gentleman seemed equally interested, and Elizabeth was surprised to realize it was Simon Vogel.

"Oops. I'm sorry." She backed up to give him room to see the press as well. "I didn't realize you were trying to squeeze in here too."

"No, no, go right ahead." He motioned to the press. "I'm just looking."

"Me too. No room for this in my office," she said with a light laugh.

He smiled and would have wandered off had Elizabeth not stopped him. "Excuse me. Aren't you Simon Vogel?"

He paused, and his brow rose quizzically. "I am. Do I know you?"

"I don't think so." She stuck out her hand. "I'm Elizabeth Classen. My sisters and I own Secondhand Blessings."

"Ah, the resale shop in Bird-in-Hand." The confusion cleared from his face, and he made a circular motion with his finger. "Looking for more inventory?"

"Not exactly. Just shopping for my birthday."

"Is it today?"

"No, it's next week, but I really wanted to come to the flea market, and it's only open on the weekends."

"Well, happy early birthday."

He seemed nice. Warm, even. Elizabeth smiled. "Thank you."

Once again, he turned as if to continue on and, once again, Elizabeth stopped him. "Listen, you have a son named Zach, don't you?"

His expression morphed from curious to slightly guarded. He slipped one hand into the pocket of his coat and rested the other atop the printing press. "I do. How do you know Zach?"

"To be honest, I don't know him well. I met him out at the Troyers' farm the other day."

"Troyer." Simon shifted, his smile frozen, his fingers white where he gripped the press. "You mean Moses Troyer? What was he doing out there?"

He didn't know? Caught off guard, Elizabeth found herself floundering for how much to say.

"From...uh...from what I understand, he was j-just helping out," she stammered. "Moses's accident has left the family a little shorthanded. Zach has been so kind, helping out when he can. I'm surprised he hasn't mentioned it."

"I see."

Actually, it was Elizabeth who saw. Simon was not happy to learn his son had been spending time at the Troyers'. In fact, "not happy" put his reaction to the news mildly. His eyes widened, his nostrils flared, even his breathing seemed labored. Simon Vogel was downright angry. But why?

"I take it you know Moses Troyer?" Elizabeth asked before Simon could attempt to move on again.

"I know him, for sure and for certain."

His response hearkened to his Amish days, the vagueness of which only further prompted Elizabeth's curiosity. "You two must be around the same age. Did you go to school together?"

"Moses is a couple of years older than I am. I'm sorry, Ms. Classen, but I must be going. It was a pleasure meeting you."

"You too," she called to his back. His long strides already carried him some distance away.

"Who was that?" John slipped in next to her, his hand light on her elbow. "Anyone I know?"

"Possibly. Simon Vogel?" She tilted her head to peer up at John, who shook his head.

"The name's not familiar. Should it be?"

Briefly, Elizabeth explained about Zach and his presence on the Troyer farm. "The trouble is, I don't think Emma has been forthcoming about him helping out on the farm, and going by my conversation with his father, neither has Zach."

"Well, they are pretty young," John said. "Both still live at home. Maybe they're worried about what their parents will say, seeing as she's Amish."

Elizabeth shook her head. "It feels like more than that—like maybe there's a history there we don't know about."

"What kind of history?"

"That's an interesting question." Elizabeth bit her lip, coming up with a dozen different reasons why Emma and Zach had chosen to keep silent, and tossing them all. Finally, she gave up with a troubled sigh. "Well, I don't suppose we'll figure anything out standing around here. Besides"—she angled her chin at him playfully—"we're supposed to be celebrating my birthday, not solving mysteries."

A teasing glint sparkled in John's eyes as he looked at her. "But you'd feel better if you knew what the connection was between Moses Troyer and Simon Vogel, right?"

She said nothing and put her hand to her lips to hide the smile begging to come out.

Giving an exaggerated roll of his eyes, John offered his elbow. "Fine, I'll see what I can dig up. Later. For now, let's see what else we can find here and then go get something to eat. I'm starving."

Letting a laugh loose, Elizabeth took John's arm and let him lead her to the next booth. "You're a good sport, John. Thank you for always indulging my curiosity."

"Your curiosity is one of the things I l—"

He cut off before saying the rest, his arm tensing beneath her touch. Elizabeth didn't push for him to finish, even though she longed to know. One of the things he...what? Liked? Laughed about?

*Loved?*

Struck by a sudden bout of nerves, she let her hand slip from the warmth of his arm. Was that why he hadn't finished? Because it was the latter? Was he afraid she would place too much stock in the word? Make more of it than he intended, which of course would make things awkward and uncomfortable?

Her stomach fluttered as another thought took flight. Maybe he wasn't worried she would put heavy stock in the word. Maybe it was him. And then what? What would become of their friendship?

She wasn't willing to compromise her beliefs.

That should have been the end of it. *Had* to be the end of it. Which was exactly the problem.

Because it wasn't.

Not by a long shot.

# CHAPTER SEVENTEEN

*Of all days for John to show up in church.*

Elizabeth squelched the uncharitable thought the instant it popped into her head. Of course she was glad John had chosen to come. She'd invited him often enough, and he was taking her up on the offer more and more frequently. It was just that, after a night spent tossing and turning over her changing feelings for him, she'd been looking forward to shifting her focus to where it needed to be—on the Lord—and off herself. And John. But here he was, looking as handsome as ever, if a tad uneasy.

"Lizzie, there's John." Martha's eyes twinkled merrily. "You two have seen each other almost every day this week."

"Really? I hadn't realized," Elizabeth said, hoping the tremor in her voice didn't sound nearly so loud in Martha's ears as it did in hers.

"Oh, there's Peggy Hockensmith, going over to tell him hello." Martha's nose wrinkled with worry as she looked at Elizabeth. "Would you like me to invite him to sit with us?"

Elizabeth hesitated. It was just for a moment but long enough to see that Peggy had already done the inviting. A tiny worm of jealousy wriggled into her heart, and just as quickly dissipated when a smile brightened John's face as he craned his neck to peer past Peggy and spotted Elizabeth watching. He said something to Peggy and then made his way over.

"Morning."

All thoughts of Peggy faded at the look he directed at her. Elizabeth's face warmed pleasantly under it. "Morning, John."

"There's Mary," Martha said, nodding toward the dais. "She's singing with the choir today." She inclined her head toward Elizabeth. "I'll go find us a seat." To John, she added, "You're welcome to join us, if you'd like."

"Thank you, Martha. I'd like that very much."

A smile teased John's lips as he offered his elbow, then led Elizabeth into the church. Elizabeth sank into the pew beside Martha, then spent the next hour wrangling her wayward thoughts, distracted by John's nearness, by his deep, rumbling voice as he joined in the singing, and by the warmth of his shoulder as it gently bumped hers.

"Forgive me, Lord," she whispered as the final amen was spoken. "Help me to make this day about You and nothing else."

The simple prayer made her feel better, even when Martha leaned close to whisper, "I'll wait for you by the car so you and John can talk."

"You don't need—" Elizabeth began, throwing her hand out to grasp Martha's, but she was too late. Her sister had already ducked out of the pew. Elizabeth had no choice but to turn and smile.

"Well, that was a good sermon this morning. Not that the sermons aren't normally good. They are. I just mean..." She fumbled to a stop, heat creeping steadily over her neck and cheeks. She'd certainly made a proper mess out of things now.

"I had a hard time concentrating on the message too," John said.

Suddenly, everything about John's presence felt right. Elizabeth relaxed her shoulders and smiled. "I'm happy to see you."

"Whew." He swiped his hand across his forehead in feigned relief. "Glad to hear it. For a second there, I thought maybe you wished I'd stayed home."

His joke helped to settle some of the nerves rattling around inside. "Never. You're always welcome."

He tilted his head to whisper in her ear. "Maybe more so when I tell you what I dug up on Simon Vogel and Moses Troyer."

"What? You found something important?"

"Maybe."

All hint of discomfort fled through the nearest window. She grabbed his arm and dragged him into a hall stretching off from the nursery. "What is it? What did you find out?"

"Turns out you were right about the two of them having a history," John said once Elizabeth quit yanking on his arm and circled around to face him. "Several years ago, our office got a call about a couple of local farmers involved in a dispute over at the Bird-in-Hand Farmers Market. Apparently, the argument was over who would set up where. They both wanted prime booth space closest to the entrance where people were sure to pass by. One argued he'd already staked his claim and had only left long enough to gather his wares. Care to guess who the farmers were?"

"I think I know," she said wryly.

John nodded. "That wasn't the only incident. Seems they've butted heads several times, and since neither one will back down, it always escalates, usually until someone calls the police."

Parents coming to collect their children passed to and fro near the nursery door. Granted, they were probably too occupied to pay any mind to her and John, but Elizabeth lowered her voice anyway.

"I admit, I don't know either one of these gentlemen very well, but public confrontations are not typical Amish behavior. They prefer to resolve their differences in private."

"I thought Simon was English."

"He is now, but at one time he was a member of the church."

Once again, the question of why he'd left floated into Elizabeth's head. She pushed it aside to focus on more recent happenings. "John, do you have any idea when the last run-in between Moses and Simon took place?"

"I do, and you'll be interested to know it was less than a month ago."

She gaped at him in surprise. "What?"

"The talk is that Moses replaced Simon Vogel as the milk supplier for Gingerich's Grocery and Dry Goods Store. The owner said with milk prices going up, he could no longer afford to buy from Simon. He claims it was strictly a business decision."

"But Simon didn't see it that way?"

John shook his head. "He accused Moses of undercutting his prices and intentionally stealing his business."

*Motive for sabotaging the Troyers' milk?*

She made a note to ask Emma about it later. "Okay, so Simon wasn't happy. What happened?"

"Apparently, Simon went by the store to talk to Gingerich about it and ran into Moses there."

"Oh no."

"Uh-huh. Things got heated, and Moses left. But here's where it gets interesting." John's eyes took on a speculative gleam. "The day all of this happened?"

"Yeah?"

"It was the same day Moses had his accident."

"Oh, John." Her voice rose a notch. Seeing a couple of glances directed their way, she forced herself to whisper. "You're kidding. Moses was leaving an argument with Simon when Beau ran him off the road?"

John's brows rose. "Did he?"

"Well, I mean *allegedly*—" she began.

John shook his head. "No, I mean, now there's a question as to whether he was run off the road at all, or if he was just so upset after the scene with Simon that he wasn't paying attention—"

"And drove off the road himself," she finished for him.

He nodded. "The district attorney's office is in a quandary. I even heard a rumor they're discussing the possibility of dropping the charges."

Elizabeth blew out a breath. "Okay, so say Beau didn't run Moses off the road. That doesn't explain the milk."

Or did it? Beau's claim that the accident wasn't solely his fault leapt to mind, followed by the idea that he might have given the cows the onions as retribution after being falsely accused. Simon too might have been angry enough to have been behind the plot to sabotage the Troyers' milk. Bottom line, Elizabeth was no closer to solving this mystery than she was before talking with John.

"You okay?" he asked, giving her a playful nudge with his elbow.

"I am. Just wish I was doing a little better figuring out who's behind this mess."

"You're doing everything you can," he replied firmly. "On a positive note, there hasn't been any more trouble out at the Troyers', so maybe it'll all just blow over and things will get back to normal."

"Maybe."

"There you are, Lizzie." Martha hurried down the hall toward them, car keys in hand. "Sorry to interrupt," she said, shooting an apologetic glance at John. "Mary's not feeling so well. I told her I would come and find you so we could get her home."

"She's sick again?" Worry gnawed inside Elizabeth's chest. "Her stomach was still upset yesterday, but she seemed fine this morning. She even ate a bowl of cereal for breakfast."

"Apparently it came on kind of fast." Martha jiggled the keys. "I'm going to get her to the house so she can lie down. You coming?"

"I can drive you home if you still have things to do around here," John volunteered quickly.

"Thank you, but I think I'd better ride along with Martha," Elizabeth said. "She might need help getting Mary settled."

Just like at the bakery, she thought she read a flicker of disappointment in his eyes, but it disappeared before she could be sure.

"All right, well, I'll keep my eyes and ears open for anything else I can learn about Moses and Simon."

"Thank you, John," Elizabeth said, already turning to follow Martha up the hall. A split second later, she wished she'd taken John up on his offer of a ride home, because coming from the opposite direction was Peggy Hockensmith, and she was making a beeline for John. Which was fine because John was just a friend, Elizabeth reminded herself as Peggy passed.

Of course, convincing her heart of that, well, *that* was another matter entirely. And no matter how many times she repeated it, Elizabeth suspected it might not be exactly true.

# CHAPTER EIGHTEEN

Light music played over the speakers in the waiting room of the Bird-in-Hand Family Care Practice early the next morning. Mary thought the place unusually busy for a Monday, or maybe that was typical for most doctors' offices after the weekend.

She wove past two rows of chairs, each seat occupied by people reading magazines or tending crying children, and made her way to the receptionist's window.

"Excuse me, I'm Mary Baxter, here to see Dr. Williams."

The young woman at the desk, Trudy, judging by her name tag, grabbed a clipboard bedecked with jewels on the clip and slid it across the counter to her. "Morning, Ms. Baxter. Go ahead and sign in. Dr. Williams will be with you shortly."

"Thank you." Mary signed her name and then went to look for a seat. Except for a worn black sofa with two bulky men anchoring either end, the only available spot was a chair next to a television set cranking out videos for kids. Mary made her way toward it.

"Well, except for this latest problem, we've been very lucky," a stout woman leaned over to say to the lady sitting next to her. "This time last year, we all had the flu. Heavens, I never want to relive that again."

The other woman tucked a lock of short brown hair behind her ear. "That is lucky. The weather has been so bad this year—gray and dreary one day, clear skies and sunshine the next."

"Well, whatever this is"—the stout woman patted her belly—"has nothing to do with the weather. I'm almost positive it's food poisoning."

The brown-haired woman's eyes widened. "Really? How can you tell?"

"I've got all the symptoms," the stout woman replied, emphasizing *all* with a knowing nod. "My husband had it too, but he got over it a lot quicker than I did. I think it's because he didn't eat as much of the cheesecake as I did." She rolled her eyes and let out a low moan. "Cheesecake is my weakness. That'll teach me, I suppose."

The brown-haired woman let out a sympathetic chuckle. "Any idea where you got it?"

"Oh, I know exactly where I got it."

Though she was eavesdropping, Mary couldn't help but be curious. Hoping to hear over the noise of the kids' show streaming from the television, she leaned toward the women and pushed her hair away from her ear.

"It was our first time visiting there. You know that secondhand store on Ronks Road?"

Mary's chest tightened. Surely, she wasn't talking about—

"Secondhand Blessings." The brown-haired woman nodded. "Yes, I know it. You mean you got sick from the cheesecake you bought there?"

"I'm sure of it." The stout woman rubbed her hand over her stomach gingerly. "I'll never go back."

Mary scrambled to grab a magazine and held it high over her face.

"I didn't even know they sold food."

"Baked goods, mostly. A friend of mine kept raving about how good their stuff was, so I figured I'd try it. Never again."

"Gosh, I'm so sorry. Is your husband going to get checked out too?"

"I don't think so. Like I said, he didn't eat as much of the cake, and he got over it a lot quicker. In fact, if it weren't for"—her voice dropped to a loud whisper—"you know, the bathroom trips, I'd probably just let it run its course. I'm dehydrated, I'm sure. This is the first time I've been able to get out of bed."

Mary sat frozen in place. Should she speak up? Explain who she was and apologize? But how could the woman possibly still be sick after so many days? Martha had thrown out the first batch of baked goods she'd made with the Troyers' milk.

"Mary Baxter?"

Mary jumped in her seat and dropped the magazine to stare at the two women. Neither one looked in her direction.

"Mary?"

She jerked her gaze toward the reception desk. Trudy beckoned to her. Mary hurried over. "Yes?"

"Dr. Williams is ready for you." She pointed to a wide door a couple of steps away. "I'll buzz you in."

"Oh, thank you." Cheeks blazing, Mary pushed through the door. What would Martha think? Should she even tell her?

More pressing were the two women in the waiting room. Mary *had* to say something. Her stomach cramped thinking about it.

"Ms. Baxter?" A nurse looked expectantly at her from a nearby exam room. "Are you ready?"

"I…yes…but…" She sighed and held up her finger. "Could you hang on just a minute? I'll be right back."

The nurse glanced at her watch. "I'm sorry, Ms. Baxter, the doctor has a very full schedule today. If you'd like, I can reschedule your appointment for you."

Mary debated a second and then shook her head. The pain in her stomach had grown steadily worse throughout the weekend and had even worked its way to her chest, making her feel tired and short of breath. She had no desire to risk a trip to the emergency room in the middle of the night. She would talk to the woman after she got through with her examination.

"No, I'll see him."

"Okay, right this way." The nurse led her into the room and shut the door. After recording Mary's weight and vitals, she crossed back to let herself out. "The doctor will be just a moment."

"Thank you."

While she waited, Mary listened for the sound of the stout woman being led back. The strain started a pounding in her head, which only seemed to intensify with each tick of the clock on the wall above the exam bed. Finally, the door swung open, and Dr. Williams stepped through.

Cheerful as always, Dr. Williams spent a couple of minutes asking for the reason behind Mary's visit and jotting down her symptoms as she gave them. When she got to the tightness in her chest, he paused, his pencil held midair over his clipboard.

"When you say there's a tightness in your chest, do you mean pain?" he asked.

Mary focused on that area for a second and then shook her head. "It's not pain, exactly. More like a dull ache."

She pushed her sleeve up to scratch her arm. Dr. William's gaze followed. He set aside his clipboard and held out his hand for her arm.

"Tell me about this redness, Mary. How long have you had it?"

Surprised, Mary dropped her gaze to the red patch of skin. "Oh, a couple of days, I guess."

"What about your eyes? Any itching there?"

She shook her head. What did her eyes have to do with her stomach?

"What about sudden onset of nausea?"

To this question, she nodded. "It comes on really fast. Yesterday, I was fine all morning, and then all of a sudden, I had to go home."

Though his expression remained calm and comforting, his gaze sharpened. "Mary, have you been swimming lately?"

"Swimming?" She laughed. "It's October."

"No, I mean, have you been in any indoor pools."

"Like the natatorium in the YMCA?"

He nodded.

Mary's smile faded. "Actually, yes. I've been taking a water aerobics class a couple of times a week to help me keep in shape."

"How long are the classes?"

"Just an hour. Why?"

Dr. Williams let go of her arm and sat back on his stool. "I'd like to test you for chlorine poisoning. I see this quite a bit in the summertime. It's unusual for October, but you're displaying all the symptoms."

Mary's heart tripped inside her chest. "Chlorine poisoning? How? And what—"

Dr. Williams shrugged and held up his hand. "Before you ask, let me reassure you, it's simple enough to treat. In fact, many times, it clears up on its own. My main concern is figuring out how it happened."

"Treat the cause, not the symptoms."

"Exactly." He tilted his head, and his brow crinkled thoughtfully. "So, if you're not spending a lot of extra time in the pool, then I would have to wonder if you've ingested something. Any major changes to your diet?"

"None to speak of," she said, and then paused. She had been drinking quite a bit of milk lately. Suspicion formed in her brain. "Dr. Williams, how much chlorine would a person have to ingest to experience symptoms of poisoning?"

"Actually, you'd be surprised. Poisoning occurs more often than people think, but because the case is so mild, they chalk it up to overexposure to the sun or simple tummy aches, things like that."

*Tummy aches.* Mary's mind raced. She wasn't the only one who'd started taking classes to get in shape. Heidi had enrolled herself and Nick in a baby swim class as a way of helping her burn off the last of her pregnancy weight and get Nick used to the water. "Would you mind putting together a little more information on chlorine poisoning for me? A list of the symptoms would be great, as well as any treatment options."

"I'll be happy to." He braced his hands on his knees and rose. "For now, let's go ahead and get some samples so I can run a few tests. If it turns out my hunch is right, then we'll look a little closer at your routine, see if we can't figure out what's going on."

Mary agreed, and a short while later, she was back in the waiting room. There were still several people scattered about, but the stout woman with the case of food poisoning wasn't among them.

Mary's stomach sank as a dreadful thought occurred to her. What if it wasn't food poisoning, but something else? Something more like what Mary had? And what if they'd contracted it from the same place?

Though she didn't want to believe it, her thoughts instantly winged to the Troyers. She grabbed her phone and looked up the symptoms of food poisoning, many of which were similar to chlorine poisoning.

"It *could* be the milk," she whispered to herself, and then looked up as the waiting room door swung open and the stout woman stepped out.

"Just see the receptionist for your prescriptions," the nurse instructed, laying one hand on the stout woman's shoulder and pointing with the other. "And give us a call if your symptoms don't clear up in a couple of days."

Prescriptions? Did that mean it wasn't food poisoning?

"All right, Mrs. Davis, which pharmacy would you like to use?" Trudy asked, her fingers flying over the keyboard as she spoke.

"I suppose you can just send it to the one here in town," the stout woman—Mrs. Davis, Mary mentally corrected—said before resting her arms on the counter with a disgusted sigh. "Another case of the flu. I could have sworn it was food poisoning."

"Well, sometimes your symptoms can mimic something else," Trudy said with a smile. A few more keystrokes and then she reached behind her to pull a sheet of paper off the printer. "Okay, you're all set. Give the pharmacy a couple of hours and then swing on over."

"I'll do that." Taking the paper from Trudy, Mrs. Davis smiled. "Thank you."

"You're welcome. I hope you feel better."

Knowing it wasn't some sort of poisoning made Mary instantly feel better. She ducked her head as Mrs. Davis passed, glad to be spared the embarrassment of having to apologize, but a little irritated that the damage had been done and the store's reputation marred.

Once again, the door opened, and the nurse called Mary back.

"Well, Mary," Dr. Williams said, swinging into the exam room with the results of her tests in his hand. "It's as I suspected. You have chlorine poisoning. The good news is, your levels are only slightly elevated."

"That's good news?" Mary asked weakly.

He nodded. "High enough to make you feel bad, but assuming we can pinpoint where the chlorine is coming from, it should clear up on its own in a couple of days." He perched on the edge of the desk, one hand propped on his leg. "So? Any idea where it's coming from?"

"It could be the pool," Mary said. "I'll give them a call, maybe ask if the chlorine levels in the water are higher than normal."

"Wouldn't hurt, though places like that usually have professionals caring for their pools." He scratched his chin thoughtfully. "If it's not the YMCA, you might want to start thinking about where else you might have come in contact."

Unfortunately, she *did* have a hunch, one she couldn't support without proof. And that meant she'd be paying another visit to the Troyers.

# CHAPTER NINETEEN

Elizabeth kept one eye trained on the Secondhand Blessings doors while she bustled about waiting on customers. Her reasons were twofold. Rachel would be coming in soon, and Elizabeth had several questions she wanted to ask, and Mary would be returning from the doctor any minute.

Thinking of Mary twisted a knot in Elizabeth's gut. After complaining of nausea yesterday afternoon, she'd woken up with a peculiar rash on her arm.

Prompted to pray, Elizabeth continued working while she communicated silently with the Lord. And as it often did, spending time praying for one person quickly recalled another need, and another, until she settled on little Nick.

Her hands stilled over the collection of hand-painted vintage pot lids she'd been carefully arranging. "Lord, please give Michael and Heidi some answers soon."

Love for the little boy and his parents swelled in her heart. But his was just one mystery to solve, and one in which she had no part to play except to pray. The Troyers, on the other hand, needed her help. But to do that, she needed answers.

The door chimed, so Elizabeth pushed the last lid into place and then went to see to her customers. Spying Rachel, she dusted her hands clean on her apron and hurried toward her.

"Thank goodness you're here. Do you have a minute to talk?"

Rachel tucked her purse under her arm before loosening the strings on her bonnet. The brisk autumn air stirred a rosiness to her nose and cheeks that was quite becoming against the blue wool fabric of her cloak. "Of course. Is everything all right?"

"Fine, fine. I just have some questions for you." She motioned toward the door. "Let's go up to the house so we can talk in private."

Signaling to Martha, Elizabeth grabbed her coat then walked with Rachel to the house, where she'd left a pot of coffee warming. Butterscotch watched them from the window with casual disinterest, but Pal and Tink were excited to receive visitors and greeted Rachel with happy yips and playful nudges begging for attention. One command from Elizabeth, however, was enough to send them back to their doggie beds. They watched with their heads on their paws and sleep tugging at their eyelids as Elizabeth hung her coat and Rachel's cloak, then poured two cups of coffee and joined Rachel at the wide table in the center of the kitchen.

For the first couple of minutes, Rachel sipped her coffee quietly while Elizabeth reviewed everything she had learned about Moses and Simon from John. When she finished, Rachel put down her cup and nodded sadly.

"It is true, there is a very long history between those two, going back more years than I can count."

"I figured as much," Elizabeth said, fingering the handle on her cup pensively. "What I don't know is how it all started, or how it affects Zach and Emma."

Rachel jerked her head up to stare at Elizabeth. "Zach and Emma? What do you mean?"

There it was again, the look of worry in Rachel's eyes every time those two names were mentioned together.

Elizabeth pushed her cup aside and rested both arms on the table. "Rachel, we never did finish our conversation the other night, after the meeting of the Dairy Farmers Association. I meant to ask you about Zach, but the meeting started and it got put off."

Rachel gave a nod to show she remembered.

"It's because you're afraid he and Emma might have feelings for each other, aren't you?" While she waited for an answer, Elizabeth studied her friend's face. Lines of worry crisscrossed her brow and fanned out from her eyes. Finally, Rachel's lips parted and she blew out a sigh.

"Ja, it is true. I have been noticing some troubling exchanges between the two of them. Nothing inappropriate," she added, holding up her hand quickly. "Emma's behavior is always above reproach. It is just a glance here and there, or an expression on her face that makes me think..." She bowed her head, the prayer kapp on her head hiding the sorrow in her eyes.

"I've seen it too." Elizabeth clasped both hands around her coffee cup. There could only be one reason Rachel would be so upset. "I take it Emma has made her vow to the church? She has decided to join the Amish?"

"Ja. Last summer, after her *rumspringa*."

Elizabeth frowned. "If that's so, then surely she doesn't have romantic feelings for Zach. She wouldn't have asked him to help out around the farm otherwise. It would be too much of a temptation."

"That is what I thought at first, but how else to explain what we have witnessed?"

Elizabeth opened her mouth to answer and closed it again when words failed her. "So, tell me about Emma," she said instead. "Is she seeing anyone inside the church?"

Rachel pressed her hand to her cheek. "Emma is very sweet. Several young men have expressed an interest in courting her, but none of them have captured her attention. She always says she is too busy for such things, and Moses does not press. I think he worries that with Emma gone, he will be lonely."

"Not to mention, he'll be forced to manage the farm on his own."

Rachel nodded. "Abel and Ezra are hard workers, but they are not family, and Moses's son has shown no interest in leaving Texas to take over the farm."

"But Emma wants to farm."

"She does, which is another reason, I think, why Moses is in no hurry to see his daughter wed."

More questions rang inside Elizabeth's head, but since all of them concerned Emma's feelings, or lack thereof, for Zach, she didn't think it fair to ask Rachel. She chose a safer topic instead.

"So, you mentioned young men have expressed an interest in Emma. Do any of them seem like the sort who might have wanted to cause trouble on the farm as a way of getting back at her for not returning their affection?"

Rachel's eyes widened, and she shook her head. "Ne, I cannot think of one who would do such a thing."

"I figured as much. Just thought I'd ask," Elizabeth assured her. She carried her cup to the sink and dumped out the coffee. "I should head out to the farm so I can talk to Emma. Maybe I'll go this afternoon, after the store closes."

"Would you like me to go with you?" Rachel motioned toward the clock. "I have several errands to run, but they can wait if you would prefer not to go alone."

Even with battery-operated headlights, the black buggies the Amish used were harder to see at night, and Rachel always liked to have her errands completed before dark.

"Thank you, but I can manage," Elizabeth said. "Besides, Emma might feel a little more free to talk if we're alone."

Rachel agreed without hesitation. Grateful for her friend's trust, Elizabeth wrapped her in a hug and then returned with her to the store.

"I'll let you know how it goes," she said as Rachel climbed back into her buggy.

Reaching for the reins, Rachel smiled. "Danki, Elizabeth. I will come by tomorrow. We can talk more then." She raised her hand in a wave, then giving a chirp to the mare, set off down the road.

As she turned to go inside, Elizabeth's cell phone vibrated in her pocket. She pulled it out, and seeing Mary's name on the screen, she swiped to answer and jerked the phone to her ear.

"Mary? Where are you? Is everything okay? What did the doctor say?"

"Everything is fine. The doctor said I'll probably be back to normal in a couple of days."

The words brought instant relief. Elizabeth closed her eyes for a brief second and pressed her hand to her heart. "That is good news. I'll let Martha know. But what did he say is wrong? Is it just a stomach bug?"

"Not a bug. Listen, Lizzie, a lot has happened, some of it involving Heidi and Nick. I'll explain everything when I see you, but first, I need to make a stop out at the Troyers' place. It can't wait."

*The Troyers?* A bit of tension returning, Elizabeth clutched the phone tighter. "I was going to head out there after work. Do you want me to meet you?"

There was a brief pause, and then Mary's voice sounded again, but with a note of strain and urgency that sent chills running down Elizabeth's back.

"Yeah, I think maybe you'd better meet me. If I'm right, and I have a strong hunch that I am, then I have some news to deliver. Emma is closer to you than she is me. It might go a little better if you're there."

"What kind of news?" Elizabeth asked, but inside, a tiny curl of dread unfurled. Mary's next words confirmed her fears.

"It's not good, Elizabeth. Not good at all."

# CHAPTER TWENTY

Chlorine poisoning." Emma's gaze skipped from Elizabeth to Mary and settled on Abel. "From our milk? You are certain?"

"I have tested it twice, just to be sure." A slight tremor shook Abel's hand as he tugged off his hat to hold it clutched in front of him. "How the chlorine got in the milk, I have no idea. We use some to sanitize our equipment, but not enough to cause the kind of symptoms Mary has experienced. So where it came from, I just…" He lifted both hands and shrugged helplessly.

Mary stepped forward tentatively. "There is another possibility."

All eyes swung to look at her. She gestured toward a group of cows meandering slowly across a nearby pasture.

Elizabeth put up her hand. "Wait, you mean from the cows, not the machinery?"

"The cows ate the onions. Maybe the chlorine got into the milk the same way."

Panic bubbled inside Elizabeth's chest. "But wouldn't that hurt the cows?"

Emma jerked her head to Abel, who held up his hand. "Ne, ne, the cows are fine. They are still drinking and have not gone off their feed. We still need to figure out how they are getting it, however."

Before Elizabeth could comment, a brown pickup rattled into the yard, and Zach climbed out. Sugarpie hurried to greet him with Emma following close behind. Mary continued questioning Abel about the possibility of the cows somehow ingesting a significant amount of chlorine, but with her conversation with Rachel still ringing in her ears, Elizabeth watched Zach and Emma instead.

Emma's hands expressed urgency as she relayed the events of the morning. Several times, Zach looked their way, disbelief written plainly across his features. Elizabeth had to admit, it was all rather unbelievable. Finally, Emma's arms dropped to her sides, and she fell silent. Zach grasped her elbow and led her toward them, his face grim. He gave a nod to Abel, then turned to Mary.

"First of all, I'm really sorry that you've been sick."

"Thank you," she said. "I know it wasn't your fault, or Emma's. We just need to figure out what's been going on so we can fix it before anyone else gets sick."

Zach agreed and looked at Abel. "We can't send out any more orders today."

Abel shook his head. "I have already made the calls."

"Good." Zach pointed toward the barn. "I'll get to work emptying all the water troughs and filling them with fresh water. We'll probably need to clean out all the stalls and feed bins too. We can put the cows out to pasture while we're doing that so we don't risk them getting into something they shouldn't."

"That is a good idea," Emma said. "I will start moving them now."

While Zach and Abel rushed off to get started, Elizabeth looked at Emma. "Anything I can do to help?"

"We could certainly use another pair of hands, but I hate to ask," Emma began hesitantly.

Elizabeth waved her protests aside. "It's no problem." She turned to Mary. "Would you mind letting Martha know where I am?"

"Of course not, but maybe I could—?"

Elizabeth cut her off with a shake of head. "Not with how sick you've been. Better if you get back to the house and rest."

Though Elizabeth knew she would have preferred to stay and help, Mary agreed with a nod.

"I'm really sorry," Mary said to Emma.

"It is all right. Thank you for letting us know there was a problem."

Mary grasped Emma's hand one last time before turning for her car. Emma waved goodbye and then looked at Elizabeth. "If you are ready, we can head down to the barn and get started."

Elizabeth glanced down at her boots, glad she'd thought to change her shoes before she came. "I'm ready. Show me what I need to do."

Moving the cows took almost an hour, but thanks to help from Sugarpie, they accomplished it with little trouble.

Zach and Abel concentrated on the troughs first. Abel took samples to make sure the chlorine wasn't coming from the pipes before opening the drains to let the water run out. Soon, muddy rivers made navigating the spaces difficult, but Zach got on the tractor and began spreading straw to make walking less treacherous. Before too long, the work was complete, and Elizabeth joined Emma on the porch steps, the kink in her back forgotten as she read the dismay brimming in the girl's eyes.

"Are you all right?" she asked softly.

Emma lifted her hands, the move encompassing the muddy mess that was left of their yard. "This is just...it will be days before we can begin producing milk for sale again and..."

She stopped, her lips pressed tightly together. Likely it was to quell the angry tears Elizabeth saw filling her eyes. She grabbed Emma's hand and gave it a squeeze.

"I'm tired. Let's sit down for a minute and take a little break." She motioned to a pair of wooden rockers on the porch. Emma didn't argue. She let Elizabeth lead her to one of the rockers and sank into it heavily and bowed her head.

"This was no prank." A hard edge sharpened her voice. "And it was no coincidence. Someone is trying to sabotage our farm."

Seeing no point in denying it, Elizabeth nodded. "It certainly does seem that way."

"Why?" She lifted her head and stared, leaving the word hanging painfully between them. Little by little, her shoulders sagged. "What have we done to anger someone so?"

Elizabeth had no answer. Only questions. "Emma, tell me about your friendship with Zach."

"Zach." Her gaze darted to the truck parked a few yards away. "We have known each other since we were kinner. Why?"

Both Elizabeth and Rachel had noticed the looks the two exchanged. Was it possible someone else had as well? "I just can't help wondering if maybe the answer to the things going on around here could be as simple as jealousy."

Emma caught her bottom lip between her teeth, her hands gripping the arms of the rocker. "I don't understand. Why would anyone have cause to be jealous?"

Elizabeth tilted her head and waited.

Emma swallowed hard and rested her clasped hands in her lap. "I admit, Zach and I are close. He has been such a huge help to me since my father's accident. But he and Lillian—" Her voice rose, and she broke off with a shake of her head.

Lillian? Elizabeth had almost forgotten about the girl from the Dairy Association Meeting. "Are the two of them dating?"

Emma shrugged. "Lillian would like that, I am sure, but Zach sees her as just a friend."

"The same way he sees you?" she asked gently.

Emma's eyes rounded but she said nothing.

"What about you? Are there any people in particular who might have reason to be jealous?"

This time, Emma shook her head firmly then rose to pace. "Ne. I have made my feelings plain in this matter. I do not attend the singings for this very reason. I do not want anyone to think I am ready to court."

"That's probably wise." Elizabeth's stomach growled, reminding her that it had been several hours since she'd had something to eat. Standing, she pressed her hand to her middle and smiled in apology. "Sorry. I should probably be going."

"Wait, I haven't thanked you for your help this afternoon." Sucking in a deep breath, Emma hitched her thumb toward the house. "I need to go in and start supper. Why don't you stay? It is the least I can do after making you work so hard."

Elizabeth looked down at her muddy boots. "Oh, but I would hate to drag all of this inside."

Emma laughed and pointed at her own shoes. "It will not take us long to get cleaned up. Unless…" She hesitated, and the smile slipped a little. "I understand if you have other plans."

In that moment, it was Elizabeth who understood. Emma was tired, and sad, and in need of a little company. Maybe by staying, Elizabeth could help in the kitchen and give her a much-needed break.

"If you're sure you don't mind, I would love to stay," she said.

Emma's face brightened, and Elizabeth breathed a grateful prayer that the Lord had opened her eyes to a need beyond figuring out what was wrong with their milk. Sometimes, a person just needed a friend.

Elizabeth stepped out of her boots and then, taking a broom, brushed away the mud still clinging to her pant legs. Emma also left her muddy shoes on the porch, but instead of sweeping the mud from her skirt, she hurried upstairs to change. When she came down, she not only looked fresher, there was a lightness to her step that had been missing before.

"Daed will be down in a minute," she said. "I told him you would be joining us for supper." She gestured toward the hall. "I have some pork chops marinating in the kitchen. I thought we could peel some potatoes to go with them."

"Sounds scrumptious." Elizabeth rolled up her sleeves and then braced her hands on her hips. "Lead me to them, and I'll get started."

Chuckling softly, Emma pulled a bushel basket of potatoes from the pantry. While Elizabeth worked on the potatoes, Emma fried the pork chops. Soon, the tantalizing smells filling the house coaxed Moses from his bedroom. Leaning heavily on his crutches, he hobbled into the kitchen.

"Elizabeth, welcome. Emma tells me you were very helpful this afternoon."

Elizabeth glanced at Emma. She'd told him? The last she knew, Emma preferred her father not be made aware of the problems she'd been having.

"I'm just glad I was around," she said, hoping the vague answer gave nothing away.

Moses shooed Emma away when she drew near to help him. He leaned one crutch against the table and wrangled a chair around to sit. "I heard a car pull in and thought maybe it was Abel getting the truck ready for a delivery. But when I looked at the clock, I knew that could not be right. It was too early in the afternoon for deliveries."

"It was either me or Zach," Elizabeth said, cutting off at the look of horror Emma shot her way.

"Zach?" Moses swung his gaze to his daughter's face. "What was Zach Vogel doing here?"

"Daed, he was just helping out," Emma began.

Flustered by her gaff, Elizabeth stared mute as a flush crept over Emma's face.

"Daughter." Color mottled Moses's face, and he pressed his palm firmly to the tabletop. "I have told you before, I do not want that *Vogel* boy on my farm."

If she could have, Elizabeth would have crawled into a hole. Emma cleared her throat and tipped her head in Elizabeth's direction. Reminded of her presence, Moses dragged in a deep breath and bobbed his head.

"We will discuss this after supper."

The way he said "that Vogel boy" left no doubt about his feelings, whether he voiced them in front of Elizabeth or not. Though the food was delicious, she found it hard to eat. Without knowing the details of the situation between Emma and her father, she dared not risk saying anything that would make the problem worse. But keeping silent felt wrong too.

With supper finished, Moses retired to the living room to warm himself by the fire, and Elizabeth set about helping Emma with the dishes.

"You need to tell him what's going on," she said, taking the washed dish Emma handed her and running a dry cloth over it. "I know you're worried about his health, but at this point, not telling him would be the same as lying."

Emma's hands stilled in the soapy water. "I know."

Elizabeth set the dish aside and twisted to rest her hip against the sink. "Emma, why doesn't your father like the Vogels? It has to be more than just that they are Englisch. What is this 'long history' I keep hearing about?"

Emma reached for another plate and slid it under the suds. "I cannot say what happened between my father and Simon Vogel. It all happened long before I was born."

It was Emma's tone, more than her words, that surprised Elizabeth. She spoke them with such adamancy, further questioning would be pointless.

Elizabeth stifled a sigh of frustration. It was much harder helping someone who refused to open up about the past. And Emma *did* refuse, because deep down, Elizabeth was certain Emma knew what had happened. She just wouldn't talk about it. Which left Elizabeth in a very hard spot.

With no idea how she would figure out who was trying to sabotage the Troyers' farm.

# CHAPTER TWENTY-ONE

The store closed early on Tuesdays. Elizabeth arranged to meet Rachel for a late lunch at the Bird-in-Hand Café. Fortunately, the weather cooperated, and the icy rain that had been forecast all weekend held off until after Elizabeth and Rachel were snug inside.

"Thank you so much for coming," Elizabeth said, draping her coat over the back of the booth next to Rachel's cloak.

"Your message sounded urgent." Rachel scooted into the booth across from Elizabeth. "What is it? What has happened?"

While they waited for their server to appear, Elizabeth explained about Mary's illness and how it had led them back to the Troyers' farm.

"Chlorine." Disbelief rounded Rachel's eyes. "And it affected the entire herd? How can that be?"

"No idea...yet." Determination built in Elizabeth's chest. "They've cleaned out the stalls and changed out all the food."

"Maybe Adam would have an idea."

Elizabeth nodded eagerly and leaned forward to rest her arms on the table. "I was hoping we could ask him."

"Of course."

Their server appeared, and Elizabeth and Rachel placed their orders. Soon she returned with their drinks, and Elizabeth grabbed a packet of sugar to stir into her tea.

"The good news is, Emma has agreed to talk to Moses about what has been going on, including the fact that Zach has been helping out in Ezra's absence." Elizabeth ripped the top off the sugar and added the sweetener to her glass. "I just wish she would talk to *me* about the problem between Moses and the Vogels. Maybe then I could get a lead on what's been going on."

Rachel stopped stirring her own tea and set her spoon aside quietly. "Emma may not know. It all happened before she was born."

"That's exactly what she said." Elizabeth pushed her glass aside to peer at her friend. "I don't believe it's just because Zach is Englisch."

"Ne, you are right. It is much more than that." Rachel thought a moment and then matched Elizabeth's posture and rested her arms on the table. "It was years ago, back when Simon was still a member of the church. He was never comfortable with the Amish lifestyle and had been thinking of leaving for some time. The problem was, he was in love with an Amish woman. I always thought he only stayed as long as he did because of her. People even said she was the reason he made his vow."

"Oh no." The Amish life was not an easy one, despite what many people thought. Without the proper motivation and commitment, Elizabeth could see how Simon's choice must have troubled him. "So, what happened?"

Sadness wrung Rachel's voice. "He asked the woman to leave the church with him. She refused. Hard as it was, Simon knew he could not live a lie. He left without her."

Hearing the news sent a stab of pain to Elizabeth's heart. "And the woman?"

Rachel swallowed hard and dropped her gaze. "She wound up marrying Moses Troyer."

"What?" Elizabeth gaped, swallowed, and repeated quieter, "What?"

Rachel nodded. "The three had always been friends, but after that, Simon soured. He directed his anger toward Moses, and it only got worse after Amelia Troyer died."

"That is so sad."

"Indeed." Rachel grabbed her glass but didn't drink from it. Instead, she ran her thumb over the drops of condensation forming on the sides. "This is just my opinion, but I always wondered if what passed between them when they were young is the reason they are so competitive now. Moses acts like he has something to prove."

"And the same for Simon."

"Ja, I suppose so."

Their food arrived, and Elizabeth sat quietly while the waitress set their plates on the table. No wonder Moses was so opposed to Zach's presence. At best, he probably feared another case of history repeating itself. And at worst…

What would he do if Emma made a different choice than the one made by her mother? A weight settled on her chest thinking of the possible ways Moses might react.

"Given this information, I think we have to consider the possibility that Simon might be behind the problems with the Troyers' cows," Elizabeth said at last. She grabbed her fork and picked at the bits of salad in her bowl. "Much as I hate to consider it, he seems to have a pretty strong motive."

Rachel rested her elbow on the table and tapped her temple with her finger. "I admit, it does not look good. But what about Beau Hegel? We still cannot be certain he is not involved. Or even that young girl you said might be jealous of Emma. Lillian, I think, was her name?"

She was right. Elizabeth took a bite of her salad and chewed thoughtfully. There had to be some way of narrowing down their suspects. But how?

With no obvious answers coming to mind, she and Rachel finished their lunch talking about other things. By the time she left, things with the Troyers were still unsettled, but Elizabeth felt better knowing she had some insight into events that had transpired in the past.

When she arrived back at the farm, she dropped her keys on the hall table and shrugged out of her coat.

Martha's voice echoed from the kitchen. "Lizzie, is that you?"

"It's me." Blowing into her hands, she walked down the hall to find her sisters. They would want to know what Rachel had told her about Simon and Moses. At the sight that met her eyes in the kitchen, Elizabeth stopped dead, her heart sinking to her stomach.

Mary sat at the table, a tissue in her hand and her eyes red from crying. Behind her, Martha patted her shoulder, murmuring words of comfort.

"What's going on?" Somehow, she managed to croak the words building in her throat. "Is it Nick?"

Martha's frozen expression said it all. With her nephew's sweet face swimming before her eyes, Elizabeth strode forward to clasp Mary's other hand. "They got his test results back? Is it chlorine poisoning? What did the doctor say?"

Choking on another sob, Mary pressed the tissue to her nose and closed her eyes.

"It's not the report we were hoping for, Lizzie," Martha said. "Michael and Heidi called. They're taking Nick in for more tests."

# CHAPTER TWENTY-TWO

Though every cell in Mary's body longed to make the nine-hour drive to Indianapolis to be with her grandchild, she knew Michael was right. Better if she waited until they got the test results back so she could be there for Heidi if she was needed. Still, she hated to think what her poor grandson was going through. His case of chlorine poisoning—which Heidi confirmed had come from the swim classes they'd enrolled in—was much more severe than Mary's.

"Father, help me to wait on You. You'll provide the answers at just the right time."

For a split second, Mary wondered if she really believed the words she said. Peace filled her along with the knowledge that yes, she truly did. God's timing. Not hers.

"How ya doing?" Martha handed her a plastic tub stuffed with vinyl records for Mary to cull. The more sought-after ones she slipped into plastic sleeves. The rest went into a cardboard box to be given away or carted off.

"I'm doing okay. Better than okay," she amended, taking the tub from Martha with a smile. She nodded to the empty bakery case Martha had spent most of the morning cleaning out. "How about you?"

Martha fisted both hands on her hips. "It's such a bummer. All that food, wasted. But we couldn't take a chance that anyone else might get sick."

Mary set the records aside to clasp her sister's arm. "I'm sorry, Martha."

Tears welled in Martha's eyes. She cleared her throat and blinked them back. "For what? If anything, I should be apologizing to you."

"Stop that," Mary said, wagging her head. "It's not your fault I got sick. There was no way you could have known about the chlorine in the milk. Besides, Dr. Williams said I was probably more susceptible because of the water aerobics classes I've been taking. Spending time in the pool meant I'd already been exposed to chlorine."

"Still." Martha shook her head. "I feel terrible about it. I just hope no one else is affected."

"I know." She gave Martha's arm one more squeeze and then picked up the tub. "I think I'll take these to the back to finish sorting later. Right now—"

She stopped as sunlight glinted off the doors, followed by a chime, and then Bill appeared. Instantly, Mary felt her knees go weak.

"Let me do that," Martha said, taking the tub with a knowing smile. "It looks like you have company."

Bill's gaze remained locked on Mary as he approached. "I heard about little Nick," he said, clasping her arms as he reached her. "Why didn't you call me?"

"I was on the phone, off and on, with Michael and Heidi most of the evening. It was so late by the time we finished up, I didn't want to risk waking you."

"Mary." Exasperation mingled with the worry in Bill's voice as he pulled her into his arms for a hug.

For several seconds, neither said a word. Content to simply rest in Bill's embrace, Mary let the tears run unchecked down her face.

"When are you going to Indianapolis?" Bill asked, pulling back to yank a handkerchief from his pocket and press it into her hand.

"I'm not sure. I won't make any plans until I hear back from the kids."

"Well, let me know. I'll take a couple of days off so I can drive over with you."

Blinking with astonishment, she said, "You'd do that for me?"

"Mary."

The gentle chiding in his voice raised a fresh wave of tears. He took her hand and pulled her toward the door. "C'mon, let's get some air."

With tears blurring her vision, Mary stumbled after Bill. Only when they stepped outside did she realize it hadn't bothered her one bit that she couldn't see. She trusted Bill. He would never let her fall.

Closing the distance between them, Bill shrugged out of his jacket and draped it around her shoulders.

"You'll be cold," Mary protested weakly. "Just let me grab my coat from inside."

"I'll be fine," he said, smiling as he took her hand and tipped his head toward where they kept their goats. "Let's go check on Wynken, Blynken, and Nod."

Mary agreed. On the way, she filled him in on her conversation with Michael and Heidi, as well as her own recent visit to the doctor.

His steps slowed as she finished. "I wish I'd known Sunday that you weren't feeling well. I would have brought you home myself."

She squeezed his hand to let him know she appreciated his concern. "You were helping with the youth. Besides, Martha and Elizabeth took good care of me."

"I'm sure they did, but—"

"But?" She tipped her head up to peer at him.

His steps slowed. "I was going to say, I wish that was my job." He pulled on her hand, drawing her to a stop. "I'm glad you're all right, Mary."

Placing her palm against his stubbled cheek, Mary smiled. "Thank you so much for coming by today. Seeing you was just what I needed."

For the span of several heartbeats, neither of them moved, until finally, reluctantly, Mary dropped her hand.

"So, tell me about the Troyers," Bill said, his rough voice sending delicious shivers over Mary's skin. "I'm sorry I haven't been able to help out more with all of that. You and your sisters have any idea yet what's been going on over there?"

Mary sighed and turned with Bill to continue walking. "Not yet, unfortunately. The chlorine proves the thing with the onions wasn't just a random prank, which is troubling." Sorrow pinched her heart. "That poor family is already going through so much. I just hate that they have this to deal with on top of everything else. I've been praying that God would show us who the culprit is so we can at least take that worry off their plate."

Bill said nothing, but his lips twitched in a small smile.

She slanted a glance up at him. "What?"

"You."

"What about me?"

"You've been sick, you're concerned about your grandson, yet you still find time to pray for someone else. It's one of the things I admire about you."

Flustered, Mary pushed her hair behind her ear and shifted her gaze forward. "Oh. Well, thank you."

"How are the plans coming for Elizabeth's birthday party?"

"Now that is one thing I can say we have under control. Martha is taking care of the cake, and I'm handling all of the invitations."

"Elizabeth still has no idea that you're planning a surprise party for her?"

"Actually, I think she's been so caught up with the problems the Troyers are having, she hasn't had time to think about her birthday."

He let go of her hand as they reached the barn to pull open the door and let her pass through. "Good, then you don't have to worry about anything ruining the surprise."

"Not yet, anyway. I sure hope she likes the party. She's been so busy, we gave up trying to get her to make definite plans." Mary tapped her temple. "But Elizabeth is a pretty smart cookie. All it will take is the smallest whisper, and she'll figure out what we have planned, like that."

A snap of her fingers emphasized her point. From inside one of the stalls, Wynken seconded Mary's opinion with a loud bleat. Elizabeth *was* smart. And intuitive. Mary had no doubt those skills would help them uncover whoever was behind the events at the Troyers' place. The only question was...

Would it happen in time to keep them from losing their farm?

# CHAPTER TWENTY-THREE

Elizabeth's grip on the steering wheel tightened as she slowed to make the turn into Jeff Thompson's driveway. After she checked with Rachel and Adam, they had all agreed that he would be the best person to talk to about the problems the Troyers were having with their cows. Even if he couldn't offer insight into how chlorine had gotten into their milk, he would at least be able to tell them what to do about it.

Elizabeth frowned and took her foot off the gas pedal. If she was honest, those weren't the only reasons she had come. Jeff was still on her list of suspects, albeit low on the list, and asking about the chlorine gave her a good reason for seeking him out.

The Thompsons' farm was set up much like the Troyers'—with long, low barns set up for feeding, another for milking, and yet another faded red building fashioned in the more typical barn style Elizabeth was used to. When she saw that the door was standing open, she circled around to park in front of it then climbed out of her car. Instantly, a mischievous wind snagged the ends of the lace scarf she'd paired with her sweater and dragged it from around her neck. She scrambled to catch it then shoved it into her pocket and turned for the barn.

In the distance, the low rumble of a tractor drowned out the lowing of the cattle. Elizabeth poked her head into the barn, but seeing no one, made her way toward the tractor. Jeff spotted her right away and killed the engine before hopping down to meet her.

"Afternoon, Ms. Classen."

"Good afternoon, Jeff. And please, call me Elizabeth."

Smiling, he tugged a hanky from his pocket and used it to mop his face and hands. "Elizabeth, it is."

She nodded toward the tractor. "I hope I didn't catch you at a bad time. I didn't mean to interrupt your work."

"No problem. I was ready for a break."

That was one thing in her favor. She smiled. "I was hoping you could spare a minute to talk?"

"Sure." He stuffed the hanky back in his pocket then held out his hand toward the barn. "Why don't we go inside, out of this wind?"

Clutching her coat collar, Elizabeth followed him into the red barn, then waited while he slid the door partially closed.

"There. That's better." He rubbed his palms together briskly. "I believe it's getting colder out there by the minute."

Shivering, she had to agree.

Jeff reached up to a light switch covered in cobwebs and flicked it on. Instantly, light from the fluorescents high over-head flooded the room and gave life to the dust motes dancing on the air. Obviously, this building wasn't depended on as heavily as the other buildings. By the look of the grit heaped on the tarps scattered around, and the amount of dirt and grime piling up in the corners, this place was for storage and very little else.

"So, what can I do for you, Elizabeth?"

"Well, this is probably going to sound a little strange," she began, and then launched into an explanation about the chlorine in Mary's system and the reason for her visit. Jeff's frown deepened as she talked, and when she got to the part about the Troyers' milk being at least part of the cause, he let out a loud "humph."

"Dr. Williams did say that Mary was extra susceptible due to the amount of time she'd been spending in the pool," Elizabeth concluded a bit uneasily.

Jeff crossed his arms, the scowl on his face giving him the look of an irritated badger. "That may be, but it still goes to prove what I've been trying to tell old Troyer all along. Just because a farm passes inspection doesn't mean they're doing things the best way possible. It only means they're following the minimum standards allowed."

Elizabeth angled her head as she listened. "Minimum standards? I'm not sure what you mean. The Troyers' weren't negligent in the processing of their milk. Their milk was intentionally sabotaged."

Jeff shook his head stubbornly. "The United States Public Health Services maintain a Standard Milk Ordinance to help prevent milk-borne diseases. It's one of the things the Dairy Farmers Association provides instruction on to area farmers. Maybe if the Troyers educated themselves on the finer points of the ordinance, their milk wouldn't have been so easily susceptible to sabotage."

"But Moses isn't a member."

"Exactly." Jeff's chin rose a notch, matching the tilt of his lips in a barely suppressed grin. "Apparently, he thinks he already knows everything he needs to about dairy farming. I guess this shows him. Maybe he'll be a little more ready to listen the next time I ask him about joining."

"I'm not too sure about that. Moses seems pretty set in his opinion."

"Well, he's in a proper muddle now," Jeff pointed out. "At the very least, he'll think twice before he spouts off against the Dairy Farmers Association again."

"Again?" Elizabeth schooled her features innocently. "When was the last time?"

Jeff blinked in surprise. "You haven't heard? It was right before he had his accident."

It was Elizabeth's turn to stare. "But…I thought he was coming from a conversation with Simon Vogel."

"He was. Troyer replaced Simon Vogel as Gingerich's milk supplier. Simon went to talk to Gingerich about it."

"Only Moses was there." At his nod, she pressed on. "Jeff, Gingerich claimed he could no longer afford to buy from Simon because he said milk prices were too high. Why didn't Simon just lower his prices to match what Vogel was offering?"

Jeff's face went from slightly smug to angry and mottled in the span of a heartbeat. "The members of the association signed an agreement. We're all local farmers. We live and work here together. We try hard to keep prices fair and equitable across the board."

A seed of understanding sprouted in her head. "But non-members set their own prices."

He didn't have to answer. His dark glare said it all. She pressed her lips together to stifle a sigh. So, if other dairy farmers also felt like Moses was undercutting their prices, there was no telling *who* might be behind the ordeal the Troyers were facing. Still, something about Jeff's attitude didn't sit right—almost like he wasn't surprised or even upset by what had happened on the Troyers' farm. Almost like...he was glad.

She licked her lips nervously. "Going back to what you said, how exactly did Moses 'spout off'?"

"He claimed the association was behind the high milk prices. He told Simon if he wanted to be angry at anyone for losing a buyer, it should be us." He waved his hand dismissively. "Then he went off on his usual rant about the association, all stuff I've heard before. I won't bore you with the details."

She sucked in a deep breath and pressed her hand to her chest. "I just recently learned that all of this happened before his accident. The argument between Simon and Moses hasn't been reported in the news, so who did you hear it from?"

Jeff's eyes narrowed in puzzlement. "Well...I didn't have to hear about from anyone. I was there when it happened."

"You were?"

He nodded. "I was in Gingerich's store when Simon and Moses began arguing. At first, I didn't think it was any of my business, but when Moses started in about the association, I felt like I had to intervene."

Elizabeth did a quick mental reorganization of the events of that day. "Jeff, do you know if anyone else was in the store when all this happened?"

He thought for a second, and then shook his head. "To be honest, I really don't recall."

"Okay. So, after Simon and Moses argued, what happened next?"

"Moses left. Simon and I stayed for a bit and talked to Gingerich. After that, I assume Simon went home. I did the same. At least, I intended to."

"Something stopped you?"

Again, he stared at her with a puzzled look on his face. "Well...yeah, the accident. You know."

Her mouth opened, and disbelief spilled out. "Wait, are you saying you saw Moses get forced off the road?"

"Well, not exactly. I mean, by the time I came up on it, the accident had already occurred. Moses's buggy was lying in a heap on the side of the road."

"So what did you do?"

"I called 911, then stayed on the line until help arrived. Fortunately, it didn't take long. I know basic CPR, but not a whole lot beyond that. Mostly, I just stayed with Moses until the ambulance got there. And when the police arrived, I gave them my statement, such as it was."

"What do you mean?"

"Well, like I said, the accident had already happened. But I did see something I knew would help the police." He stopped for a second, and Elizabeth was of the opinion he did it for dramatic effect, as though he'd already told the story several times and knew that what he was about to say would shock his listener.

"It was the decal. As the car drove off, I saw the decal in the back window. I knew immediately who it belonged to."

"Beau Hegel."

"That's right. It was Beau Hegel." The confident smile returned. "I was just glad I came along when I did—to help Moses, of course, but also to catch a glimpse of the car before he drove away. We might never have known who caused the accident otherwise."

"Well, except for Moses, of course. He would have—"

Jeff shook his head before she could finish. "He was unconscious after the accident, and since the car came up from behind, he didn't see who forced him off."

Elizabeth was shocked to realize that in all the excitement, she had never really asked Moses about the accident. She'd just assumed he was the witness who'd told the police about the decal, and was stunned to hear it was Jeff.

"Wow, that is…very interesting."

"Sure is." He pushed up his sleeve to check his watch and frowned. "Listen, I really should…" His eyebrows rose as he trailed off, his implication clear.

"Oh, yes. Of course. You need to get back to work. Thank you so much for talking with me, Jeff."

"No problem." He crossed to the door and slid it open for her, then followed her outside without bothering to close it again. "If I can be of any more help, please don't hesitate to ask."

"I'll do that. Thanks again."

Jeff nodded then turned and walked back to his tractor. Elizabeth started toward her car, but mindful of being buffeted by the wind, paused to reach for her scarf. Her pocket was empty. A check of the ground revealed nothing, which meant she'd likely dropped it in the barn.

Grumbling to herself, she ducked inside the barn and quickly spotted the scarf on the floor where she'd been standing. She hurried to pick it up and shake out the bits of dust and straw clinging to it. Not *dust*, she realized, but a strange, white powder. She brought it to her nose. It smelled like...

Her head swiveled back and forth as she searched for the source of the powder. A trail of it led back to the tarp she'd noticed when she entered. Drawing closer, she realized it wasn't grit that coated it, but more of the white powder. Pulling back one corner revealed buckets with labels that confirmed what her nose had already told her.

The powder on her scarf and all over the tarp and floor... was chlorine.

# CHAPTER TWENTY-FOUR

Elizabeth steadied the two jars on the seat next to her to keep them from tipping over as she turned in to the parking lot of the East Lampeter Township Police Department. Her heart patted nervously inside her chest as she pulled to a stop, climbed from her car, then crossed the walk toward the red double doors to make her way inside.

Two people eyed her from a bench just inside, one nervous and watchful, the other wrinkled with age but apparently at peace, judging by her closing eyes and folded hands.

A few feet away, the receptionist filed paperwork into a cabinet that screeched loudly when he closed the drawer. Behind him, Officer Gavin Price spotted Elizabeth and circled his desk to greet her at the counter.

"Elizabeth, this is a surprise. What brings you by?"

Gavin and John were friends, so Elizabeth felt comfortable calling him by his first name. "Hey, Gavin, I'm looking for John. Is he around?"

He hitched his thumb over his shoulder. "He's walking someone down to holding. It shouldn't take him long." He pushed open the gate that separated the reception counter from the desk area. "You wanna come on back and have a seat?"

"That would be great. Thank you." She walked past him, the jars cradled carefully in her arms.

Gavin eyed them curiously. "Whatcha got there?"

"Actually, that's why I'm here. I'm hoping John can tell me."

"Tell you what?"

At the sound of John's voice, Elizabeth set the jars on his desk and turned. As usual, seeing him looking so handsome and smart in his uniform did strange things to her pulse. She wondered if she'd ever tire of it.

"S-sorry to bother you at work," she stammered. "Do you have a minute?"

"Of course." He grabbed one of the jars and held it up for inspection. "I assume it's about this?"

At her nod, he grabbed the other jar and turned to Gavin. "We'll be in the interview room." Then to Elizabeth, he said, "Come on back."

A wide hall right down the middle separated the station into two halves. They passed a room marked BOOKING and then a bathroom and a break room, and arrived finally at the Interview Room.

After pushing open the door, John flicked on the lights then stepped aside to let her pass. "So, tell me about these," he said, walking to a table in the center of the room to set the jars down. He pulled out a chair for her then crossed to the wall to grab another for himself and swing it alongside hers.

"Those are water samples from the Troyers' farm."

His eyebrows rose. "Two?"

"One is from their well. The other is from a cistern I spotted in the pasture behind their house."

John looked down at her crusted boots. Elizabeth smiled. "It was a little muddy."

"Okay." He settled against the back of his chair, his arms crossed. "So, tell me why we're collecting water samples."

While Elizabeth explained, John scribbled notes on a notepad. He looked up when Elizabeth mentioned the chlorine and Mary's illness.

"Is she okay?" he asked, his brow furrowed.

Elizabeth nodded. "The doctor says it should clear up on its own."

"Good." John flipped the notepad closed and picked up the jar labeled CISTERN.

"I'm surprised you went to the trouble to get a sample from their rainwater."

Elizabeth shrugged. "Rachel's son, Adam, told me if someone wanted to taint the milk from an entire herd, putting the chlorine in their water source would be the easiest, quickest way. I figured whoever did it might have chosen the cistern because putting it in the well would mean the family would drink it too. Even though it's not a large amount, they might have noticed the difference in the flavor."

He nodded, his gaze bright with admiration. "I'll get this sent off for testing. Hopefully, it'll only take a week or two."

"A week!" Dismay flooded Elizabeth's heart. "That's much too long."

He lowered the jar to look at Elizabeth. "Don't the Troyers have a lab on their farm? I thought they used it to test their milk for bacteria."

Elizabeth bit her lip. "They do, but since I can't be sure it's not one of their hired hands behind this mess, I figured I'd better get the samples tested somewhere else."

"Abel and Ezra? Do you have reason to suspect it might be one of them?"

"Abel, possibly, but Ezra is out of town. A young man named Zach is filling in until he gets back." She frowned. "Not that I think either of them is guilty. I'm just trying to take every precaution."

"Good thinking." He set the jar down again and clasped her hand. "There's got to be another way. Since we're just checking the chlorine levels, maybe a pool supply store can help. Don't worry. I'll see what I can find out."

"Thanks, John."

He held her hand a moment longer before pushing up from the table. Elizabeth rose with him, then walked to the door.

"I'll call you as soon as I have an answer," John said.

Elizabeth thanked him again and returned to her car. The short drive back to Secondhand Blessings gave her plenty of time to think over her list of suspects, Jeff Thompson high among them after their last conversation and the chlorine she'd found in his barn. Rachel's buggy was parked outside the store when she arrived, so Elizabeth hurried inside to look for her. She found her deep in conversation with Martha and Mary. Otherwise, the store was empty.

"There she is." Martha nodded in Elizabeth's direction the moment she entered, then waved her over. "We were just telling Rachel about the water samples you collected to take to John."

"It is so unbelievable." Rachel tsked sadly. "Who would do such a thing to the Troyers, especially now, with Moses injured?"

"Actually..." Elizabeth took off her coat and draped it over the counter next to the cash register. "I may have a lead on that."

"You what?" Martha asked. She looked at Mary, who shrugged and looked at Elizabeth.

"Sorry, I didn't have a chance to fill you in before I headed to the police station." Elizabeth told them about her visit to Jeff Thompson and the chlorine she'd found in his barn.

Rachel listened quietly, and when Elizabeth finished, pursed her lips doubtfully. "I do not know, Elizabeth. Adam mentioned just the other day that many of the area farmers were implementing footbaths. Don't they use chlorine in them?"

She was right. Adam had mentioned that. "Maybe a small amount," Elizabeth admitted.

Mary frowned. "Then you're saying it wouldn't be unusual for farmers to have buckets of chlorine in their barns?"

"I guess not." Disappointment settled like a stone in the pit of Elizabeth's stomach. Just when she thought they were making headway. She drummed her fingers on the countertop, thinking.

"So, if it's not Jeff Thompson, then who?" Martha's question echoed Elizabeth's thoughts exactly.

Beau, Abel, even Lillian was suspect, though she seemed only a remote possibility. Images of Zach rushing to empty the water troughs popped into Elizabeth's head. She tilted her head. Rushing? Yes, that was an appropriate description. Maybe because he knew there was something in the water and he wanted to replace it before anyone found out?

"I know that look." Mary shook her finger at Elizabeth. "You're thinking about something."

"I was just wondering about Zach." She looked at Rachel. "How well do you know him? What's he like? Is he dependable?"

Martha laughed. "Wow, that's a lot of questions."

Elizabeth chuckled. "I know. Sorry."

Rachel shook her head. "I do not mind. Unfortunately, I do not think I know Zach well enough to say what kind of person he is. I only know what I have seen from the few times we have met."

Elizabeth nodded encouragingly.

"Well, he is a hard worker. That much I know. And he has always seemed willing to help out in times of need. Not just the Troyers. Last summer, after the Michaelsons' house flooded, he and a few other men went over to tear out drywall."

"Oh, I remember that." Martha rubbed her chin and nodded.

Mary lifted her brows questioningly. "Why do you ask, Elizabeth?"

"I'm just trying to focus on all the possible suspects, and Zach *did* go about emptying the troughs the moment we realized the cows might have ingested chlorine."

Martha perked up, interest shining from her eyes. "How did he know it was in the water?"

Elizabeth held up her hand to stop Martha's train of thought. "To be honest, it wasn't just the water troughs. He suggested cleaning the feed bins and stalls too."

"Oh." Her frown hinted at disappointment. Apparently, she felt as frustrated with this mystery as Elizabeth.

"It might still be worth talking to him," Mary suggested. "If Zach isn't guilty, he might at least be able to shed some light on who is."

Elizabeth agreed. "I'll head over to the farm and talk to him tomorrow afternoon, after the morning rush is over."

"I will meet you there," Rachel said. "The ladies from the quilting circle have been busy preparing freezer meals for me to take over."

"Good, then I'll see you tomorrow."

With a time decided upon, Rachel left. The store doorbell chimed, and Elizabeth and her sisters went to help some customers. Though they still didn't have answers, Elizabeth felt better. Hopefully, tomorrow would see some questions answered, and then she could relax and focus on more pleasant things.

Like her birthday.

# CHAPTER TWENTY-FIVE

The ladies of the quilting circle finished early on Thursday, and the store seemed oddly quiet without their chatter filling the air. Mary tidied the shade on a Tiffany desk lamp then pushed the dustcloth into her apron pocket with a sigh. It wasn't the absence of the quilting circle that had her feeling so anxious. It was Nick and not knowing what his test results revealed.

She checked on the two women perusing the fall display. They were still looking. Another couple browsed the vintage toys section with several wooden trucks already in their arms. A third sorted through a stack of *Farmer's Almanacs*. They all looked engrossed. Maybe it would be a while before they were ready to check out.

Mary slipped her cell phone from her pocket and headed toward a quiet corner to call Michael and Heidi. Just hearing Heidi's voice when she answered brought a sense of relief.

"Good morning, sweetheart. How is the baby doing?"

"Better today. And before I forget, please thank Rachel for me. I think adding a tiny bit of peppermint to the cream I've been rubbing on his tummy helped. He actually got more than just a couple of hours of sleep last night."

Which meant Michael and Heidi did as well. Mary blew out a bit of the anxiety knotting her stomach. "I'm so glad to hear that. I'll let Rachel know." She pushed farther into the corner to lean her shoulder against the wall. "What about you and Michael? Are you two doing okay?"

"Believe it or not, we are. I think it's all your prayers. We're really feeling them."

Tears of relief welled in Mary's eyes. "Thank You, Lord."

"Amen to that. We still don't have Nick's test results back, but at least we don't feel so sleep deprived. Amazing what just a few hours can do."

"Oh, I remember." Mary chuckled wryly as she swiped her finger under her lashes.

"How are things at the store?" Heidi continued. "Any idea yet what's been going on with the Troyers?"

Mary had told her all about the things going on in Bird-in-Hand the last time they talked. Now, she filled her in on the most recent developments then sighed. "Unfortunately, we still don't have any idea who's behind these attacks. Elizabeth went out to the farm this morning to talk to Zach. Maybe we'll have more answers then."

"I'll be praying so." Heidi paused and then changed the subject. "So, about Elizabeth's surprise party on Saturday? Needless to say, if Nick still isn't feeling better, we won't be making the trip. It's just too hard when he's in the middle of one of his crying spells."

"I sort of figured that." It hadn't even occurred to Mary that they would try, but hearing Heidi say it sparked another idea. "What do you think about doing a video call during the party so you can see her face when we yell surprise?"

"Mmm, I don't know. One of us has to be holding Nick almost constantly. Even then, he doesn't always calm down, so it might be more trouble than it's worth. Thanks for asking though."

"Of course, sweetheart," Mary said, fighting to keep the disappointment from showing in her voice. Video calls weren't the same as having someone with you, but they were better than nothing. "Don't even worry about it. I'm sure Elizabeth will understand."

"Okay, well, tell her happy birthday for us, and let her know we would have loved to be there."

"I will. Give Nick a kiss for me."

"Will do."

They disconnected, and Mary went back to waiting on customers, but her smile was forced and she caught herself more than once looking at the clock and wishing they could close early. Today, her heart just wasn't at the store. It was several hundred miles away with her grandson.

"You ready for a break? It's almost lunchtime."

Martha's voice startled Mary out of her daze. She looked down at the wooden baby rattle in her hand and smiled. Apparently, she'd picked it up subconsciously. She put it back in the bin with several other handcrafted Amish toys then reached behind her to tug her aprons strings loose.

"I think I do need a little time to myself. Thanks, Martha."

Reading compassion in her sister's gaze, Mary gave her hand a squeeze before grabbing her coat and slipping out the door.

Driving always gave Mary a sense of calm. Before long, she found herself outside of Greta's Coffeehouse and decided to turn in for a cup. Few guests lingered inside the quaint shop, but with lunch approaching, Mary knew it wouldn't be long before people began filing in. She grabbed a muffin and a large coffee and headed toward a quiet corner where she could eat and drink in peace.

While she nibbled her muffin, Mary pulled up pictures of Nick on her phone, praying over each one as she scrolled. Was this what the Lord meant when He told His disciples to "pray continuously"? She had to think so, since every thought of her grandson brought an instant plea to her lips and heart.

*Lord, watch over my grandson.*

*Help me to trust in You.*

*Remind me how much You love my children.*

The last one felt especially poignant. As much as Mary loved her family, she had to remind herself sometimes that God loved them more.

*"And I love you too."*

The thought was so familiar she instinctively pushed it away to concentrate on Nick.

*"I love you too."*

The still, small voice became more insistent. More urgent. When it tugged on her heart in this way, she'd learned to listen. She put the phone down and closed her eyes, drowning out the quiet conversations going on around her, the ringing of the bell over the entry, everything but the voice of the One trying earnestly to capture her attention.

"I hear You, Lord." She whispered the words, not caring if anyone watched, if anyone saw. "I know You love me—"

She broke off, sensing this time was not for her to speak, but to hear. And yet it was oh so difficult to calm the clamor inside her head. Finally, one verse broke through. No, it was more like one part of a verse, or many, if she really thought about it.

*Fear not.*

That was it? Her eyes blinked open. In the midst of everything, the Lord's only message to her was not to fear? What about Nick? What if the chlorine had caused lasting damage? What would Michael and Heidi do? What would she do?

The idea was too awful to bear. Was God telling her not to fear, promising that her grandson would get better?

She dismissed the idea as quickly as it came. People didn't always recover from their illness, even if they prayed in faith to get well. So then...

God was simply reminding her that He was in control, even if the storm continued to rage. Mary could trust Him, because He already knew the outcome. And He *loved* them. Intimately. Completely. Fervently.

Fear. Not.

Suddenly, it occurred to Mary that He meant *all* her fears. Not just the ones plaguing her today. Her heart broke, and her eyes welled with tears. "Okay, Lord, I understand what You're saying. No more fear. I'm giving it all to You."

"I'm sorry, what did you say?"

Mary's attention snapped to a young waitress standing near her table, her hand outstretched toward the plate full of crumbled bits of muffin.

"You want me to take it all?" the waitress asked, a hint of impatience making her words crisp.

Mary drew back a little as the girl's face triggered a memory. "Hey...don't I know you?" She shook her finger as the memory slipped into place. "The Dairy Farmers Association. Lillian, right? Didn't I see you at the meeting last week?"

The girl's hand rose to touch the name tag pinned to her shirt. "Yes, I'm Lillian." She angled her head at Mary. "But I don't think—"

"I'm Mary Baxter. My sisters and I own Secondhand Blessings."

Recognition flickered in Lillian's eyes, but not in a good way. Her head tilted back, her chin rose, and she braced her hands on her hips. "I know that place. I read a review about it online."

The review again. Mary squelched a scowl. "Yes, well—"

"Can I ask you a question?" Not waiting for Mary's answer, Lillian stepped toward the table and placed her hand flat against it. "Are you all still buying milk from Emma Troyer?"

"Uh, well..." Caught off guard, Mary stumbled for words. "My sisters and I...we...we have bought milk from them, yes."

Lillian reached up to coil her finger through her long hair. "I heard several of your customers got food poisoning. Was it from the milk?"

"I'm not aware of customers getting food poisoning," Mary replied carefully. Which was true. The one customer who thought she'd contracted a case was instead diagnosed with the flu.

Lillian dropped her hand and kept her eyes pinned to Mary's face. "But people are getting sick, and the talk is that the Troyers' milk is what caused it."

She said it with enough glee to make Mary think the "talk" Lillian referred to may have come from her. Mary put her hand on the table and slid to the edge of the booth. Unfortunately, with Lillian standing where she was, getting out completely was next to impossible, unless Mary wanted to push past her.

Mary lowered her voice to keep from drawing the attention of the other customers in the coffeehouse. "The Troyers test all of their milk and milk products on site. If something is wrong, I tend to think it's because someone is tampering with their milk."

She said it with just the barest hint of challenge in her voice. It was a long shot. She, Elizabeth, and Martha all thought so. But what if Lillian knew something about the tainted milk? Something she could be coaxed into giving away? She held her breath while she waited for Lillian's response.

Disbelief widened Lillian's eyes a split second before she released a grunt and leaned back on one foot. "Tampering? Really? Is that supposed to be some kind of joke?"

Put off by her forthrightness, Mary frowned. "I wish. Unfortunately, we know someone is messing with the Troyers' livestock, and my sisters and I intend to find out who."

Mary grabbed the edge of the booth and hauled herself out, forcing Lillian to retreat a step or stand nose to nose with her. Now that Lillian was no longer looking down on her, she no longer seemed so confident. She licked her lips nervously and glanced over her shoulder toward the counter.

"Well, I should probably be getting back to work."

Mary put up her hand to stop her. "If you don't mind, I have a couple of questions for you."

Uncertainty darkened Lillian's brown eyes to almost black. She crossed her arms and gave a nod for Mary to continue. "I guess that's all right."

Mary softened her stance and hoped that doing so would subconsciously encourage Lillian's trust. She started with an easy question. "How long have you and Zach known each other?"

"Since we were little. Zach grew up around here, but my parents moved when I was three."

"Ah, I see. And your dad's a dairy farmer too, right?"

"Yeah, that's right." Lillian's frown deepened. "I'm not sure I understand these questions. Why are you so curious about Zach?"

Mary's only choice was to be honest. "I wasn't kidding earlier when I said my sisters and I are trying to figure out who's tampering with the Troyers' milk. Zach has been helping out on the farm, which means he's had plenty of opportunity. Elizabeth is heading out there right now, hoping to ask him a few questions."

Something that looked an awful lot like panic froze Lillian's features and turned her lips white. "Your sister is heading out to the Troyers' farm to talk to Zach?"

"That's right. Actually, she left the store before I did. I'm sure she's at the farm by now."

Lillian grabbed a pen from her apron pocket and rapped the end in a furious rhythm against her palm. "Sorry I can't talk anymore. I need to check on my customers now."

She whirled and left, her long ponytail swinging.

"It was nice seeing you again," Mary called after her, but Lillian didn't turn, and she didn't go around to tables to check on customers. Instead, she went straight to the back, but didn't quite disappear from view. If Mary leaned just so she could peek through the order window and catch a glimpse of Lillian's profile, what part wasn't hidden by her phone.

Mary frowned and settled back against the booth. Just who was Lillian trying to call, and why was she in such a frantic rush to do it?

# CHAPTER TWENTY-SIX

Except for the occasional call of a crow perched high in branches of an oak next to the farmhouse, an odd stillness had settled over the Troyers' farm. There was no rumble of machinery, no noise of trucks rolling in or out, no lowing of cattle. Where was everybody?

Elizabeth frowned and left the milking barn to head toward the processing plant. Expecting to see Abel, she was surprised that even here, the lights were out and an odd silence prevailed. That only left the house.

Perplexed, she turned and made the short climb up a small hill toward the main house. At least here, there were signs of life. Smoke rose from the chimney, a white column that curled away on the brisk air.

She knocked on the front door and only had to wait a few seconds before Emma opened and welcomed her in.

"I was not expecting to see you this morning," Emma said, holding out her hands for Elizabeth's jacket.

"Actually, I was hoping to see Zach," Elizabeth said, speaking softly so as not to alert Moses and upset Emma. "I have some questions I'd like to ask him."

Emma shook her head. "I am sorry, Elizabeth. I told Zach and Abel not to come in today."

Elizabeth lifted her eyebrows in surprise. "But what about the milking?"

"I can manage that on my own." Emma's shoulders lifted, and a glum frown pulled at her lips. "I did not see the sense in having Abel and Zach here since we are dumping out all the milk until the chlorine is cleared up. It will be two days, at least."

Elizabeth's heart sank. "Or possibly a little longer." She motioned toward the living room. "I have some news to share with you. Maybe we should sit down."

Emma's eyes widened with apprehension. She nodded and led the way. Once they were seated, Elizabeth explained about the water samples she'd collected and John had taken to a pool store to be tested. She reached into her purse and pulled out a sheet of paper and passed it to Emma.

"I'm sorry, Emma. I probably should have talked to you about collecting the samples before I did it, but this was just a hunch, and I wanted to have something concrete before I told you about it."

Emma shook her head. "I asked for your help. It is fine."

"These are the lab results," Elizabeth continued. "As you can see, the chlorine levels in the cistern were much higher than the levels in the water troughs."

Emma's gaze roamed the paper and then flew back to Elizabeth. "So, what this means is that someone put chlorine in the cistern?" She jumped to her feet. "But...we didn't empty that. And the cows..."

Her glance skipped to the window and back to Elizabeth. "I put all the cows out to pasture after the morning milking. They can reach the cistern."

The air left Elizabeth's lungs in a rush. She scrambled to her feet and waved Emma toward the door. "You go start rounding them up. I'll call Zach and Abel and see how fast they can get here. Do you have their phone numbers?"

"Zach, yes. Abel only has a phone shack." She hurried to a drawer, pulled out a tablet, scribbled down a number, then tore off the sheet and handed it to Elizabeth. "This is Zach's number."

Elizabeth nodded and waved her out. "Go. I'll get ahold of him and join you outside."

Emma grabbed her coat, heels flying as she threw open the door. Elizabeth placed the call, but Zach didn't answer. In the end, it didn't matter. Within an hour, she and Emma had all the cows rounded up, but Elizabeth knew that was the least of their worries. All she could think of as they worked was Moses. His farm. His cows. She *had* to tell him what was going on, no matter what Emma said.

Emma seemed to sense what was on Elizabeth's mind. As they trudged back to the house, she hung her head low, not even questioning when Elizabeth mentioned speaking to Moses.

"I know you are right, Elizabeth. It is time Daed knew what has been going on. But I would like to be the one to tell him. I was the one who insisted we keep it from him, after all."

Elizabeth rubbed Emma's arm in sympathy. "Of course. Would you like me to wait outside while you talk to him?"

Emma shook her head. "You do not need to do that. Come, sit down in the living room. I will fetch Daed."

While Elizabeth waited for Emma and Moses to return, the rumble of a buggy sounded outside. She rose to answer the door, a bit relieved when it was Rachel's face she saw. She had no doubt that Moses would be more than a little upset once Emma told him what had been going on, so having Rachel here was welcome support. They sat side by side on the couch while Elizabeth explained in quiet undertones what had taken place that morning.

Rachel listened, hands clasped in her lap, nodding now and then, and letting out a troubled sigh when Elizabeth finished.

"I am very glad Emma has agreed to talk to her father. It is long past due."

A thump sounded on the stairs, drawing both their gazes upward. Moses did indeed look angry, his face pale as he bumped down the stairs, clinging heavily to the handrail. Behind him, Emma followed, one hand outstretched as though to catch him if he stumbled.

Almost as one, Elizabeth and Rachel rose and waited until Moses's foot hit the bottom step. He looked from Elizabeth to Rachel and back, then surprised Elizabeth with a grateful nod.

"Emma has told me all you have done to help. I give you my thanks, Elizabeth. She could not have managed without you."

Elizabeth's gaze flitted to Emma, who kept her eyes downcast. So, Emma had told Moses that she helped but not that she'd also kept her secret?

She stepped forward, determined to clear her conscience. "Moses, I think you should know—"

He held up one gnarled hand before she could finish. "Emma is a grown woman. I put the farm in her hands. She did what she thought she must, as did you. For now, it is best that we turn our attention to the cows, and to figuring out who is behind all of this."

Elizabeth nodded. "In that case, would you mind if I asked you a few questions?"

After giving a curt nod, Moses clutched Emma's arm and lumbered toward the living room, heaving a breath when he reached a battered brown armchair. He sank heavily onto the cushions, grabbed his injured leg, and lifted it with both hands onto a footstool that Emma dragged close. "What is it you would like to know?"

Elizabeth glanced at Rachel, and the two of them moved to sit across from Moses.

"Well, for starters, can you think of anyone who might have a grudge against you or the farm? Anyone who might want to harm you in this way?"

"Beau Hegel," he replied, staring steadily at Elizabeth. "I have no doubt."

Elizabeth leaned forward and grasped both knees. "He's been out here a couple of times to talk to you about the accident."

"Bah!" He waved his hand in front of his face in disgust, his white whiskers trembling. "You mean he has come to threaten me."

Elizabeth inhaled sharply and heard Rachel do the same. "Threaten you? Is that what he's done?"

"He has claimed his uncle will help him get out of all the charges and hire a lawyer to make me look a fool. He has said he will push to have laws created limiting access to roads for all Amish." He spread his hands wide. "Are these not threats?"

"Have you tried explaining your side of things?" Elizabeth asked.

Moses looked away and ran his thumb under his nose. "What is the sense? That young man is unruly and arrogant. He will not listen to reason if he thinks he is right."

Remembering what Jeff Thompson had said about Moses being hit from behind, Elizabeth bit her lip. "Is it possible that he *is* right?"

All three stared at her, their eyes wide with disbelief.

"Moses, did you actually see Beau Hegel force you off the road?"

Anger flashed in his pale blue eyes, turning them to ice. "Ne. He hit me from behind and then did not bother to stop. But a witness said—"

"Which witness?" Elizabeth interrupted. "Are you talking about Jeff Thompson?"

His head bobbed.

"You and he have had problems in the past, haven't you?"

Rachel's and Emma's heads swung back and forth between the two, like observers at a ping-pong match.

"One thing has nothing to do with the other," Moses stated, squaring his chin and folding his hands across his stomach. "This is something separate."

"I would certainly like to think so," Elizabeth assured him. She sat back and laced her fingers in her lap. "Unfortunately, I think we have to consider every possibility. Like Abel or—"

"Ne." Moses grabbed the arms of his chair and pulled himself forward. "Abel would never do this. It is not him."

Elizabeth blinked, caught off guard by the adamancy in his tone. "All right, then what about Simon Vogel?"

It was Moses's turn to blink. "Simon?"

"You two argued right before the accident. Is it possible he was more upset than you realized?"

Moses's gaze skipped to rest on Emma. For a moment, he said nothing, sadness filling the lines and creases around his eyes and mouth. Finally, he sighed. "Simon and I have a history. But before that, there was nothing we would not have done for each other." He tore his gaze from his daughter to look at Elizabeth. "Nothing. I would have given my life for him, and he for me."

Elizabeth softened her tone, certain that her next question was sure to sting. "If that is so, why are you so opposed to his son?"

Except for the ticking of a cuckoo clock counting the seconds on the wall behind Moses's head, quiet fell. Of the four people gathered, all knew varying degrees of the "history" he spoke about, yet had anyone ever talked about it aloud in front of him? For Emma's sake, and for his, it was time.

"Zach is a good man, Daed, and a good friend." Emma's quiet words hung heavily in the silence. Elizabeth nodded encouragingly. Emma licked her lips then clasped her hands and lifted her chin. "You told me to do whatever I thought best to keep the farm running. I know you do not like it, but Zach is a big help, and we need him."

Moses mulled her words for a long moment, his fingers cupped tightly around his chin. When he finally nodded, Emma's shoulders sagged with relief.

"I...could use your help figuring out what to do now," she said hesitantly. "Besides testing the milk, I have no idea what to do next."

Moses's head lifted, and his eyes lit with gratitude and something closely resembling joy.

Understanding filled Elizabeth's heart. Yes, and why not? Everyone wanted to feel needed, Moses probably more than most after the last few days spent cooped up in his room.

"Have you put the cows on a strict food and water schedule?" he asked.

Emma shook her head. "Just their usual feedings. But we did change all their food and water."

"Ne, we need to do more."

Moses's voice rose as he told Emma exactly what to feed the cows and when. He also suggested they move all the cows into the pasture closest to the house so they could keep an eye on them, something he could do from his second-floor bedroom window. Watching the two of them work and plan together filled Elizabeth with gladness. Maybe this was the silver lining around all of this mess. Maybe, just maybe, Moses and Emma would finally be a team.

# CHAPTER TWENTY-SEVEN

Elizabeth hopped from foot to foot while she waited next to the cistern in the far corner of the Troyers' pasture for John to arrive. The cows had access to this cistern, had probably rubbed against it, bumped against it, or even licked around the rim. Chances were slim she and John would find fingerprints, but since no one else's cows had been affected, this had to be how the culprit was tainting the Troyers' water supply. Elizabeth thought it worth the possibility to look, and John and Moses had agreed.

Flapping her arms against her sides, Elizabeth fought to keep warm. The sky had darkened to a slate gray as clouds rolled in from the north, threatening wind and rain that would wash away the evidence that remained on the cistern, if any. Elizabeth couldn't do anything about that. She was standing guard against other kinds of interference, namely, people. Guilty people, to be exact.

Moses's words replayed in her head while she waited. He was quite certain Jeff wasn't the culprit, or Simon or Abel either. So then, who did that leave? Beau seemed the most likely candidate, but did he even know enough about cows to sabotage the farm in this way? She didn't think so. Lillian's father was a dairy farmer, so she might have the knowledge, but hauling buckets of chlorine across a muddy pasture seemed an awfully big task for such a slight girl. And Zach?

Elizabeth chewed her lip, thinking. Mary had texted about her encounter with Lillian earlier that day. Lillian *could* have been calling to warn Zach. But why? He had access and ability, but motive? What would compel him to do such a thing?

Hearing voices, Elizabeth turned to watch John and Emma navigate the same muddy path she had taken.

"Thanks so much for coming, John," she said.

"Ja, danki," Emma said.

"Glad to help." He held up the black plastic case he kept in his car. "Guess this thing comes in handy again, eh?"

John cracked open the fingerprinting kit and set to work dusting the rim of the cistern, starting with a spot closest to the road, the most likely place a person would have put their hands while pouring chlorine into the water. For several minutes, he worked in silence, until he was more than halfway around the cistern. The farther he got, the more Elizabeth despaired of finding anything, until John stopped and motioned her and Emma over.

"Look here." He pointed to a dark smudge on the outside edge of the rim and three nearly perfect ovals lined up next to it. "I think we might just have gotten lucky."

"Fingerprints?" Elizabeth asked, excitedly.

"That's what it looks like," John said.

"How will we know who they belong to?" Emma asked. "Daed, Abel, Ezra, and I have all worked in this pasture."

"Ezra hasn't been here for several days," Elizabeth reminded her. "It's not likely the prints are his."

"I'll need the rest of your prints for comparison," John said, "but once I have those, it will be easy to determine if these prints belong to one of you or someone else."

"But will they tell us who put the chlorine in the water?" Emma persisted.

"Only if their prints are already in the police database," Elizabeth said. She realized that Emma might not know what that meant, so she explained the record of fingerprints that were collected and stored and why.

"So unless these prints belong to a person who has been arrested or fingerprinted for a job, we still might not have our answer," she finished, then rubbed Emma's arm. "But it's worth a shot."

Emma nodded in agreement, but her face wasn't quite as hopeful as before. She and Elizabeth watched in silence as John lifted the prints onto a thin plastic film. When he finished, all three turned to walk back toward the farm.

"So? What happens next?" Walking through the muddy field was difficult. The words stuttered from Emma's lips.

John's long legs ate up the distance much easier. "I head back to the station and see what I can pull up. It won't take long, if you'd like to ride along."

Emma mulled John's offer a long time and finally gave up with a shake of her head. "The cows will need milking soon. I cannot go."

"I'll go," Elizabeth said, reaching for John's arm as she stumbled over a patch of earth furrowed with hoofprints. Instantly, his free hand steadied her. She flashed him a smile of thanks then turned to Emma. "Keep an ear out toward the phone shack. I'll call as soon as we have some answers."

The ground smoothed some as they reached the edge of the pasture. Emma grabbed Elizabeth for a quick hug before turning toward the barn. Elizabeth and John veered toward the cars.

"What do you think?" Elizabeth asked when they reached them.

John grabbed her door handle and pulled it open. "I didn't say anything before because I didn't want to get Emma's hopes up, but there's a distinctive scar across two of the fingers. Whoever these prints belong to must have had a pretty serious cut at one time."

"Will that help us narrow down who they belong to?"

"Maybe." John glanced up at the sky, which seemed to have grown even more foreboding. "For now, let's just get these to the station before the weather turns nasty."

Elizabeth climbed into the driver's seat and jammed the key into the ignition. "I'll follow you."

John closed her door and strode back to his own vehicle. Soon, they were back at the station, but despite Elizabeth's hopes, the prints they'd taken from the cistern did not pull any matches.

Sitting next to John, staring at the blank computer screen, Elizabeth couldn't help but feel disappointed. "Nothing. Those prints tell us nothing."

"Actually...they do rule out one person." John raised his eyebrows and waited.

Elizabeth pulled her gaze from John to think, and then it hit her. "Beau. His prints would be in the system."

John nodded. "Looks like he's not your guy after all."

"No, though I was starting to think that anyway since he wouldn't have known how to taint the milk without hurting the cows."

John leaned forward to rest his elbows on the desk. "So, who does that leave?"

Elizabeth blew a heavy breath from her lips. "I know Moses doesn't agree, but I have to think it's either Simon Vogel or Jeff Thompson. Both of them are nursing grudges. It makes sense that it would be one of them."

She reached down to pick her purse up off the floor. "I'm going to call Emma. She and Moses need to know that Beau is innocent."

She moved away from John's desk to make the call. When she finished, he joined her at the entrance.

"Shoot me a text when you get home, okay?" He cast a worried glance outside. "They're predicting a bad storm tonight."

Elizabeth laid her hand on his arm. "What about you?"

A corner of his mouth lifted in a grin. "There are cots in the back. If it gets too bad, I'll sleep here."

"That should be comfortable."

He chuckled. "I've slept in worse places." His gaze softened as he covered her hand with his own. "Sorry we didn't get more information from the prints."

"It's okay. Thank you for checking."

With John's hand so strong and warm on hers, Elizabeth wanted to linger, but she knew she needed to get going. Reluctantly, she pulled her hand from his arm.

"I'll text you when I get back to the farm."

John reached for the crash bar and pushed the station door open, letting in a swirl of rain and wet leaves. Elizabeth clutched her coat around her neck and hurried toward her car. Though it was only four o'clock, the lights in the parking lot had already flickered on, thanks to the early dusk cast by the clouds overhead.

Apprehension crowded Elizabeth's chest as she climbed into her car and peered at the sky through her windshield. There was trouble brewing. She felt it in her bones and the aching of her joints. But something told her it was more than just the weather she needed to worry about. This went deeper.

And it might only be a matter of time until she found out how bad it could get.

# CHAPTER TWENTY-EIGHT

The wind that had only whispered that afternoon had whipped to a full roar by the time Elizabeth and her sisters settled down for coffee in front of the fire.

"Looks like John was right." Martha nodded to the rain pinging off the windows. "It's really kicking up out there."

"Poor John." Mary cupped her hands around her coffee mug. "I hope he made it home before the weather got too bad."

Though it was too dark to see much, Elizabeth eyed the dark leaves splatting against the glass. "I doubt it. When I texted him earlier, he said he was going out on a call."

Repeating the words aloud ramped up the tension she'd felt in her chest ever since hearing he would be out driving.

"He'll be all right," Martha said in response to her unspoken question.

Elizabeth smiled at her gratefully then took a sip from her cup. "So, about Lillian?"

Mary had told them more about her run-in with the young woman the moment she got home. Elizabeth still wondered if it was Zach she'd called, and why.

"Any idea what the call was about?"

"None. I wish I could have gotten just a little closer before she hung up, but no chance." Mary tapped her index finger lightly against the side of her cup. "She sure did look suspicious though. You think maybe she has something to do with what's been going on at the Troyers' farm?"

Elizabeth lifted her eyebrows. "You know, come to think of it, I've kinda been dismissing Lillian because she's so small, but size can be deceptive. Or what if she had help dumping that chlorine into the cistern?"

"Like who?" Martha asked.

Who, indeed? The only person Elizabeth had seen her around was Zach. Besides him, she had no idea who Lillian's friends were or who she hung around with.

Shrugging, she motioned to Mary. "You said she asked you some questions about the Troyers' milk?"

Mary set her cup on the coffee table then rubbed her hands together briskly. "She was awfully curious about whether or not we were still buying milk from them. And she knew people had gotten sick."

Elizabeth's gaze jumped to Martha's red face. "Claims to know them," Elizabeth corrected gently, sympathy for her sister flooding her heart.

"Anyway," Mary continued, "she mentioned the review *and* she seemed a little too glad about the rumors regarding the Troyers. I think we need to check into her a little further."

"Why?" Martha cleared her throat. "I mean, a lot of people take perverse pleasure in spreading gossip. Lillian could just be one of them. That doesn't make her guilty."

"We mentioned the possibility of Lillian being jealous of Emma and Zach's friendship," Elizabeth said. "Maybe we need to look a little closer at that."

Martha considered this a moment and then shrugged. "You're right. Jealousy has been motive enough before. Maybe it is again."

"All right, then who do we talk to about it?" Mary asked. "Lillian wasn't very forthcoming with me this afternoon."

"And probably won't be, now that she knows we're working hard to figure out who's messing with the Troyers' milk," Martha added.

"Maybe Zach?" Elizabeth frowned. "I sure wish he'd been at the farm the first time I went out there to talk to him. Maybe I'll get another chance tomorrow."

"We can cover for you if we have to. You'll have plenty of time," Mary said.

Martha humphed. "Maybe, if this storm ever lets up."

Being reminded of the weather instantly made Elizabeth think of John.

"Martha." Mary frowned a warning, but Elizabeth held up her hand.

"It's all right. I'm sure John is fine—"

The ringing of the doorbell startled them all. Elizabeth set her cup down next to Mary's and jumped to her feet. "I'll get it."

Hurrying down the hall, she let out a gasp at the familiar figure she saw outlined in the front door.

"John!"

Rain dribbled from the brim of his hat onto his cheek and off the end of his nose. Elizabeth grabbed his arm and pulled him inside before shoving the door shut behind him.

"What on earth are you doing all the way out here?"

"Actually, your place was on my way back."

"On your way back from where?" Martha asked, as she and Mary joined them in the hall.

John nodded to her and Mary in turn. "The Vogels' farm."

"What?" Elizabeth held out her hands. "Here, give me your stuff, and then come warm up by the fire."

Instead of arguing as she half expected he would, John shrugged out of his coat and laid it in her arms.

"I'll get you some coffee," Mary said, disappearing toward the kitchen.

"Now, what's this about a visit to the Vogels' farm?" Elizabeth asked as she led the way back to the living room.

"I wish it was just a visit." John grunted, his expression sour. "I got a call to go out there."

"A call...as in an official call?" Mary ducked back into the living room just as John sat down. She put the coffee cup in his hands and then sat down on the couch next to Martha. Elizabeth took the chair opposite John's.

"It was official all right." John voiced his thanks to Mary then took a sip from his cup. "Just after you left the station, Elizabeth, a call came in about a dispute."

She winced, already dreading the news. "Oh no. Please tell me it wasn't—"

"Moses." He nodded before she could finish. "Apparently he got very upset when Emma told him the fingerprints didn't belong to Beau. He went straight out to the barn and hitched up the buggy."

"In this storm?"

"By himself?"

Martha and Mary's questions overlapped one another. John set down his coffee and held up his hand.

"John, how?" Elizabeth's softly spoken question silenced the others.

He turned to look at her. "Emma begged him not to go, but Moses was so furious he wouldn't listen. He took off in the buggy before Emma could get to the phone shack."

Martha's eyes widened. "So she was the one who called the police? Was it really so bad she thought Moses meant to harm Simon?"

"Not Emma," John cut in. "Vogel's son, Zach. Apparently, Moses showed up in a rage, demanding that Simon confess to what he'd done. Simon swore he had no idea what Moses was talking about. Fearing things would escalate, Zach called the police."

"Did Moses say why he assumed Simon was the culprit?" Elizabeth asked. Granted, he had reason to suspect him, but Jeff Thompson could be guilty as well. Why had Moses immediately concluded it was Simon?

"They were still arguing when I showed up," John said. "Moses kept ranting something about Simon never getting over his feelings for Amelia." He glanced around the room at them. "That name mean anything to any of you?"

"Amelia was Moses's wife…and Simon's first love," Elizabeth said, then shook her head sadly. "I hate that Zach had to hear all that."

John bobbed his head in agreement. "Me too. Zach looked pretty upset by it all. I actually think he was the only reason Moses finally calmed down enough to let me drive him home. I think he felt bad."

"Thank goodness he had that much sense," Martha said, swinging her gaze to the darkened window. "In this storm, he might have ended up in another wreck...or worse."

She shuddered, and Elizabeth couldn't help but do the same, thinking of all the horrifying possibilities.

"I think he realized that," John said. "Zach offered to return the buggy tomorrow, after the weather clears. Moses agreed without too much argument."

Elizabeth blew out an anxious breath. "Thank you so much for stopping by to let us know what happened, John." Her heart thumped painfully in her chest. "But what about you? Should you be driving in this?"

"I'll be fine." He rose, and all three Classens stood with him. "I probably should get going though, before things get any worse."

He said his farewells, then grabbed his coat and headed out the door. Elizabeth bit back a sigh. Protecting their community was his job. She realized this, but it didn't make watching him back out of their driveway any easier.

"Lord, please watch over him," she whispered.

"Amen," Martha whispered next to her.

Elizabeth locked the door then turned to her sister. "I didn't realize you were standing there."

"Of course you didn't." She nodded to the taillights disappearing slowly into the pounding rain in the distance. "Your attention was somewhere else. Or should I say on *someone* else?"

Arguing was pointless. What could she say that wouldn't be a lie at worst, or at best, a half truth? Much as Elizabeth dreaded admitting it, as hard as she'd tried to deny it, John was more than a friend.

Her heart told her he was much, much more.

# CHAPTER TWENTY-NINE

By early Friday morning, the worst of the storm had passed, leaving behind a glittering blanket of red, green, and gold that draped the hills leading out to the Troyers' farm. On both sides of the road, piles of leaves formed colorful banks that whipped and swirled as she drove past. To her surprise, it was Moses, and not Emma, who greeted her when she reached the house.

"Elizabeth, come in," he said, holding the door wide.

Elizabeth glanced down at the cast on his foot as she stepped inside. "Thank you, but are you supposed to be standing on that foot? Where are your crutches?"

"Bah." Moses gave a wave of his hand as he closed the door behind her. "Doctors do not know everything. It is time I began doing more. Come, I have coffee brewing."

He motioned her to the kitchen then hobbled along ahead of her.

"I can't stay long," Elizabeth said. "I just came by to see how you and Emma are doing. That storm last night was pretty rough."

"*Ach*, so it is the storm that has you checking on us?" Moses lifted a shaggy brow.

Elizabeth chuckled wryly and pulled out a chair at the table. "Not exactly. John told me about what happened at Simon Vogel's place."

Moses's hands slowed as he pulled two cups from the cupboard. Slowly, he set them down and turned to Elizabeth, his face a bright, embarrassed red.

"My actions are not befitting one who claims to walk with Gott." He heaved a sigh and reached for the coffeepot. "I will make my apologies to Simon and his son." His shoulders drooping, he motioned to her with the cup. "Your friend, John, as well. I am grateful he arrived when he did, before I could say more things I regret."

So he *did* regret his words. Elizabeth couldn't help but feel sorry for him. "We've all had our emotions get the better of us from time to time. I'm sure Simon and Zach will understand."

"You are kind." Moses poured the coffee then balanced the cups in one hand while he shuffled to the table. "And perhaps more generous than I deserve." He dipped his head ruefully and rapped his knuckles against his skull. "One day, I will learn to control my anger, instead of letting it control me. Until then—"

A rumble sounded outside before he could finish. Through the window, a bit of black flashed by. Zach must be bringing back the buggy.

A weary sigh puffed from Moses's lips. After taking his crutch from a corner next to the stove, he lumbered toward the door, cupped his hand to his mouth, and hollered for Emma. When she appeared, he nodded toward the door. "Your friend is outside."

"Zach?" Emma's gaze flashed to Elizabeth, and then to the window. She hurried to the door, grabbed a cloak, and tossed it over her shoulders. "I will only be a moment. I will thank him for bringing the buggy then ask him to go—"

"Please ask him to come in so I can speak to him," Moses interrupted quietly, but with a firmness Emma didn't defy. She nodded, her lips pressed tightly together.

Elizabeth rose, leaving her coffee untouched on the table. "Why don't I walk down to the barn with you?" she said to Emma.

Outside, Emma slipped over to speak to Zach. He looked a little confused as he glanced past her at the house, but then squared his shoulders and headed up the steps to the porch. Elizabeth couldn't fault his courage. After what had happened last night, facing Moses couldn't be easy. She started with Emma to the barn. Emma spared several glances over her shoulder as they walked. Elizabeth could almost hear the worried questions that rattled around in her head.

"If it makes you feel any better, I think your father wants to apologize to him," she offered gently.

Emma's brows lifted with surprise. Still staring toward the house, she ran her fingers over the strings of her prayer kapp, again and again.

They had reached the barn. Elizabeth grabbed the handle and yanked it open then followed Emma inside. "You really care about him, don't you?"

Emma whirled to stare at her.

"It's pretty obvious." Elizabeth pointed to Emma's prayer kapp. Instantly, her fingers stilled and she dropped her hands to her sides. Elizabeth smiled. "I take it he feels the same about you?"

She waited, her eyes locked with Emma's—steady, but not condemning. Only questioning. Finally, Emma's lips parted, and she nodded.

"Have you told your father?" Elizabeth asked.

Emma shook her head, wildly at first, and then slower. "There is no need," she said, her tone as adamant as any Elizabeth had heard Moses use. Emma crossed her arms and thrust out her chin. "I will not leave the church."

Elizabeth licked her lips. "Is…uh…is that what Zach is asking you to do?"

Emma nodded, her eyes wide and soaked with misery. "I told him when I took my vow, I would not break it, and I meant it. But Zach…"

"Won't take no for an answer?" Elizabeth crossed to clasp Emma's fingers. "So then why did you agree to let him help on the farm? Surely, spending so much time together has only made things harder for you both?"

"Zach…insisted we could be friends and I…" She spun and paced the cold wood floor. "I was desperate to prove to my father I could run the farm. Zach was there when I needed him." She stopped to look at Elizabeth. "Like a friend would be. Nothing more."

"But is that really fair to him, or to Lillian for that matter?" Elizabeth demanded bluntly. Though she wasn't intentionally trying to hurt Emma's feelings, sometimes direct was best. She sensed this was one of those times.

Emma held her gaze a moment longer then lowered her eyes to stare at the floor.

"Zach does not care for Lillian the way she would like," Emma said.

"But he might, if he didn't already have feelings for you, or if he thought there wasn't a chance between you," Elizabeth insisted. She stepped closer to peer intently into Emma's face. "I know you don't see it now, but what you're doing isn't fair, to either of you. It might even explain what has been going on around your farm."

"What?" Emma lifted her head to stare, her mouth agape. "Zach wouldn't—"

"Not Zach. Lillian."

Emma's eyes narrowed with disbelief, and then suspicion.

"Is Lillian the type to meet jealousy with anger?" Elizabeth asked.

Emma's chest heaved, and she lifted both hands in a helpless gesture. "Lillian has spoken poorly of me before, but to take it further and try and sabotage my family's farm? That I cannot say for certain she would do."

She wrung her hands, her despair evident. Elizabeth sucked in a deep breath and blew it out slowly. There was no sense pushing Emma further. She was sad and upset and unlikely to provide any more information that would prove useful.

"Never mind," she said, patting Emma's arm. "We'll figure it out later. For now—"

The screech of the screen door drew their attention to the house. Zach stepped out onto the porch, his head swiveling this way and that until he spotted Emma.

"You need to talk to him, Emma," Elizabeth prompted.

"I know." The hollow words hung sadly in the air. Emma took one step and then stopped and looked back at Elizabeth. "Please do not say anything to my daed until I have had a chance to work things out with Zach. I will tell Daed everything when the time is right."

She meant it. Elizabeth could read the conviction in her eyes. At her nod, Emma turned to go, her plain brown shoes crunching on the gravel drive. Rather than return to her car, Elizabeth waited just outside the barn. Zach would need a ride home. Better she gave it to him than Emma.

Zach and Emma didn't talk as long as Elizabeth expected, but whatever was said did not sit well with him. His face resembled last night's dark storm clouds when Elizabeth offered him a ride, and he spoke nary a word the entire drive home. Though Elizabeth longed to talk to him, now wasn't the time. She dropped him off then drove back to the store, her mind humming with unanswered questions.

Filling in Mary and Martha didn't take long. By the time she finished, both appeared just as worried as she felt.

"You did the right thing convincing Emma to talk to Zach and her father," Martha said. "Even if it has nothing to do with what's been going on, it needed to be cleared up."

Elizabeth picked up a wrinkled newspaper and dropped it into the trash next to the register. "I sure hope so."

But deep down, uncertainty burned like a hot coal in Elizabeth's belly. Emma *needed* to put an end to things with Zach, and she *needed* to be up front with her father. Those were good things. Honest things.

Why then did Elizabeth feel like the situation would get a whole lot worse before it got better?

# CHAPTER THIRTY

Mary pushed the cash drawer closed then cast a worried glance at her sister. Elizabeth had been very quiet all afternoon. Granted, the store had been unusually busy. It could just be she hadn't had a moment to talk—except Mary didn't think so. She'd seen that distant look in her sister's eyes before, the one that said her thoughts were somewhere and on something else. Or someone.

Zach and Emma.

Mary sighed and circled the counter. She couldn't help but feel sorry for them. It couldn't be easy feeling the way they did...or thought they did. But true love would never be so selfish as to expect one of the members to compromise their faith. Hopefully Emma would realize that, before she and Zach wound up hurting each other further.

The doors whooshed open, and Mary looked up just as Bill stepped through. His ready smile instantly lifted her spirits.

"Hey, this is a busy place," he said, looking around. "Did I come at a bad time?"

"Actually, it's a great time." Mary pointed to a stack of boxes she'd been about to unpack. "How would you like to help me carry those to the stockroom?"

Bill's grin widened as he pushed up his sleeves. "I'm all yours. Lead the way."

*All yours.* The sound of that warmed her heart. She hefted the first of the boxes and veered down one of the aisles toward the back of the store. Bill followed behind with the other two.

"So, I wasn't expecting to see you today," Mary said, balancing the box on her hip so she could switch on the light. She grinned at him over her shoulder. "Not that I'm disappointed."

The gleam in his eyes robbed her of breath. Bill eased past her to set his boxes on the floor, then turned and took Mary's hand—or started to. His hands lingered over hers and he stared at her, with just the box between them. "Where do you want this one?"

Mary swallowed nervously. "Just on top of the others is fine." Who did that breathy whisper belong to? She cleared her throat. "I need to go through them."

He smiled, his eyes crinkling at the corners in that endearing way Mary found more and more attractive. He set the box on top of the others then straightened and braced both hands on his hips.

"Anything else you need me to do?"

"That'll do it," she said, resisting the urge to press her hand to her heart to steady her pulse.

"Good, then we can talk about why I came."

"Okay."

"It's about Elizabeth's birthday party."

"Oh." She had to mentally switch gears. "Right. We're all set on our end. Is everything okay with the reservation at the Stockyard Inn?"

His answering grimace struck a note of dread in Mary's heart.

"What is it?"

"The owner called. Apparently they're experiencing some problems with their pipes. They're getting the repairs done now, but he's a little worried the restaurant won't be ready by Saturday."

"Oh no!" Afraid Elizabeth would overhear, Mary pushed the stockroom door closed and lowered her voice. "But we've already sent out all the invitations."

"I told him that. He apologized and offered to return the deposit if the repairs aren't finished in time."

"Except that doesn't help us locate another place." Mary groaned and slapped her palm to her forehead. "How on earth can we reschedule everything by tomorrow?"

Bill rubbed her shoulder soothingly. "There is still a chance it'll all work out. I just wanted to let you know what was going on in case you didn't want to risk waiting to see if the work got done."

"I appreciate that, Bill." Mary raised her eyes to the ceiling, her hands lifting and falling to her sides. "This week has just been…"

"Come here."

Before she knew it, Bill had pulled her into his arms. With one hand, he patted her back. With the other, he smoothed her hair. She could have rested there all day, except…

"Still no word on Nick, huh?"

She pulled back to look up into his face. "How did you know?"

He smiled softly and tucked her head under his chin. "I've been praying for him. You, Heidi, and Michael too."

Goodness, but he was making her want to cry. "Thank you."

"Anything else I can do for you?"

She sniffled and shook her head.

"All right, then I'll head over to the restaurant and see if I can help out there. I'll call you tonight and let you know how it's going."

"Okay."

She felt him start to pull away, so she wrapped her arms around his waist and gave him a firm hug. "You're a good man, Bill Richmond. My family has always been able to count on you in a pinch. I appreciate that more than you know."

His jaw tightened then relaxed into a smile. "I do it all for you."

He said it so soft and low, she almost missed it. Her heart rate sped as he cupped her chin and tilted her face up. Slowly, gently, he placed a small kiss on her forehead and then another on her lips.

For a moment, words failed her, which was perhaps a good thing. Bill pressed another kiss to her forehead and then slipped out the door before she could recover enough to speak.

Seconds after he disappeared, Martha poked her head into the stockroom. "Was that Bill?"

Mary had to remind herself to breathe. "Yeah. There's a problem with the restaurant for Saturday, but Bill is taking care of it."

Martha didn't bat an eye. "Well, if Bill's taking care of it, I'm sure everything will be fine." She pointed to the boxes on the floor. "Do you need help with any of that?"

Mary's gaze followed her pointing finger. "No, thanks. I've got it."

"Okay, well just holler if you change—"

Raised voices cut the words from her mouth. Her eyes wide, Martha jerked her head toward the sound.

"What on earth is that?"

Mary skirted the boxes on the floor to join Martha at the door. "It sounds like Emma Troyer." She grabbed Martha's arm and slid past her out the door. "C'mon. Let's go see what's going on."

Indeed, it was Emma Troyer they heard. Her face was red but not from the wind, if the tears welling in her eyes were any indication. In her hand was a piece of paper that she waved and fluttered at Elizabeth like a flag.

Mary skidded to a stop. All around them, the faces of their customers reflected the same shock she felt.

It had been a long week. Apparently, it wasn't over yet.

# CHAPTER THIRTY-ONE

Elizabeth held up both hands, trying in vain to calm a distraught Emma before they drew any more attention.

"Emma, this has to be a misunderstanding. I don't know what you think I've done, but I can assure you, I haven't betrayed your confidence."

Emma shook the paper in her hand. "Then how do you explain this?"

"What is that?" Mary strode forward, her hand outstretched. "May I see it?"

Mary's interruption could not have been more timely. Emma looked at her askance, for a moment lost for words.

Elizabeth motioned Emma away from the door and toward a quiet corner. "Please, Emma, let's go over here so we can talk."

Though she still appeared reluctant, Emma followed Elizabeth and Mary. Once they were no longer the main focus of attention, she took a couple of deep breaths and handed the paper in her hand to Elizabeth. "Someone dropped this off at the house just after you left. I assumed it was you."

Quickly, Elizabeth scanned the few lines then handed the paper to Mary. Written on it was everything Emma had shared with Elizabeth that morning, including Zach's attempt to lure her away from the church. The letter was not signed.

Elizabeth shook her head. "Emma, you can't actually think I wrote that?"

Emma's face flushed redder. "If not you, who? I have spoken to no one else about my feelings for Zach."

The doorbell rang, and Mary turned to Emma. "There's Rachel. Would you like me to get her? Maybe she can help."

For a moment, Elizabeth thought Emma would refuse, but then she nodded, sending Mary scooting away. She returned in a flash with Rachel in tow and just as quickly disappeared again.

"What is this?" Rachel asked, looking from Elizabeth to Emma. "What has happened?"

When Emma refused to answer, Elizabeth filled her in, then held up the paper and looked at Emma. "May I?"

Emma ducked her head in reply. Elizabeth handed Rachel the note and waited while she read.

"It is not signed," she said when she finished. She flipped it over to scan the back, then flipped it again and handed it to Emma. "Where did it come from?"

"Someone left it tucked inside the door. Daed found it before I could."

"Oh no," Elizabeth groaned. "Emma, I'm so sorry."

Things between Moses and his daughter were already troubled without adding this. She reached out to squeeze Emma's fingers. "I promise you, it did not come from me."

Emma searched her eyes then blew out a sigh. "I believe you. To be honest, I did not really think you would do such a thing. I was just so upset and angry, and you were the first person I thought of. Forgive me?"

"Of course." Elizabeth looked at Rachel. "Emma does bring up a valid point, however. She hasn't spoken to anyone else about her and Zach, so who could have written this note?"

"Zach also knows of the situation between you, ain't so?" Rachel asked quietly.

"He did not write this," Emma said, shaking the letter. "It is not his handwriting."

"Perhaps not, but maybe he talked to someone?" Rachel pressed.

"What about his father?" Elizabeth asked.

Rachel shook her head. "I cannot see Simon doing this. He would have faced Moses, not left an anonymous note. Ne, it is too..." She lifted her hands, at a loss for words.

*Immature.*

Though Elizabeth thought the word, she didn't say it. Instead, her mind winged to a jealous young woman with a thing for Zach. She looked at Rachel, who conveyed the same worried message with a glance.

"Emma, perhaps you should go on home," Rachel suggested gently. "Elizabeth and I will try to figure out who is behind the letter."

"But it is about me," Emma protested. "I should be the one figuring out who left it."

Rachel met her gaze steadily. "You are upset and angry. Not without cause, but it is not goot to accuse without proof."

She paused to let her meaning sink in. Emma shot a glance at Elizabeth then ducked her head.

"Let us ask some questions. We will talk with you later," Rachel urged.

Finally, Emma gave up with a nod. "Fine. I will wait until I hear from you. Again, I am sorry for blaming you, Elizabeth."

She spun and scurried toward the entrance, her cloak and skirt flapping behind her. Elizabeth waited until she'd hurried through the door before turning to Rachel.

"Well? Are you thinking what I'm thinking?"

"Lillian?"

Elizabeth nodded. "Mary said she works at Greta's Coffeehouse." She arched an eyebrow. "Feel like grabbing a cup?"

Hugging her coat tight, Rachel smiled. "Coffee sounds goot on such a chilly day."

A chuckle bubbled in Elizabeth's throat as she went in search of Mary and Martha to tell them where they were going. That done, she and Rachel made the short drive to the coffeehouse. Within minutes, they were snugged into a booth, but with no sign of Lillian, Elizabeth wondered if maybe they'd wasted a trip.

She motioned to one of the waitresses. As she'd feared, Lillian wasn't scheduled to work until later that day.

"Maybe we could come back?" Rachel suggested, splaying both hands against the tabletop.

Elizabeth thought a moment, then lifted her head as something behind the counter caught her eye. She leaned forward to whisper to Rachel. "Look over there. Do you see those hooks?"

Rachel craned her neck to look in the direction Elizabeth indicated. Behind the cash register, aprons hung from several hooks. White tape on the wall marked the owner of each.

"Lillian's apron is on the end."

Rachel frowned. "I do not understand. Why do we need her apron?"

"Not her apron…her guest check pad." Elizabeth slid out of the booth. They didn't really need Lillian—just a sample of her handwriting. And more than once, Elizabeth had seen waitresses sign the back of their guest checks. Maybe Lillian did the same.

She crossed to the cash register and waited until one of the other waitresses spotted her. Smiling, the woman walked over to her.

"Yes, ma'am, can I help you?"

Elizabeth gave her a timid smile. "I hope so. I have an odd request." She pointed to the apron and the guest checks peeking out from one of the pockets. "Could I possibly have one of those?"

The waitress looked at the apron, her brow drawn in confusion. "The…?" She pointed.

Elizabeth nodded.

"I…suppose that would be all right?" Her voice lifted with hesitation, but she reached for the guest checks and ripped one off the top.

"Thank you," Elizabeth said, scrambling back toward the booth with her prize before the woman grew bold and asked too many questions.

She slapped the check on the table. As she'd hoped, Lillian had written "Please come again" on the back and signed her name. Elizabeth fumbled in her purse for the letter left at the Troyers' door and laid it next to the check.

Rachel leaned in close.

"What do you think?" Elizabeth asked.

"They are very similar."

Excitement built in Elizabeth's chest as she traced a couple of letters on the check and compared them to the note. "I think so too. John might be able to tell for sure. I'll call him and ask him to come by the house this afternoon."

Rachel agreed. Though they hadn't ordered, Elizabeth left a dollar on the table then pushed out of the booth.

*Finally.* Finally she felt as though they'd begun making headway. The only thing that remained now was to tie Lillian to the chlorine and then the onions. Then, maybe, they could put this mystery to rest.

# CHAPTER THIRTY-TWO

Elizabeth bit her lip anxiously while she waited for John to finish examining the guest check she'd gotten from the coffeehouse earlier that day. At his elbow lay the letter left at the Troyers' farm.

"They're very similar, right?" she asked, when she could no longer bear the silence.

John smiled at her and went back to studying.

"Especially the tail on the *g*." In case he hadn't noticed it, Elizabeth pointed to it on the guest check.

"Elizabeth—"

"I know." She got up to pace. John was meticulous. It was part of his job. But just this once, she wished he'd give her a clue as to what he was thinking.

From the back of the house, the kitchen door rattled, and Elizabeth ducked into the hall in time to see Mary and Martha hanging up their coats.

"Well?" Mary didn't bother removing her boots the way Martha did. She hurried down the hall, leaving a trail of muddy footprints.

"Mary," Martha scolded.

After setting her own boots aside, Martha reached for a broom. Mary ignored her and continued toward Elizabeth. "What did John say?"

"*John* hasn't finished yet," he called from the dining room. He emerged a moment later with both pieces of paper in his hand. "But he does agree that there are some pretty incriminating similarities. We'd have to take it to a handwriting analyst to be sure."

"I knew it," Mary said, slapping her palm against her thigh.

Elizabeth took the letter from John's hand, her gaze flitting from the page up to his face. "So, it may have been Lillian who wrote this?"

"Looks like it."

"But what does that mean?" Martha asked, coming up behind them all. "It isn't a crime to leave notes on people's doorsteps."

"No, but it may help us know where to look for answers to the hijinks at the farm." Elizabeth looked at John. "What do you suggest we do next?"

"I could talk to her, if you'd like," he said, slipping his hands into his pockets. "We don't have enough evidence to make it in an official capacity, but if she is guilty, it just might put enough of a scare into her to keep her from trying anything else."

Elizabeth thought a moment and then nodded. "She works at Greta's. She's scheduled to come in this afternoon."

"If you leave now, you'll probably catch her," Martha said.

Elizabeth looked at John. "I've got time," he said. "I don't have duty until later this evening." He tugged his keys from his pocket and held them up. "I'll drive."

A cell phone jangled, and Mary tugged hers from her pocket and glanced at the screen. "It's Michael. I need to take this." She waved to John. "Thanks again for coming."

"No problem."

Mary nearly dove into the dining room in her haste to answer.

John glanced at Elizabeth. "Do you think maybe he's calling with some answers to the baby's illness?"

"I sure hope so."

"We've all nearly worried ourselves sick," Martha added, "but Mary especially. Not that worrying ever helps. At this point, it's our prayers that are most effective."

"I couldn't agree more," John said. Reaching out to take Elizabeth's hand, he added, "Why don't we say a quick prayer for them right now? I'm sure they could all use it."

Elizabeth's heart swelled to near bursting as they circled around and closed their eyes. While John prayed, he squeezed her hand tightly. She squeezed back, offering silent support. How far he'd come in his faith over the last few months! How much he'd grown. Elizabeth couldn't have been prouder. Or happier.

John said "amen," and then Mary reentered the hall, interrupting the awkward moment of silence that had fallen.

"That was Michael. He just called to let me know the test results are in. The doctor was worried the chlorine poisoning could have caused fluid to build up on Nick's lungs. He ordered a chest X-ray, which came back clear."

"And the blood work?" Elizabeth asked hopefully.

Mary nodded, tears brimming in her eyes. "Also clear. Michael and Heidi were both so relieved."

"Praise the Lord," Martha said, grabbing Mary's hand.

With her free hand, Mary swiped the tears from her lashes. "I know. I've been praying they would get the results quickly."

"And God answered," Martha said, a wide smile blooming on her face.

Mary covered Martha's hand with her own. "Michael asked if we would continue praying for them. Nick is doing better, but it'll still be a couple of days before they know for sure if all the chlorine is out of his system."

"Of course," Elizabeth said, and Martha quickly agreed. They wrapped Mary in a hug, and then Elizabeth walked with John out to his car.

John was subdued on the way to the coffeehouse, somber even, as they pulled into the parking lot. Elizabeth fumbled with her seat belt while he circled around to open her door.

"I'll clear things with Greta before we get started. You see if you can find us a quiet table, out of the way of people passing by."

"Okay."

Elizabeth hastened into the coffeehouse while John veered in search of Greta. This time of day, only a few people sat scattered about sipping lattes, their noses buried in an assortment of handheld technology. While this was good for Elizabeth and John's purpose, it was maybe not so good for business.

Elizabeth sidled past them and chose a table farthest from the cash register. Here, bright sunlight streamed through an oversized window. She took off her coat and draped it over the back of her chair. A couple of minutes later John approached with Lillian close behind. John stopped and signaled to her, then waited until Lillian sat before claiming the chair next to Elizabeth.

"Thank you so much for talking to us today," Elizabeth began, leaning forward eagerly.

Lillian swallowed, her breaths coming in shallow gasps through her parted lips. "I wasn't sure I had a choice." Her gaze darted to John and back to Elizabeth. "Isn't he a cop?"

"This isn't an official visit," John clarified. "We just have a few questions we'd like to ask, if you don't mind."

Lillian squirmed in her chair. "I...don't have a lot of time. My shift is about to end, and I need to get home."

"Hopefully, this won't take long," Elizabeth assured her.

Though she still looked reluctant, Lillian nodded. Elizabeth reached into her purse for the letter and laid it on the table. "This was left at the Troyers' farm earlier today. Do you know anything about it?"

Lillian barely glanced at the letter. She folded her hands in her lap and shook her head.

John clasped his hands on the tabletop, his fingertips touching. "Don't you want to know what it is?"

Lillian clamped up so tight her lips turned white.

"It's a letter to Moses Troyer." Elizabeth took out the guest check and laid it alongside the letter. "We compared it to the handwriting on the back of this check."

A tic started at the corner of Lillian's eye. "Where"—she paused and licked her lips—"where did you get that?"

"I stopped by here earlier this morning, before your shift began." Elizabeth pushed both pieces of paper toward Lillian. "The writing is very similar."

Over time, Elizabeth had learned that people hated silences. Sometimes, saying nothing at all was the most efficient way to encourage a person to talk. She pressed her mouth shut and forced herself to be patient.

Lillian's fidgeting increased as the seconds ticked by. She pressed her fingers to the twitching of her eye, opened and closed her mouth several times, and finally jerked forward and thrust out her chin. "All right, fine. I wrote the note and left it for Moses to find. He deserved to know what was going on under his roof."

"And what exactly would that be?" John asked, his eyes narrowing.

"Emma Troyer." Lillian bit the name out then slammed against the back of her chair and crossed her arms. "She has a thing for Zach and has been stringing him along trying to get him to help her run her father's farm."

"It's my understanding that the feelings between them are mutual," Elizabeth corrected gently.

Lillian snorted and slapped her palms on the table. "Zach only *thinks* Emma loves him. The truth is, she's a scheming, manipulative—"

"All right." John held up his hand, cutting short her tirade.

Lillian's shoulders slumped, but her chin still jutted mutinously, and fire sparked from her glare. John had his work cut out for him.

"Tell us about the onions," he continued, his voice firm but steady. Obviously, he was up for whatever challenge Lillian cared to throw at him.

"What are you talking about?" Lillian blinked, her gaze bouncing from John to Elizabeth.

Elizabeth angled her head, stunned that Lillian could still act so innocent. "The Troyers' milk? Someone fed their cows onions and put chlorine in their water supply."

Lillian gaped, both her mouth and eyes wide. "Is that what your sister meant when she said somebody was tampering with their milk?" She swiveled her head back and forth. "Uh-uh. That wasn't me. I had nothing to do with any of that."

Elizabeth frowned. "Lillian, we found fingerprints on the cistern. Right now, the worst offense you're looking at is trespassing, but if—"

"It wasn't me!" Her face flushed as cups at the next table over clattered and fell still. She shot a look that way and then lowered her voice. "Fingerprint me if you want. I wasn't anywhere near that cistern, or even the Troyers' farm. Well, except for today."

Elizabeth sucked in a breath. Lillian wasn't kidding.

"You carry a fingerprint kit around with you, right?" Lillian looked at John and stuck out her hands, palms up. "You can check right now."

John glanced down at her hands and then at Elizabeth. "I don't think that will be necessary. No scars."

A memory clicked. The prints John found had a scar across two of the fingers.

"Sc-scars?"

The hitch in Lillian's voice drew both Elizabeth's and John's attention.

"The f-fingerprints you found had a scar across them?"

Elizabeth's gaze dropped to Lillian's hands. The fingers of her right hand lay cradled in her left, her thumb running absently over the pads...almost as though she were rubbing invisible scars.

What did she know? And who was she protecting?

"It's a very distinctive mark," John said. His gaze too followed the motion of Lillian's hands. "It'll make figuring out who put the chlorine in the water pretty cut-and-dried."

Except he'd already run the prints through the police database and come up empty. He leaned forward to peer at Lillian.

"Is there something you would like to tell us about those prints?"

She cleared her throat, and her jaw worked. Elizabeth narrowed her eyes. Lillian was nervous.

She stopped rubbing and dropped her hands to her lap. "Sorry...I...no. I was just surprised when you mentioned the scars...because...that's unusual, right?"

If she'd had any doubts before, it was clear now that Lillian was lying, and badly. Elizabeth returned to her original questions. Why? Who was she protecting? Her gut said it was Zach. She glanced sidelong at John. He didn't appear any more convinced by her poor explanation than Elizabeth.

"Lillian, so far, there's been no permanent damage to the Troyers' livestock, but the family has lost revenue. That, combined with trespassing, could lead to some serious trouble if the family decides to press charges."

Lillian's chin rose. "They won't. They're Amish."

Elizabeth's mouth dropped at her boldness. "Lillian—"

She gripped the edge of the table, her jaw hard and voice firm. "Look, I'm really sorry, but I need to finish stocking the tables before my shift ends."

She scraped her chair back and stood. As much as Elizabeth wanted to stop her, she knew saying more was futile. Lillian's mind was made up. Tossing her hair over her shoulder, Lillian whirled and flounced away.

"Well?" Elizabeth scooped up the letter and the guest check and stuffed them into her purse. "One guess at who she was protecting?"

John grimaced and reached for his coat. "I think I know."

"Me too. Have time to ride out to the Vogel's farm with me?"

A smile twitched John's lips as he held out his hand. "Lead the way."

# CHAPTER THIRTY-THREE

Across the dining room table, Simon Vogel's face looked carved from stone as he listened to Elizabeth and John explain the reason for their visit.

"Bottom line, we both got the feeling that Lillian was lying to protect someone," John said.

"That 'someone' being Zach," Elizabeth finished, "based on the flashes of jealousy she's displayed whenever his name is mentioned, especially if it's in conjunction with Emma."

Simon's brows winged upward. "Emma Troyer?"

At Elizabeth's nod, he twined his fingers together, his gnarled knuckles punching against the skin, turning it white. "Ach, I have feared that might be the case."

"You know about his feelings for Emma?" Elizabeth asked.

"He has never spoken of it, but I have long had my suspicions." Simon grunted and got up to pace. "That boy. I have tried to warn him about such things. Emma is a nice girl, but she is Amish. Their differences are too great."

Elizabeth swallowed hard at his words and resisted the urge to look at John. "I, um, heard that you chose to leave the Amish church yourself."

Simon sighed wearily and rubbed his palm over his face. "Likely, you heard more than that, ain't so?" He didn't wait for her response, and continued pacing the floor, his steps slow and methodical. "It is true, I was once in love with Amelia Troyer, but it was not meant to be. I had hoped to spare my son the same heartache, but Zach can be like a dog with a bone when he gets an idea into his head. Just can't let go."

Suspicion grew in Elizabeth's head—of a young man who saw himself and Emma as star-crossed lovers, who was stubborn to the point of pigheaded, who knew as much about cows and dairy farming as Simon himself, and finally, who wanted nothing more than to show Emma how much she needed him.

Elizabeth inhaled deeply. "Simon, where is Zach now?"

He stopped pacing to look at her. "At the Troyers' farm helping Emma."

"Has Zach ever hurt himself?" John slashed his finger across his other hand. "Maybe cut his fingers here?"

Simon squared to the table and gripped the back of one of the ladder-back chairs. "When he was a boy. He ripped his hand on a length of barbed wire chasing after a calf. Nearly lost two of his fingers." He held up his right hand and wagged his middle and ring fingers. "Why?"

Nostrils flaring, John shot a glance at Elizabeth. Much as she would have liked to leave the explanations to him, she couldn't. She was the one pursuing this investigation. It was her job, distasteful as it might be.

She drew in a steadying breath and lifted her gaze. "Simon, we have reason to think that Zach may have tampered with the Troyers' milk."

She told him about the onions and chlorine, and finished with the fingerprints they'd found on the cistern.

Simon listened silently right up until Elizabeth mentioned the fingerprints. At that point, he sliced his hand through the air and shook his head.

"No, no. I will not believe it. Zach has been helping at the Troyers' place for several days. The fingerprints may just be from him taking care of the cows, something Emma *asked* him to do." He jabbed his finger against the table to emphasize his point.

"That is true," Elizabeth said, then glanced out the window toward the barn. "We do need more proof."

She turned her gaze back to Simon. "Would it be all right if we took a look around?"

He followed the direction of her stare and waved his hand, his brow lowering. "For what? Like a lot of other farmers, I keep chlorine out there for use in the footbaths for my cows."

"What about onions?" John asked.

When Elizabeth and Simon turned to look at him, John gave a nod toward the window. "Let me be clear: I am not here in any official capacity. I don't have a warrant, and you don't have to show me around."

Simon remained silent, the expression on his face changing from agony to indecision in the span of heartbeat.

"But we would know once and for all if Zach had anything to do with these events," Simon said, at last.

It wasn't a question, which perhaps said more about his reason for agreeing than his actual words. Elizabeth nodded.

Simon relaxed his grip on the back of the chair. "I will go with you. I will see for myself what is there."

"Of course." John rose and circled the table to stand face-to-face with Simon. "Thank you, Mr. Vogel." He swept his hand out toward the door. "After you."

Simon's breaths came in deep, ragged heaves as he plowed through the dried grass toward the barn. Inside the dim interior, the temperature actually felt colder than it had outside, or perhaps that was just the added nip of dread that shrouded Elizabeth's shoulders as they dug through stall after stall.

If they found nothing, it would mean she'd been wrong about Zach and would find herself back on square one. The opposite was no more charming. If they found something, it would mean that Zach was their culprit, a fact that would no doubt break his father's heart. But what else could she do except keep looking and hope that—

"Elizabeth."

Something in John's voice chilled her to the bone. She jerked upright and spun to stare at him. He stood in the tack room door, his expression dark with concern. She threw a look at Simon, who stepped forward, his hands hanging limply at his sides.

"What is it?" he asked, taking another step closer. "What have you found?"

Instead of answering, John stretched out his hand. Sitting on his palm, white and almost gleaming in the dim light, was a pale, round onion.

# CHAPTER THIRTY-FOUR

The ride to the Troyers' farm was completed in near silence. Every now and then, Elizabeth craned her neck to peer out the rear window of John's car.

"Is he still back there?" she asked, for what had to be at least the sixth time.

John reached out to grip her knee. "He's there."

Elizabeth sighed and sank into her seat. "Poor Simon. I can understand his insisting he come with us to speak to Zach, but all of this has to be so hard for him."

John's gaze flicked to the rearview mirror. "It really is. He seemed to be handling it well though."

Elizabeth blinked back a sudden wash of hot tears. By "handling it," John meant Simon had prayed—a short but heartfelt plea for wisdom and discernment that had John clearing his throat repeatedly and Elizabeth reaching for a tissue.

As though he sensed her roiling emotions, he turned his head. "You okay?"

Her lips twitched in a smile. "I'm okay. Just thinking. And in case I forget later, thank you for coming with me today. Simon and Moses don't have a very good track record when it comes to confrontations, so having you there will be a big help."

He smiled back at her, his gaze warming. "No problem. It's my job."

"No, I mean…"

A flutter started in her belly. Suddenly, she needed more air. She reached for the seat belt and pulled it away from her neck. "John, you go above and beyond what's required for your job. I want you to know I don't take you for granted. You're a good man and…a good friend, and I appreciate you always being there for me. It means more than you know."

"Right. About that." John gripped the steering wheel in both hands and shifted his gaze to stare straight ahead. "I know this probably isn't the best time, but since you brought it up…"

He cleared his throat, and Elizabeth had the strangest sensation that he was nervous. "John?"

"Yeah." He rolled his fingers across the wheel, then took his foot off the accelerator and glanced at her. "It's the 'good friend' thing. I mean, I'm glad you think of me that way, because I want to be your friend, but I also want more."

"More," she repeated, the word a ragged whisper on her lips.

He nodded, shot her another look, and then returned his gaze to the road and sped up. "I'm not asking for an answer from you this second. I just want to be clear about my intentions, in case, you don't, you know, feel the same way."

"I do." She said quickly, without thinking.

John stared at her in surprise. "You…do?"

She nodded. She'd known for weeks that her feelings were deepening where he was concerned. Growing. Changing. She just hadn't told him because, really, she'd been too afraid to admit that she might be falling in love with him. All of that and more remained clogged in her throat, silencing her until they pulled into the Troyers' driveway and the moment for saying more was lost.

She reached for the door handle but hesitated when Zach sauntered around the corner of the barn with Sugarpie loping at his heels.

"Before we get out, I should warn you about the dog," she began, and then stopped and looked. Really looked. "She barks," she said, thoughtfully.

"What?" John's gaze shifted from Elizabeth to the dog.

Elizabeth pointed. "Sugarpie, the Troyers' basset hound, raises a terrible ruckus whenever a stranger shows up at the farm. But look at her now. She just loves Zach."

"Well, he has been here quite a bit lately, right?" John asked.

"That *could* explain it."

Elizabeth pushed open the door and got out. On cue, Sugarpie's voice rose in a low howl that echoed off the barn and a nearby stand of pines. It grew louder when John moved to Elizabeth's side, and reached a crescendo when Simon's car also rolled to a stop.

"That's some alarm system," John said, lifting his fingers to his ears with a grimace.

Elizabeth nodded and cupped her hand to her mouth. "Told you. But guess who doesn't draw the same reaction?"

She shifted to face Zach as he approached. His gaze was curious at first, but became wary when Simon exited his car and joined them.

"Miss Classen? Dad? What...uh...what's going on?" He reached down to curl his fingers around Sugarpie's collar. "Is everything all right?"

"I hope so, Zach." Elizabeth motioned toward the house. "Are Moses and Emma home?"

"Yeah, they're down at the barn, actually. I'll let them know you want to talk to them." He turned to go. His father's voice stopped him.

"Son, we need to speak with you as well. Come back with them, please."

Zach's gaze slid to John and just as quickly skittered away. "Okay. I'll just be a second." He clapped his mouth closed, his Adam's apple bobbing as he swallowed hard and turned.

A few minutes later he returned, Emma at his side and Moses hobbling along at the rear. Emma's face reflected confusion. Moses's was full of concern, especially when he spied Simon with them. He drew to a halt, his gaze skipping over all three of them.

"What is this? What has happened?" He shuffled to a stop, his crutches braced out wide on either side for balance. With his footing secure, he angled his head to peer up at Simon. "What are you doing here, Vogel?"

Elizabeth spoke out. "He came because of us. We have a few questions for Zach."

Emma stepped forward with a confused frown. "Elizabeth, what is this about?"

"It's about everything that has been going on with the milk, Emma. John and I were out at the Vogels' farm today. We found several bags of onions in one of their feed bins."

Zach's mouth fell open. "Dad?"

Simon eyed his son steadily. "Where did the onions come from, Zach?"

Zach glanced at Emma and then shook his head. "I have no idea."

"You didn't purchase them?" John asked.

"No, I didn't." Zach's attention jumped from John to Elizabeth. Running his palms up and down over his jeans, he said, "What is this? Why are the police here?"

Before she could answer, John spoke. "Zach, I need to tell you fingerprints were found on the cistern in the Troyers' pasture. Two of the prints were marked with a pretty distinctive scar."

Zach stopped rubbing his hands on his jeans and stuck them in his coat pockets. "So? What does that have to do with me?"

John's eyes narrowed. "Your father says you cut yourself pretty badly when you were a kid."

Beads of sweat formed on Zach's brow and rolled down his temples. "That's right. It was a long time ago."

John took a step closer, but stopped as Zach stumbled back. "Mind if we see your hands?"

Elizabeth held her breath. They'd never be able to prove otherwise if Zach claimed his prints had gotten on the cistern when he was caring for the cows. She and John both knew that. The question was, did Zach?

He was dancing now, his feet shuffling through the mud beneath his boots.

"Zach?" Pain made Emma's voice waver. She stared at him, begging for answers they all knew only Zach could give.

"Emma...I can explain."

"Zachary!" The name exploded from Simon's lips.

Simon strode forward, and for a second, Elizabeth stood frozen, wondering if he would strike his son, or tell him to keep silent until they could talk to an attorney. He did neither. The big bear of a man put his hand out to clasp his son's shoulder, his chin trembling as he battled the emotions welling inside him.

"Why, Zach? The onions and the chlorine. You tainted the Troyers' milk?"

Zach's face crumpled at the hurt and shame throbbing in his father's voice. "I'm sorry, Dad. It was stupid, I know. I'm so sorry."

He moved to cover his face with his hands. Simon stopped him, grabbing both of Zach's hands in his much larger ones.

"Ne, Son. It is not me to whom your apology is due. Or your explanation." He sucked in a deep breath, then threw his arm around his son's shoulders and turned with him to face Emma and Moses. "Tell them."

At first, only sniffling filled the silence, and then Zach began, brokenly at first, to explain.

"I never meant to hurt the cows." Head bowed, he looked up at Moses through his lashes the way a boy who'd just been scolded might, not straight on like a man. "I thought at most, you'd lose a day or two of milk. I wanted Emma to ask for my help, wanted..."

He trailed off, licked his lips, and began again. "Emma was better at running the farm than I gave her credit for. She knew what to do to without having to ask me."

"And that's why you had to try something else?" Elizabeth asked.

Zach nodded. "The chlorine was a last-ditch effort. I thought if I could prove to her that she needed me, maybe...I thought just maybe..."

His face flushed almost purple. Emma shook her head sadly.

"It was never about needing you, Zach. That place belongs only to God. I just couldn't make you understand that."

"I know that," he muttered. "Now." He dropped his head into his hands and groaned. "Lillian was right. I should have listened to her."

"Lillian knew about this?" Elizabeth asked. "She knew what you were doing?"

"She suspected I would try something," Zach said. "I never told her what."

So, it was Zach that Lillian had been protecting all along. And it must have been Zach she tried calling the day Mary spoke to her in the coffeehouse—a warning that apparently had fallen on deaf ears.

Silence fell as the words Zach had spoken sank in. Finally, Simon stepped forward, his face solemn. "Officer Marks, what my son has done is a crime, ain't so? What will happen to him now?"

"I suppose that depends on the Troyers." John turned to Moses. "If you choose to press charges, I can take Zach down to the station with me now."

"Daed." Emma's gaze turned pleading as she looked at her father.

Elizabeth bit the inside of her cheek as she too waited anxiously for his answer. Despite everything, Emma cared about Zach. What Moses decided could either cause further division between their two families or possibly begin to heal the rift.

Moses lifted his eyes to Simon. "The feud between me and thee has lasted long enough, ain't so?"

Simon blew out a shuddering breath then ducked his head in shame. "Zach and I will pay back everything you have lost, and we will work your farm while you recover. Rest assured, I will keep a close eye on him. There will be no more mischief while I am present."

Moses's head bobbed once, then twice. "That sounds like a goot deal to me, except for one thing." He hobbled closer to stand in front of Zach. "My daughter has taken her vow. You will honor her choice?"

This time, Zach met Moses's gaze head-on. "Yes, sir, I will."

"Goot. Then it is settled." He turned to John. "There has been enough discord between our two families. It is time we extended grace to each other, instead of harsh words or deeds."

John nodded, but a flicker of amazement shone in his eyes as Moses turned and stuck out his hand to Simon.

"You can start tomorrow. Today, I think perhaps there is much you and your boy need to discuss."

"Ja, that's so." Simon shook Moses's hand, the slight smile on his lips reminding Elizabeth of the friendship the two men had once shared and, given time, perhaps might again.

"Come, Son." Simon clapped his hand on Zach's shoulder, his stern face saying Zach would be in for a long night. Still, it was better than what might have happened, what *would* have happened had not Moses and Emma found it in their hearts to forgive. And wasn't that what the world needed, after all? A bit of grace and forgiveness to mend wounds, both old and new?

Elizabeth's heart felt light as she walked with John back to his car. Zach wasn't getting off scot-free. He'd have consequences to face, and probably more guilt and shame than he realized now, but in the end, it was the lessons Moses taught that she hoped would sink in.

Those two things—mercy and kindness—were lessons they all needed to learn.

# CHAPTER THIRTY-FIVE

Elizabeth shook her head as John walked her to the door of the Stockyard Inn. "You didn't have to do this, you know. You already took me out for my birthday. I wasn't expecting you to feel like you had to take me out again."

"I didn't have to, I wanted to," he said, smiling as he reached for the door handle. "Besides, with all the commotion that's been going on at the Troyers' place, they haven't even had a chance to celebrate your birthday with you yet."

"No, but I don't mind. Really."

John moved behind her and helped her out of her coat, something that made Elizabeth smile every time he did it. Chivalry wasn't dead. It was just waiting for women to appreciate the men who still practiced it.

Elizabeth glanced around her at the many packed tables. "Wow, this place is busy tonight. Are you sure we'll be able to get in without a reservation?"

"Oh, we have a reservation."

John nodded to the hostess, who smiled brightly and held out her hand.

"If you're ready, I'll show you to your table."

"Well." Elizabeth grinned up at John. "Aren't you full of surprises tonight?"

He smiled in a secretive sort of way that piqued her curiosity. "Just wait."

She leaned toward him to bump his shoulder. "You mean there's more planned after this?"

"A lot more."

What he meant by that, he wouldn't say. Knowing it would be futile to attempt to coax the information out of him, Elizabeth smiled and walked after the hostess. They passed several empty tables along the way, including one next to the massive stone hearth where a blazing fire crackled invitingly.

Elizabeth glanced over her shoulder at John. "Where on earth are we going?"

"Just keep walking," he whispered in her ear. "You'll see."

A private table? A quiet corner? Elizabeth imagined all sorts of things, but was surprised when the hostess stopped at the entrance to the large room at the back of the restaurant typically reserved for parties.

"What—?"

She got no further. The hostess threw open the doors, and Elizabeth was instantly bombarded with cries of "Surprise!" Near the front, Martha and Mary shouted the loudest.

Behind her, John stepped in close to wrap his arms around her waist. "Happy birthday."

"John!" Elizabeth twirled in his grasp. "You knew about this?"

"Of course he did," Mary said, laughing as she moved forward to pull Elizabeth into a hug. "How else would we have gotten you here without you guessing what was going on otherwise?"

"Though you have to admit, pretending like we'd been too busy to plan anything was a pretty good idea," Martha said, tugging Elizabeth from Mary's grasp into her own. She hugged Elizabeth tightly and then pulled back to look into her face. "Were you surprised?"

"Surprised?" Elizabeth shook her head. "Shocked is more like it." She looked around at the familiar faces of friends and family. "How did you manage to put all this together with everything we had going on?"

"It wasn't easy," Mary said, and then gestured toward the back of the room. "But we're not done yet. We've got one more surprise for you."

Following the direction of her stare, Elizabeth gasped as Michael and Heidi stepped forward, little Nick cradled tightly in Heidi's arms.

Elizabeth rushed forward to meet them, her gaze bouncing from Heidi, to Michael, and down to Nick. "Wh—How did—? Is the baby all right?"

"He's much better," Heidi said, smiling brightly as she shifted Nick to her hip so Elizabeth could wrap them both in a hug.

Mary rubbed her grandson's head lightly. "He won't be going to baby swim classes any time soon, but the doctor didn't think he'd have any lasting effects from the chlorine."

"Oh my goodness, that's wonderful news." Elizabeth pressed a kiss to Nick's forehead, and then another to Heidi's and Michael's cheeks for good measure. "I'm so happy you got an answer."

"We got answers all right," Michael said.

"Answers to prayer," Heidi added. Tears standing in her eyes, she looked around the room at all of their friends. "Thank you all so much for praying for us."

She and Michael moved away, back toward their table. Mary and Martha followed, leaving Elizabeth and John alone. She took his hand, wanting to savor the brief moment before she would need to attend to the rest of her guests.

"Thank you," she said quietly.

John smiled. "For what?"

"For everything." She motioned around the room. "For this."

"You're welcome."

Instead of letting go of her hand, he brought it to his lips and pressed a light kiss on the back. So featherlight was the contact, Elizabeth might have thought she'd imagined it, except for the delicious little shivers that followed.

"So, a miracle?" John nodded toward Heidi and Michael and the members of their family all gathered around.

"More like an answer to prayer," Elizabeth said, and then frowned playfully. "And anyway, I thought you didn't believe in miracles?"

John shrugged and gave her fingers a squeeze. "Maybe I'm beginning to? It was sort of a miracle what happened between Simon and Moses, wouldn't you say?"

"I guess I would," Elizabeth agreed.

The chatter filling the room grew louder. She knew their time was up, but that was okay. They could talk after. Right now, she wanted to enjoy this moment with their friends.

A happy sigh built in her chest as John's hand slipped to the small of her back. Here too was another answer to prayer, or rather, a partial answer. But it was enough to prompt her to keep hoping. And praying. Because God had a plan. She had no idea how much it entailed, but she didn't need to. Because He was in control.

And knowing that was enough.

# A NOTE FROM THE AUTHOR

Though I have called Texas home for over twenty years, I was not born here. My childhood was spent running barefoot through the fertile fields of the Midwest. I ate fruit directly from the trees and heard cows lowing through the open bedroom window of my first house. I played in barns and swam in lakes. I attempted downhill skiing through a pear orchard—an escapade that did not end well—and just like any other kid, I suffered my share of cuts and scrapes. Those days are a dim memory now, but the lessons I learned about respect, integrity, and hard work have stayed with me. Writing this book was a return to a simpler time, a reason to linger there for a brief season. I remembered what it was like to race through pastures, tripping over clumps of mud and dirt, and experience the smells and sweat that come with working a farm. Years and distance have softened some of the sharper edges, made the memories somehow sweeter. I hope you have enjoyed returning there with me, and that this story has stirred pleasant memories of your own.

Sincerely,
Elizabeth Ludwig

# ABOUT THE AUTHOR

Elizabeth Ludwig is a *USA Today* bestselling author and speaker, often attending conferences where she lectures on editing for fiction writers, crafting effective novel proposals, and conducting successful editor/agent interviews. Book three in her popular Edge of Freedom series, *Tide and Tempest*, was named a finalist for the Gayle Wilson Award of Excellence. Elizabeth was also named a Selah Awards finalist for her novella "One Holy Night," part of the bestselling anthology collection, *Christmas Comes to Bethlehem, Maine*. Most recently, she was honored to be awarded a HOLT Medallion for her book *A Tempting Taste of Mystery*, part of the Sugarcreek Amish Mysteries series from Guideposts. Her latest releases include *Pride and Pettiness* and *A Bitter Brew*, part of the Mysteries of Lancaster County and the Tearoom Mysteries series respectively, also from Guideposts. To learn more, visit ElizabethLudwig.com.

# MORE TO THE STORY

I was very fortunate to have knowledgeable friends I could reach out to when researching this story. Though many of the circumstances were very different, the staff at Country Dairy in Shelby, Michigan, was a huge help in getting some of the facts straight regarding the processing of milk, and I am very thankful for their willingness to share information. Country Dairy is a family-owned business whose history stretches as far back as the 1880s. Today, the business employs about 125 people in the production of cheese, milk, ice cream, and other dairy-related products. In 2004, they opened their first retail store on the farm—an interesting tidbit that I incorporated into the writing of my story. Country Dairy's Farm Store and Moo School have become field trip destinations for school children and a tourist stop for guests from around the world. If you'd like to learn more, please visit countrydairy. com and schedule a tour. Tell them I sent you.

# FRESH FROM MARTHA'S KITCHEN

## *Martha's Cinnamon Muffins*

**Ingredients:**

½ cup flour

½ cup sugar

2 teaspoons baking powder

½ teaspoon salt

½ teaspoon ground
  nutmeg

½ teaspoon ground
  allspice

1 beaten egg

½ cup whole milk

⅓ cup melted butter
  (salted or unsalted)

**Topping:**

2 tablespoons granulated
  sugar

½ teaspoon ground
  cinnamon

¼ cup melted butter
  (salted or unsalted)

**Directions:**

For muffins:

Preheat oven to 400 degrees.

Mix together dry ingredients: flour, sugar, baking powder, salt, nutmeg, and allspice.

Stir into the dry ingredients the egg, milk, and butter, just until moistened batter is formed.

Spoon into greased or paper-lined muffin cups.

Bake for 20 minutes, or until done.

For topping:

Mix sugar and cinnamon together until well combined.

Brush top of each warm muffin in butter, then dip top of muffin into sugar/cinnamon mixture.

Read on for a sneak peek of another exciting book
in the Mysteries of Lancaster County series!

## *Not Her Type*
by Beth Adams

Mary Classen Baxter had just finished setting up the
cash register when the doors of Secondhand Blessings
opened, and four women walked inside.

"Cold enough out there for you?" Della Bradford asked as
the sliding glass doors closed behind her. The scent of smoke
hung in the air, and Mary knew someone nearby was burning
leaves.

"It's too early for weather like this," Linda Marten said, rubbing her hands together, jostling the plastic carrier bag that
was draped over her arm. Her glasses fogged up as the warm
air inside the shop surrounded her.

"You say that every year." Nancy Van Slyke was wearing a
cheerful red wool coat and a knit hat, and she carried a large
cardboard box in her arms. "But it seems there's always a cold
snap before Thanksgiving. It's not too early, it's just how it goes
in Pennsylvania."

"Well, maybe it isn't too early, but that doesn't mean I have
to like it." Linda pulled off her glasses, wiped away the moisture,
and then rested them back on her nose.

"But it feels lovely in here." Beverly Stout started across the open space at the front of the store, and the others followed behind. "I'll never understand how you make an old barn feel so warm and cozy. Our barn is full of drafts."

"It's magic," Mary said. "Magic and good heaters." She was happy to see her regulars in here, just like they were most Saturday mornings. Della, Nancy, Beverly, and Linda hit up the garage sales and estate sales in the area each week and brought their finds to resell at Secondhand Blessings, the shop Mary ran with her sisters. They always brought in the most interesting items, and Mary looked forward to seeing what they'd found this week.

"Well, whatever it is, I'm planning to stay here until I die so I never have to go back out into the cold," Linda said as she placed her bag on the counter.

"Make way. This thing is heavy." The others cleared a path for Nancy, who set the cardboard box on the counter next to Linda's plastic bag.

"What do you have in there?" Mary stood on her toes to peer over the side of the box.

"You're going to love this. I found it at the estate sale over in Lititz we hit up first thing this morning." Nancy reached into the box and hoisted out something made of molded red metal. She turned it around as she set it down on the counter, and Mary gasped.

"A typewriter!" She clapped her hands together. This wasn't a delicate nineteenth-century model, with round keys and graceful pins. This was a serious typewriter that would take up half a desk. Judging by the boxy metal body and the red color, it was probably from the late sixties or early seventies. "We had one just like this when I was growing up."

"It's an IBM Selectric," Nancy said, pointing at the logo on the top of the machine. "These things were once on the desk of every secretary in America."

"I typed all my high school papers on one like this," Mary said. "Only ours was the plain old beige color." She leaned forward and looked down at the square keys and the ruler affixed to the front of the machine. How many times had she used that ruler to line up her papers perfectly?

"Go ahead," Nancy said, pointing at the sheet of copy paper that had been rolled around the barrel. "Plug it in and give it a whirl."

Mary uncurled the plastic-coated cord and plugged it into an outlet behind the counter. There was a low hum, and she placed her fingers on the keyboard. Mary Frances Classen Baxter, she typed. Each keystroke resulted in a satisfying click as the letters appeared on the paper.

"Ooh. This is fun!"

"Why did we ever move to computers?" Della asked, leaning in to get a closer look. "There's something about that sound that is so satisfying. You just don't get that from a computer."

"I, for one, don't miss having to use correction fluid," Beverly said. "And spending so long lining up my papers to get the perfect margins."

"And you can't get on the internet with a typewriter," Linda added.

"Is that such a bad thing?" Nancy asked, and they all laughed.

"I checked eBay to see how much these things are going for, and if they're in good working condition, they can be worth several hundred dollars, but I got this one for a song," Nancy said. "I don't have the patience to list it online and ship it to the seller. I figured I'd let you handle the hard part."

"I'm delighted to." Mary looked the typewriter over carefully, and she and Nancy soon arrived at an agreeable price.

Mary moved the machine to the side and turned to the bag Linda had placed on the counter. Linda had brought in a copper Revere Ware pan, probably from the 1930s, Mary guessed. It had some nicks and dents, but it was old and beautiful, though likely better used for decoration than for cooking these days. Della had found four crystal water goblets and a gravy boat, while Beverly had brought in a collection of women's winter coats.

"From the same estate sale where Nancy found the typewriter," Beverly explained. "The woman had a thing for coats, apparently."

"I have no doubt these will find good homes," Mary said, looking them over. They were a small size, with a few minor stains and moth holes, but they were well made and would likely sell quickly in the shop. Beverly agreed to the price Mary named, and after chatting for a few minutes, the four women went toward the door, ready to spend their earnings on brunch.

Once they left, the shop was quiet, and Mary looked around. She knew her sister Martha was spending the first part of the morning getting started on the two dozen pies she'd promised to make and donate for the local Community Thanksgiving Meal, which fed the area's hungry for the holiday. Mary knew

Martha was hoping to get much of the baking out of the way before her family started arriving for the holiday on Tuesday, so she would be occupied for a while this morning. And Elizabeth had promised to come over after she'd fed the animals. Mary would have thought she'd be done with that by now, but then, it wasn't like they had a flood of customers.

There were plenty of things she should do. There was always straightening and rearranging of the merchandise to be done, and she needed to inventory and price the items that had just come in.

But instead, Mary turned to the typewriter. She was like a kid with a new toy; she just wanted to play with it for a while. She scooted the machine closer and sat down on the stool. She poised, her fingers hovering over the keys. What was that sentence that used every letter of the alphabet?

THE QUICK BROWN FOX JUMPED OVER THE LAZY DOG, she typed. This was such a different experience than typing on a computer, and there was something so satisfying about seeing your words appear on the paper instantly.

ONCE UPON A TIME, she typed next. Wouldn't it be fun to write a story on one of these things? She pictured herself huddled over the typewriter, her fingers picking out the words as quickly as her mind thought them. She could be like Hemingway or Fitzgerald. She'd always wanted to write a novel. Ooh, maybe this typewriter would be the thing that finally got her to sit down and do it.

But what would she write about? She'd never quite managed to settle on a story line, or even a genre, really. Maybe she should start by making a list of ideas that had caught her fancy over the years. It would be a long list, she felt sure about that. She had started a couple of novels, one a story about an artist who found a long-lost work by Van Gogh in a secondhand shop, and once a fantasy novel set in a world with dragons. She never got very far.

But could this thing handle a novel? Mary stood up and studied the machine. She knew there was a ribbon inside the typewriter; that was where the ink came from. How much ribbon was left? Could she get another one if she needed it? Could you even buy typewriter ribbons these days?

Mary saw that there was a seam, so she lifted the top portion of the machine off, exposing the insides. She found a round ball imprinted with letters, and remembered that this kind of typewriter had been revolutionary when it came out. Unlike older models, which relied on long thin pins etched with the letters that struck the paper when a key was pressed, the IBM Selectric had introduced a single central type ball, which rotated and moved around to imprint the paper. It had been seen as a huge advance in the technology, as you could switch out the type ball to introduce different fonts and alphabets.

But Mary was looking for...aha! There was the ribbon, and it spooled and unspooled from a cartridge just behind the type ball. She studied the cartridge. How could she tell how much ribbon was left? She noticed a red lever on the side of the cartridge. She pulled it back, and then it was easy to pop the cartridge off. Mary studied the cartridge, looking for a way to tell how much of the ribbon had been used. She noticed the words she had just typed imprinted there, clear as day, in the ribbon. True, they weren't easy to read as the letters had landed in two rows, so you had to read one letter, then the one below it, and then the one above and to the left, and then the one below *that*. It was cumbersome, but since Mary knew what she'd just typed, it wasn't hard to make it out.

What *else* had been typed on this ribbon over the years? She pulled at the ribbon, and more of it came out of the cartridge. She went beyond her own words and found a streak of random letters—people trying out the typewriter, just as she had, she quickly surmised—and then what seemed to be a string of letters that looked purposeful.

Mary grabbed a notebook and a pencil, pulled a long string of ribbon from the cartridge, and copied down the letters, going right to left, up and down, trying to make out what the ribbon revealed. Once she'd copied down a sizeable chunk, she wrote the letters on her paper in reverse order.

HER EYES MET HIS ACROSS THE ROOM, AND SHE FELT LIKE A YOUNG GIRL IN LOVE FOR THE FIRST TIME. HE WAS AS HANDSOME AS HE'D EVER BEEN, BUT HE HAD MATURED, AND HIS SAD SMILE REVEALED THE STRAIN THE PAST FEW YEARS HAD TAKEN.

It was a story! Whoever had used this typewriter last had been writing a love story. Mary was delighted. She looked back at the ribbon, copying down the letters one at a time.

"What are you doing?"

Mary looked up to find her sister Elizabeth standing in front of her, her brows raised.

"Oh. Hi." Mary had no idea when Elizabeth had come into the shop and no clue how much time had passed. She saw that there were a few customers browsing in the aisles, and realized she hadn't noticed them enter. "Sorry. I was kind of engrossed."

"I see that. In what?"

"Reading a romance novel."

"What?" Elizabeth was narrowing her eyes now, and her face showed concern.

"Check this out." Mary showed her older sister the typewriter and how she was reading the letters from the ribbon. "Whoever owned this typewriter last was writing a romance novel," she said. "I'm reading it backward from where the writer left off, of course, so I have no idea who these people are or how they met or whether the author intended for them to get together in the end, but I can tell she really likes him."

Elizabeth pressed her lips together and tilted her head but didn't say anything.

"We got this typewriter," Mary explained, gesturing at the hunk of red metal.

Elizabeth nodded. Mary could tell that Elizabeth thought she was nuts. What else was new?

"Come see." She gestured for her sister to come closer, and Elizabeth obediently stepped around the counter and looked at the typewriter ribbon Mary held up. "See, you can read the letters the previous owner typed on this ribbon," Mary said. "I was intrigued."

"You can read that?" Elizabeth leaned in closer. "It looks like gobbledygook to me."

"It's really hard to make sense of it just by looking at the ribbon," Mary admitted. "So I'm copying down the letters and working it out on paper."

"It sounds like a lot of work," Elizabeth said hesitantly.

"It's a glimpse into someone's mind," Mary said. "I think it's fascinating."

"Better you than me."

"It's like a puzzle. I think it's fun."

Elizabeth stood there a moment longer, and Mary realized there was probably a reason her sister had come over to her in the first place.

"Did you need something?"

"I was going to ask if you needed a break." Elizabeth gestured around at the shop. The few customers were browsing quietly. "It's quiet so far, and you've been here alone since we opened."

"That was thoughtful. But if you don't mind me working at this a bit longer, I'm fine here. I'll keep an eye on the counter."

"Have at it." Elizabeth gave her a smile. "I'll go straighten the clothing racks."

"Great." Mary turned back to the ribbon. In a few minutes she reached the beginning of the novel, and then the writing on the ribbon changed. It was no longer fiction, but business letters and memos. It took Mary a while, but she worked out that this typewriter must have been used in 1968 by a secretary at an insurance company called Patterson Insurance, which had been located in Lancaster. She gathered that from the return address as she reconstructed memos about claims and actuarial reports and liability. She was fascinated. All those years ago, someone had typed these words on this typewriter, and here she was reading them now. It was like reading the words of a ghost. Only, Mary reasoned, that ghost probably had a fabulous midcentury wardrobe. She imagined chic dresses with pencil skirts and flared A-line dresses and loose mod dresses. The men probably wore skinny neckties and drank in their offices on fabulous low couches with Sputnik lamps hanging above.

Mary glanced up again. She knew she should get up and help Elizabeth. And she would. Soon. She just wanted to read a little bit more.

Then she came to something very different. But when she finally made it out, she stared down at her notebook, trying to make sense of what she was seeing.

DROP THE SUIT OR YOU'LL BE SORRY. YOU WILL NOT WIN AND MANY PEOPLE WILL BE HURT IN THE PROCESS.

The note was not signed, but it was followed by several more entries of the same note—only these were riddled with errors—and then what must have been an envelope, addressed to a Herb Palmer in Lancaster.

Someone had threatened Herb Palmer. She felt her hackles rise. What had Herb Palmer ever done to anyone?

"Discover the secrets of the universe?" Elizabeth had brought Dottie Spencer to the counter to ring up a purchase of mixing bowls. Dottie owned a beauty shop in town and did the hair of most of the women in the Bird-in-Hand area.

"Just that someone threatened Herb Palmer."

"Who's Herb Palmer?" Elizabeth rang up the bowls one at a time.

"I have no idea."

"Maybe he did something terrible. Maybe he deserved to be threatened." Elizabeth nested the bowls on the counter.

"Maybe he owed someone money," Dottie said, joining in. She was smiling, though it was clear she didn't know what was going on.

"Or was dating someone's daughter," Elizabeth added.

"It says 'Drop the suit or you'll be sorry.'"

"So it was definitely a fight about fashion," Dottie said, grinning as she handed Elizabeth a twenty-dollar bill.

Mary laughed, and Elizabeth made change and then bagged up the bowls. Elizabeth explained what Mary was working on, and Dottie said it sounded very interesting and then turned to go.

"You're wondering about Herb Palmer, aren't you?" Elizabeth was watching Mary after Dottie walked away.

"Of course." Mary shrugged. Her mind had already worked out elaborate scenarios for who had a vendetta against Herb Palmer. She couldn't help it. She loved stories, and her brain just made things up on its own. She knew her sisters thought she was flaky because she got so lost in her head sometimes, but could she help it that it was a fascinating place to be?

"So why don't you look him up?"

"Huh?"

It took a minute for Mary to realize that Elizabeth was pointing at the computer on the counter. She blinked, and then understood. She'd been so lost in the world of typewriters that she'd momentarily forgotten about Google.

"Good idea," Mary said. She stepped in front of the computer and pulled up a search window, and then she typed in the name Herb Palmer. She knew it was doubtful anything would come up. The threatening note had been written several decades before the invention of the internet. If Herb was still alive, he was in his seventies now, at minimum. Older people often didn't have online footprints. But still. It didn't hurt to look.

And then she sucked in a breath.

"What is it?" Elizabeth was glancing at the screen.

"This can't be the same Herb Palmer," Mary said.

"What can't be? Why not?" Elizabeth moved closer to get a better look.

Mary was looking at an abstract from a local newspaper published in 1968. She clicked on the link. All she could see was the headline and the first few sentences, but they were enough. "This says Herb Palmer was killed. And the police were looking for suspects but didn't have many leads."

"Wait. What?" Elizabeth narrowed her eyes. "Really?"

"That's what it looks like." Could this be true? Mary didn't see how, but there it was. She turned to Elizabeth.

"It could be a different Herb Palmer," Elizabeth said.

"I'm sure it could be. But this Herb Palmer was supposedly found in a yard outside a house on Hickory Lane in Lancaster." Mary looked away from the computer screen and back at the typewriter. "And someone typed out an address on Hickory Lane on that typewriter. If we're talking about a different Herb Palmer, that's an astonishing coincidence."

"Did the police ever solve the case?" Elizabeth asked.

Mary turned back to the computer and returned to the search page. There was another headline that read SUSPECTS STILL SOUGHT IN THE PALMER MURDER, and, below that, a headline that read, POLICE NO CLOSER TO SOLVING AD EXEC MURDER. But only the first sentence of each article showed up on the web page.

"I don't see anything that says they caught the guy," she said, scanning down the page. "I can't read the full article for any of these, but I can see enough to say that there's nothing about an arrest or anything about a trial."

"Huh." Elizabeth frowned, and she glanced back at the typewriter.

Mary knew what Elizabeth was thinking, but she also knew her sister wasn't going to say it. Mary said it instead. "Do you think there's any chance whoever wrote that note killed Herb Palmer?"

"It's hard to say." Elizabeth was hedging. She didn't like to think about gory things like this. But Mary wasn't so hesitant. "It seems fair to say someone was threatening him, but I don't think we can assume that person had anything to do with his death."

"You're totally right," Mary said. "We shouldn't assume that."

"But...?"

"But we could try to find out, right?"

"Oh, Mary." Elizabeth sighed. Mary recognized that sigh. It said that Elizabeth didn't want to get dragged into another one of Mary's wild goose chases. Well, she couldn't help it that she was intrigued by so many things, could she?

"Don't you want to know what happened to him?" Mary asked.

"We don't know anything about him."

"We know whoever killed him got away with it," Mary said. "It's not like you to want to let an injustice like that stand."

"We don't have the first clue how to find out what happened," Elizabeth said.

"That's the thing," Mary said. "We *do* have the first clue. We have the first new clue in more than fifty years. All we have to do is figure out who typed that threatening note, and we'll be able to solve the case."

"Even if that's true—which, let me be clear, I'm not saying I agree with—but if it was true, how in the world are we supposed to find out who typed that note?"

"Well, I haven't figured that part out yet," Mary admitted. "I'll have to think about it. But I bet we can." She paused for a moment, thinking through the implications. "And if I'm right, if the person who typed this note was the person who killed Herb Palmer, this typewriter ribbon may be the clue that could help solve his murder."

# A NOTE FROM THE EDITORS

We hope you enjoyed this volume of the Mysteries of Lancaster County series, created by the Books and Inspirational Media Division of Guideposts. We are a nonprofit organization that touches millions of lives every day through products and services that inspire, encourage, help you grow in your faith, and celebrate God's love in every aspect of your daily life.

Thank you for making a difference with your purchase of this book, which helps fund our many outreach programs to military personnel, prisons, hospitals, nursing homes, and educational institutions. To learn more, visit GuidepostsFoundation.org.

We also maintain many useful and uplifting online resources. Visit Guideposts.org to read true stories of hope and inspiration, access OurPrayer network, sign up for free newsletters, download free e-books, join our Facebook community, and follow our stimulating blogs.

To learn about other Guideposts publications, including the bestselling devotional *Daily Guideposts*, go to ShopGuideposts .org, call (800) 932-2145, or write to Guideposts, PO Box 5815, Harlan, Iowa 51593.